UNRAVELLING

ESSENTIAL PROSE SERIES 183

Canada Council   Conseil des Arts
for the Arts   du Canada

ONTARIO ARTS COUNCIL
CONSEIL DES ARTS DE L'ONTARIO
an Ontario government agency
un organisme du gouvernement de l'Ontario

Canada

Guernica Editions Inc. acknowledges the support of the Canada Council
for the Arts and the Ontario Arts Council. The Ontario Arts Council
is an agency of the Government of Ontario.

We acknowledge the financial support of the Government of Canada.
Nous reconnaissons l'appui financier du gouvernement du Canada.

UNRAVELLING

Josephine Boxwell

**GUERNICA
EDITIONS**
TORONTO · CHICAGO · BUFFALO · LANCASTER (U.K.)
2020

Michael Mirolla, general editor
Lindsay Brown, editor
David Moratto, interior and cover design
Guernica Editions Inc.
287 Templemead Drive, Hamilton, ON L8W 2W4
2250 Military Road, Tonawanda, N.Y. 14150-6000 U.S.A.
www.guernicaeditions.com

Distributors:
Independent Publishers Group (IPG)
600 North Pulaski Road, Chicago IL 60624
University of Toronto Press Distribution,
5201 Dufferin Street, Toronto (ON), Canada M3H 5T8
Gazelle Book Services, White Cross Mills
High Town, Lancaster LA1 4XS U.K.

First edition.
Printed in Canada.

Legal Deposit—Third Quarter
Library of Congress Catalog Card Number: 2019949246
Library and Archives Canada Cataloguing in Publication
Title: Unravelling / Josephine Boxwell.
Names: Boxwell, Josephine, author.
Series: Essential prose series ; 183.
Description: Series statement: Essential prose series ; 183
Identifiers: Canadiana (print) 20190177373 | Canadiana (ebook) 2019017742X |
ISBN 9781771835442 (softcover) | ISBN 9781771835459 (EPUB) |
ISBN 9781771835466 (Kindle)
Classification: LCC PS8603.O97675 U57 2020 | DDC C813/.6—dc23

For Erica

CHAPTER 1

1 9 9 4

Elena remembered everything. Not just the street names and the blackboard lessons and the number plates of every vehicle her parents had owned. She remembered the stories. There were stories everywhere: rolling out of people's mouths, blowing in the summer dust, printed on the walls of the tiny village museum. She collected all of them, whole or in pieces, and she was sure there was a way to fit them together.

Mamma had to raise her voice—something she tried to avoid—to be heard. "Turn that down! You'll damage your ears!"

They were on their way home from church, the three of them. Rob thumped his leather shoes on the tarmac while Mamma kept pace in her floral print dress and kitten heels. Elena trailed behind, shaking gravel out of her sandal. Rob removed his headphones to taunt Mamma. The tinny beats from his mixtape crackled out of the foam ear pads.

"I don't have to listen to you anymore. I'm getting out of this dump."

Rob always lost his temper on hot days. Sooner or later, he would boil over. He marched ahead of them with his thumb stuck out, kicking up dust that stuck to his sweating face, looking for vehicles heading out of town toward Stony Creek. The collared shirt Mamma bought for him two months ago was already tight around his shoulders. He was 14 and desperate to be his own man. Mamma dismissed him with a wave of her hand. She didn't believe he'd really do it.

Her expression hardened when a pale blue truck appeared on the horizon. It wasn't one they recognized. There was only one way in or out of Stapleton. (The old highway ended at the railway tracks.) No one new arrived in town except by mistake, or in Mamma's mind, to do something nasty, like dump garbage or steal things.

"Roberto! Aspetti!"

Mamma couldn't keep up with her son, especially in her church outfit. Her mouth opened into a little "o" when the truck's indicator started flashing. It pulled over right in front of Rob's outstretched arm and he addressed the open window as Mamma clip-clopped toward them as fast as she could. She pulled her lips up into her sort-of-smile, slid her shades up and latched onto Rob's shoulders with a firm grip.

Bony, black-haired Frank leaned out of the window but Mamma showed no pleasure at the sight of a familiar face. Frank ran the Stapleton Inn and Mamma didn't much like either of them.

Frank stared at Mamma a bit too long without speaking. Mamma was pretty, Elena knew that. Dad said Mamma could stop traffic (if there was any). Her hair was naturally dark like Elena's, but she had highlights and layers done at the Stony Creek salon and people often commented on how she looked so fashionable. Mamma never appeared in public with what she called her "plain face". Elena wanted people to think she was pretty too, but Mamma said 10 was too young for lipsticks and lash curlers.

Elena guessed Frank was older than Mamma but she couldn't decide his actual age. Sometimes he giggled like a kid. He wore ripped jeans and tie-dyed t-shirts and she thought he cut his own hair because it was always shaggy and snarled at the back.

Frank stretched his palm out of the window toward Elena as she skipped up to the vehicle. "Gimme five."

Beaming, she slapped his hand. Mamma was frowning but Elena liked him.

"New truck, Frank?" Mamma's words were friendly but her voice was flat. That's how she spoke when she didn't want to.

"It was … a couple decades ago." He patted the door like it was his dog. "I bought it for parts."

Elena had never seen Frank fix cars but he was always collecting new hobbies. She liked that about him. Whenever she saw him around town, he was fired up about a new project, or he'd picked up something unusual.

Frank flashed Rob an apologetic look. "I can't drive you to Stony Creek. How 'bout I drive you all home instead?"

Rob and Elena both turned to Mamma, Rob wiping the beads of sweat from his forehead, Elena pressing her palms together as she begged. "Please!"

Mamma also found the heat unbearable yet today she had a shawl draped around her shoulders. Maybe she thought God would be offended by her bare, sweaty armpits.

"Thanks, but we're nearly home."

"Mom! Please!" Rob said, moaning.

Frank was still leaning out of the driver's window. "It's no trouble, Giulia."

Mamma made a last-ditch attempt at a smile before turning away. Rob offered Frank one more desperate look. "Sorry, dude," Frank said, stepping on the accelerator. Elena and

Rob slowed to a crawl as they watched the truck stutter away. Mamma was right; home wasn't that far but it seemed so much further now.

⌁ Every week on the way home from church, the three of them passed an abandoned graveyard. Only Elena paid any attention to it. It wasn't visible without crossing the concrete barrier that separated the road from the steep slope, but she knew the old Chinese cemetery was down there. It sat on a scrap of land just above the river. Dad had cautioned her there was no easy, or safe, way to reach it. The trail that cut along the eroding base of the riverbank was completely overgrown.

Dad had told her about the cemetery after he swaggered into the house one morning swinging two dead grouse by their ankles. Mamma shooed him outside. Elena followed.

"It ain't easy getting down there but the birds sure like it," he explained as Elena brushed her fingers against the soft feathers.

"Isn't it spooky?"

"Nah. Grouse don't care about ghosts. They like the gravel. They swallow it to help them digest their food."

Dad said the gravestones in that cemetery were marked with fancy dashes, that's how the Chinese wrote. They'd come during the gold rush and Elena wanted to know where they'd all gone. Almost everyone she knew in Stapleton was white and the rest were mostly Native. Dad told her that Stapleton's Chinatown burned down ages ago. Dad wasn't from Stapleton and didn't care much about history, but he'd do his best to find out about things when she asked. He drove her down to the gas station one afternoon and they bought cans of orange pop and drank them at the picnic bench beside a Moments In History signboard for the visitors that never came. She thought about how Chinatown's ashes had been absorbed into the ground, leaving no trace. The sign didn't explain how their cemetery ended up down by the river, so close it was practically falling in, but now those souls were trapped on the edge of their nowhere town forever.

Mamma strode off down the highway, determined to prove how easy it was to walk home in 30-degree heat. Elena hesitated beside the barrier that came up to her hips and casually examined the tiny bumps and grooves on its surface. She glanced ahead to see if Mamma had noticed. She hadn't.

Straddling the concrete barrier was easy enough, even in the pale yellow dress that ended just below her knees, but something shifted when her jelly sandals sank into the coarse earth on the other side. She had moved from feeling safe to being aware, and she could feel every speck of her being twitch. She was like a small animal testing the air for danger, her heart pumping hard in her chest.

Tiptoeing on the cusp of the slope, she could still only make out the shapes of the headstones. From up here, there were no visible markings, no inscriptions written in a foreign language. She shuffled her right foot half an inch further and squinted at the stones as hard as she could.

"Elena!"

Mamma screamed. Elena swung around, too quickly. She slipped out of balance and her heart hit her throat.

The scree shifted rapidly beneath her feet, rushing around her ankles and carrying her with it as though she had been caught in a river current. She dug her heels in and it slowed her a little. Her shaky legs gave in about two-thirds of the way down and her back hit the dirt. She cried out as sharp edges shaved her skin.

When she first hit the ground, all she could hear was the

river, noisier than she thought it to be. Then Mamma's screams rang down from the highway.

Elena's body throbbed with the aches of a thousand scrapes and twists. Her palms pulsated as she pushed them into the dust and sat upright. She craned her neck and looked up through the dusty clouds of her descent. There was the imprint of her journey written in the scree—light where she slid, heavy and compacted where she had stomped into it.

Rob stepped gingerly onto the top of the slope. "You alright?" His voice squeaked under the pressure of his breaking vocal cords. "Yeah," Elena called back. Beside him, their trembling mother had come as close to the edge as she dared, which wasn't very far at all. She kept one hand on the low barrier.

"I'm okay, Mom."

"Stay there!" Mamma shouted. She reached her other hand out to Rob but he found his own way back onto solid ground.

Elena curled up into her bruises, bloodied skin and self pity, wrapped in dull brown cotton that was supposed to be yellow. The strap around her left ankle had snapped and one purple jelly sandal lay broken at the base of the slide.

As the shock subsided, she remembered where she was. She pulled the remaining sandal off her right foot, hauled herself up and shook off some of the residue that clung to her dress and skin. Around her were small grey stones with symbols that ran up and down in black or white. She could see them clearly now that she was actually down in the place, covered in its dirt. The markings of people who'd lived there once. Dad was right; it wasn't spooky. It was sad.

Stapleton's other graveyard was still in use. It also had a river view but it was part of the village. A row of houses stood between it and Main Street but one of the grand willows was visible from the post office. The Stapleton Cemetery was well cared-for; mown grass shaded by huge trees. People left colourful bouquets on those stones.

There were no manicured trees to admire here. Yellow and brown grasses had overtaken the dirt between the grave markers. Sagebrush and taller, spindly bushes took root near the plateau's edge, then spread across one side. Somewhere in there was the overgrown trail Dad had mentioned, running parallel to the highway.

Elena could hear the water but she wanted to see it. She grimaced as she limped across the graveyard and pushed her way through the sprawling bushes until she could see the wide, bluish-brown river a few feet below. She found a large rock to perch on and listened to the water, her aches pounding away at her thoughts. A salmon jumped. It flew into the air and re-entered the water in the next instant, barely making a sound.

A short distance upstream, men were waiting to catch salmon just like that one. Every August, they camped under blue tarpaulins north of the village where the river narrowed and the sockeye were easier to seize from the violent water. The fishermen stood on the rocks and used nets with long poles to lift out the thrashing fish. The carcasses were split open and hung to dry on wooden beams, the bright red meat interrupted by lines of pale skin where they'd been sliced widthways at regular intervals. Elena had seen the men at work only from a distance—Dad said that was their land, and their way of doing things. They didn't need little girls interfering. It didn't stop her from being curious.

"What happens to the salmon that escape the nets? Are they free?"

"They are until the bears swipe 'em up."

"What if they get past the bears?"

"They make their way upstream to lay their eggs."

"Then what?"

Dad hesitated. "Then they die."

"All of them?" Elena's mouth had gaped in horror.

"It's a cycle," he said, trying to reassure her. "It's natural."

They would die anyway, even if they escaped the bears and the nets. It didn't seem right for nature to be so unkind.

A sound cut across the noise of the river, like the crunch of a footstep on dry grass, but it was difficult to make it out against the roar of the rushing water. Her spine shivered. She crept off her rock and wriggled through the bushes. Turning toward the graves, she caught a shadow of movement. Then nothing.

She must have imagined it. This cemetery had been still for many years, since the time people referred to as "long ago." It wasn't a spooky place. The grouse didn't think so.

Another noise; her body tensed. This sound was worse, because it had a weight to it that couldn't just be part of her imagination, and it wasn't the light crackle of leaves disturbed by a mouse or the flutter of a bird's wings. It belonged to a larger animal, like a coyote or a bear. She grabbed a small rock from the dust and held it tightly. The headstones were much too small to conceal her, so she squeezed into the bushes near the water's edge, hoping that the animal wouldn't hear her against the river's clamour. She stood so still she barely even breathed.

Swoosh, swoosh, then a pause. She listened to it a few times until she realized it was too consistent for a wild animal. As she peered across the cemetery, fat sticks rose and fell in the brush beyond. Someone was clearing a path.

Ken was a big man who might have been strong once but was now mostly soft. He cleared the bushes and loped toward her until he was close enough to scoop her up. Ken wasn't family but Dad said he was like a brother. Brothers that looked not at all alike.

Rob emerged from the trail behind Ken and dropped his path-clearing stick. The sweat from his efforts stuck his floppy hair to the sides of his face. Rob looked a lot like Dad. They both had square heads and small brown eyes and a few pale freckles on their cheeks. Elena had the freckles too but her hair was dark like Mamma's, not dusty like theirs. Dad's hair was always shaved, except in the few photos they had of him as a kid.

Rob heaved a big sigh. She could tell she'd scared him but she didn't say anything. He'd only deny it. She had Mamma's green eyes and short stature and he had all her worries. He must have sprinted to the village to get Ken. Dad would have had to drive all the way from the mill.

Mamma was waiting at the point where the freshly beaten path met the road. Flustered, she asked Elena so many times if she'd hit her head that Elena wondered if she had. Mamma turned over her arms and legs, examining all the scratches. She eventually decided nothing was serious enough to disturb the doctor on a Sunday.

"I'll drive you to the café," Ken said. "I've got a pretty good first aid kit."

The potholes jolted Elena's strained muscles and made her wince. No doubt Ken was trying to distract her by ramping up the radio, which was playing Alan Jackson's Gone Country. Elena had seen him on TV in his cowboy hat and blonde hair and blue overalls. Ken knew all the words and sang them with extra twang, just to make her laugh. His scrawny blonde ponytail switched back and forth as he bobbed his head with the music. That's what he and Dad had in common. They both made her laugh.

Elena was perched on one of Ken's plastic-wrapped chairs, reeking of pink antiseptic when Mary wobbled in. She threw Elena a suspicious glare as Mamma applied even more ointment to her scrapes. Mary sat down and dropped a dollar on the table. She didn't look that old, but she moved as slowly as the oldest old people in town and talked like there was nothing she hadn't seen before. Ken brought over the pot of coffee, poured her a cup and picked up the coin. The mounted fan clicked and whirred as Mary dabbed her forehead with wispy napkins from the dispenser.

"Getting into trouble, are you?" Mary barely turned her head, so it took Elena a moment to realize she was being addressed. Mamma responded for her.

"Too much trouble, Mary. Her head's always in the clouds."

"In my day we pounded it out of 'em." Mary gave Elena a stern look. Elena shrank back in her chair but Mamma just smiled.

Mary glared at Elena's bloody knees, scrutinizing the damage. "How did you get those?"

"I went to see the Chinese cemetery and ..."

"How the hell did you get down there?"

Mamma looked up but didn't say anything.

"I fell," Elena said quietly.

"From the road?"

She nodded. Mary shook her head.

"Dad goes there to shoot grouse sometimes."

"I bet he does."

"He went down there once, Elena. Don't exaggerate." Mamma dabbed at her stings with a little more force, making her squirm.

"Who's buried there?" Elena asked.

Mary leaned back in a pose that pushed her large stomach into the table. She was the village historian, in charge of the local heritage society and a room in the village hall that was referred to as the Stapleton Museum.

"Those bones are old ... but they ain't that old," she replied. "The first Chinese migrants would've had their bones sent back to China. The folks buried in our cemetery were most likely miners, labourers and small business owners who lived here when Stapleton's Chinatown was established. The Chinese mined a lot of jade in this area. They figured out it was here before the Europeans did."

Mamma got up with a handful of dirty tissues and Band-Aid peels. She disappeared behind the counter to tidy up the first aid kit. Mamma always seemed to feel better when she tidied things, regardless of the reason for the mess.

Mamma had different glosses and powders for every occasion but most women in Stapleton wore makeup as though it had become part of their faces; the same look every day. Mary wore very soft pink lipstick that gleamed against the white ceramic mug as she took another sip of coffee.

"Can you read the writing on the stones?"

"My grandparents were Japanese."

Elena took that to mean no but wasn't completely sure. Mary was Asian but without an accent, just like Mamma was Italian without sounding Italian. Mary's straight black hair didn't quite reach her shoulders and she wore billowy blouses, sometimes with shawls and brooches.

"Why did they send their bones back to China?"

"So their families could pray for them. You gotta take care of the ones who came before you, even after they're gone."

That made sense. Elena hated being forgotten about. She had fought back tears from beneath her tea towel headdress when Dad didn't show up for the nativity play.

"If you don't take care of them when they die, they'll come back and haunt you," Mary said.

Elena's eyes widened: "But the people in the cemetery ..." Mary leaned in and lowered her voice. "Nobody's been praying for those bones, have they?" Elena thought back to the over-grown trail that Ken and Rob had to cut their way through to reach her, and the strange noise she'd heard near the grave-stones. Dad would have told her if it was haunted, wouldn't he?

"The Chinese call them hungry ghosts. They've got long, skinny necks because nobody's been feeding them. In the seventh month of the Chinese calendar, the hungry ghosts come into our world, looking for trouble."

"When is the seventh month?" she asked timidly.

"It's right now."

Elena's eyes and ears were locked onto Mary's words. "Stay away from that cemetery," the older woman said.

"What cemetery?" Logan burst in, skateboard tucked under one arm. Elena had been so engrossed in Mary's tale she hadn't noticed him enter the café. Her best friend had a new haircut; bleached tips ready for the start of grade 5. The hint of intrigue lit up his blue eyes. He was small for his age, like she was, but his energy always put him front and centre.

Logan pointed at Elena's bloody shins and she opened her mouth to tell him all about it but Mary set her cup down loudly and gave Logan a stare that sent him on his way to the ice cream counter.

Mary shook her head silently, but Elena would tell Logan everything at the first opportunity. The ghost in the cemetery would become their mystery to unravel.

⁓ Elena loved her house. They lived close to the river where the land dropped swiftly almost to water level. It was a mobile home with a yard that ran around all four sides of it. Mamma called it their paper house; she worried they would lose it in strong winds or a forest fire or a flood. Mamma said that, when she was little, she lived in a house with stone walls. She said houses like that lasted forever, but Dad wasn't impressed. "Why didn't you stay there, then?" Mamma went quiet and disappeared into the bathroom.

Dad bought 14 Juniper Drive because he fell in love with the view. He reminded Elena of that often, proudly, as he surveyed the land beyond them. The windows at the back of the house looked onto the river and the hilly banks of the reserve. A few hundred people lived on the Stapleton Reserve, but from the windows of their living room Elena found it hard to imagine that anyone lived there at all. The reserve housing was over a ridge further up the hill, so they never had to look at the town, and the town residents never had to look at them.

Elena was curled up next to Mamma, numbed by the television, when Dad came home. Her aches had diminished to dull throbs and the whole room stank of Mamma's healing cream.

Just the sound of Dad opening the door brought his warmth into the house. Elena could hear him in the hallway, taking off his jacket and throwing his keys onto the table. "Elena is grounded again," Mamma said, her eyes still on the screen. "You remember why we moved here, Curtis? You told me it would be safer for the kids." Dad didn't respond.

"Go tell your dad what you did today."

Elena unfolded her body and limped awkwardly into the hallway. Her legs had seized up while she was sitting. She knew how he'd look before she saw him; tired, annoyed. She didn't want to see his disappointment, so she stared at the ugly linoleum—swirly patterns in greys and browns. He'd already removed his heavy boots so she focused on the scruffy bottoms of his jeans as he approached. He came down to her level and cradled his big hands around hers. She brought her eyes up to his.

"Elena", he said softly, "why do you have to get me into so much trouble?"

"Sorry," she whispered.

He cupped her chin gently and brushed his thumb against her cheek, just under a prominent scratch. The delicate links of his gold necklace poked out of his t-shirt, and she hoped that he'd pick her up and pull her to him like he did when she was little.

"What did you do this time?"

He almost laughed when she told him. He probably would have if Mamma weren't listening from the next room. "At least she didn't get hit by a car on the highway," he said, calling through to her. "That's what they call an accident in Vancouver."

"Don't even joke about that," Mamma said. Dad went into the living room and gave Mamma a kiss and she didn't seem so angry anymore.

〜 "I told Mary you shot grouse in the Chinese cemetery."

Elena's betrayal of her dad gnawed at her more than the guilt of having traumatized her mother. The two of them kicked back on rusty lawn chairs with cracked plastic straps,

Dad swigging from a can, relaxed. Mamma drank out of mugs and glasses but Dad always drank out of long cans. Sometimes they slowed him down and he fell out of time and Mamma snapped at him, but that didn't happen very often. He and Elena watched the yellow remains of the sun glint on the shadowy river as it sank behind the reserve hills.

Elena shuffled uncomfortably. "Mary was angry you shot those grouse."

Dad chuckled to himself.

She had more to say, but Dad scrunched his emptied can with one thick hand, laid his head back and closed his eyes. He didn't like to discuss the ins and outs of everything.

CHAPTER 2

Vivian drinks coffee that is too bitter. The first sip always makes her squint. She admires sharpness in tastes, in people. Cutting through the blandness that surrounds her. They are conspiring against her. Whispering in the kitchen corner. Her husband and her son. But they won't win. She always wins.

"Vivian, are you ready to go?"

Her husband. Todd. He sidles up to her and rests his weary old hand on the back of an oak chair. Sometimes she calls him Tom or Tim as though she has forgotten his name. When he corrects her, the wrinkles on his forehead mat together like tangled threads.

She has forgotten his name, really forgotten it, once or twice. A patch of white appeared where it had been, obliterating even the familiar letters. She chose not to blame herself. It is his own fault for being such a pointless human being. She had admired him once, but that was a very long time ago.

"Why do you insist on being so early?" she asks him. "I haven't finished my coffee."

"It's a council meeting. There are procedures."

"Procedures are only for show. You know that."

Todd slowly exhales his frustration. Stuart, wisely, stays

out of it, hovering closer to the door, waiting for his opportunity to make an escape.

Stuart has become quite stocky with age while his father has remained sinewy, but the thick curls he inherited from Vivian will last much longer than Todd's hair, thinned enough to reveal the freckles on his scalp. The boy takes after his father in nature if not in looks; reticent, has to be pushed to act. He can't even leave without seeking her permission.

Vivian hasn't allowed her natural curls or colour to frame her face since her youth. Grey hair on an older woman invites doubts around her competency. Curls are too soft. She keeps her hair short and medium blonde, straight or with a sophisticated wave.

Todd checks his Rolex.

"Do the seconds move more slowly when you watch them?" She can't resist baiting him.

"Please, Vivian, let's not hold everything up."

"But I do hold everything up. That's the point. I have to hold up some very dense walls." She glances across at her son. "Stuart, you would be amazed by the sheer lack of ability in Stapleton nowadays. There's simply no talent here anymore."

"No one can meet your standards, Mom."

Vivian checks her charcoal grey blouse and ivory pants for creases. No pearls; she must remember to put those on.

Todd continues to admire his precious timepiece, a not-so-subtle declaration to the world that he had done well for himself. She, of course, was the one who'd done well for them. Their magazine-page home—with its custom cabinetry, marble countertops, high end appliances and heated bathroom floors—is a drop in the ocean of her success. The crystals on the watch face scatter light across the wall as he checks it again.

"You know I think I admire that watch more than I admire you," she says. "It could sink a few hundred metres and keep ticking, whereas you would just stop."

"Thank you, dear. It's nice to know I'm valued."

Stuart's phone buzzes. He leaps to that thing like a love-struck teenager. If he had any backbone, she'd suspect him of having an affair. She wouldn't judge him for it. His wife is a horror.

Vivian glares at her son. "We could drown that device in a teacup, couldn't we?"

"This is business nowadays, Mom. You would have been glued to yours if they'd been around back then."

She shakes her head and returns to her slow sips of coffee, each one sure to infuriate her husband a little more. These simple pleasures are what keep her going these days.

"Well, it's time I got on the road," Stuart announces finally.

He kisses her on the cheek and she holds his hand tight-ly before releasing him. Todd follows him to the front door as if he needs escorting. Vivian has been playing the hard-of-hearing card for years, so she catches clearly their softly-spoken words.

"She seems like her normal self, Dad."

Vivian doesn't need to look at them to know Todd's reaction. A little shake of the head and a furrowing of wrin-kles. "Sometimes she's fine. Sometimes she isn't. If you saw her more often ..."

Their voices fade, until Stuart utters a dishonest "see you soon" and Todd sends him on his way with best wishes to his family, who they see even less frequently than Stuart. His wife and daughters have no interest in visiting little old Stapleton.

∽ The councillors have waited, as they should. Vivian en-listed every one of them; handpicked them for their malle-ability, coached them and ran their campaigns.

Mayor Kirk George, 65, is the youngest of the group. He owns the gas station. "Business First" was the slogan she chose for him. Not that it mattered. No one else stood for the pos-ition, so he won by acclamation. He's slurping his diet coke as Vivian enters but puts it down the second he spots her. He glances pointedly at Hazel.

Councillor Hazel Carter, aged 76 (who has been having an affair with her neighbour's husband since 1997), dabs the corner of her eye with a tissue. "I only just found out," she mumbles as Vivian and Todd take their seats across the table.

Vivian straightens her brass nameplate and looks at Todd. "Frank," he says, as though that is an adequate explanation. Whatever is going on between Hazel and Frank is presum-ably a personal matter that Todd can update her on after the meeting.

Beside Hazel, Councillor Gerry Martin, 71 (former dealer to the restless youth in his rural Saskatchewan hometown) has a dead look in his eyes, but that is nothing new. Vivian places a hand on her collarbone to touch her pearls, the one constant in all the council meetings she has attended over the years and discovers they aren't there.

The room is stifling and the start of the meeting is de-layed while windows are opened and attendees hit the water cooler before shuffling back to their seats. The large ceiling fan was declared unfixable several years back and deemed unnecessary for replacement. Stapleton's financial situation is precarious, to say the least. Potholes have to become sink-holes before a discussion arises about dipping into the min-uscule maintenance budget.

Vivian and Todd Lennox, both now in their eighties, are the oldest councillors and undoubtedly the wealthiest people in town but Vivian has always strongly resisted Todd's wish to provide the community with any form of financial relief. "A community cannot survive on handouts," she always tells him. "We could at least replace the fan in the council chamber, Vivian." He returns to this point only because of his own personal discomfort during the Monday night meetings. He sweats like a man three times his body weight, even in light-weight chinos and a short-sleeved shirt.

No. One thing leads to another.

Vivian will give back to Stapleton in a much more meaningful way. She can see it as clearly as if it has already come into being. Open doors on Main Street. Contemporary storefront signage with eye-catching window displays. Customers coming and going and chit chatting. A café with a patio and decent coffee. Before she dies, she will turn around the fortunes of this community, not by replacing an old ceiling fan but by once again bringing back industry and jobs to the town. That will be her legacy, as it was always meant to be.

Nonetheless, she can't deny that it's overly warm on this particular evening. The heat creeps into her old body and sticks to her brow. Discomfort turns to drowsiness, and the chattering of the room morphs into indistinct background noise.

Kirk clears his throat and addresses the handful of residents in the public seating area, the predominantly white-haired councillors, the village administrator, the minute-taker and the journalist who is there every week representing the Stapleton Herald (est. 1901). The journalist has gone down in Vivian's estimation since developing the irritating habit of taking notes on a laptop, her manicured fingernails harassing the keys every thirty seconds. Very distracting, particularly for someone like Vivian, who is not nearly as deaf as she pretends to be.

"Before we get into this week's meeting, I would like to say something on a personal note." Kirk clears his throat for a second time. Vivian's jaw clenches. She hasn't been briefed on this little detour.

"We are all deeply saddened by the death of Frank Buchanan who lost his fight with cancer. We would like to send our heartfelt condolences to his family. He has left quite a mark on our community and he won't be forgotten."

Frank isn't … he can't be.

Hazel sniffles loudly. He can't have died. Vivian would've heard. She clears her throat and reaches for her absent pearls, casting her eyes across the room. Heads lowered in respectful silence. She will not let them see her shock. That is one thing she can control. Why did no one tell her?

She visited Frank at the hospital. He was hollow-cheeked and hairless from the failed treatments. A tear fell from her eye. "The ice queen is melting," he said. Then he turned on her, the man who would rather lie with a smile on his face than give an honest opinion. "You'll suffer too, Vivian. Your time is coming." She didn't visit him again.

Kirk moves the meeting along and words bounce around the table—leftovers from the last session, motions to be dealt with—so-and-so's concerns. More keyboard tapping as minutes are recorded. She can't seem to focus. Frank is dead. Did he hate her, in the end?

"All in favour?" Kirk asks.

Vivian hasn't the slightest idea what she's voting on. She mimics her husband because she will have briefed him carefully beforehand. Sweat prickles her brow. Her throat is dry.

The mundane decisions of a typical Monday night are suddenly too much.

Her thoughts of Frank are clear. His sharp green eyes set against his narrow face. Body odour and dirt clinging to his t-shirts. Jeans with worn-out knees. A rule breaker who could be relied upon, most of the time.

They weren't colleagues, not exactly. Nobody in the town would've described them as friends, though few people knew her as well as he did. Frank was much younger but they were both Stapletonians born and raised. It was what they went through, the two of them, that brought them together and then broke them apart.

They would all hate her if they ever found out. They wouldn't understand that everything she did was for their own good. Frank hadn't forgiven her, but at least he understood the difference between what is right morally, theoretically, and what is right in a particular moment in time.

CHAPTER 3

1 9 9 4

"MAYBE WE COULD go inside first? He might be in there."
Elena desperately wanted to know what lay behind the walls
that made Mamma lift her nose up and hurry by.

"No, he'll be around the back."

"But what if we just check inside first …"

Logan was already making his way through the side gate,
NO FEAR stamped on his t-shirt and his neon green baseball
cap on backwards. Elena's hair was pulled back in a scrunchie
of the same shade. She followed him around the building and
into the sprawling mess of Frank's yard. They had to tread
carefully to avoid the metal bones of long-lost machines.

At the far end of the yard, a rickety saw rigged to an old
generator moved mechanically back and forth, rocking its
wooden frame and cutting a perfect line through a large boulder. It wasn't like the industrial equipment Elena had seen at
construction sites, or even the shiny blades that Dad fixated
on at DIY stores. This contraption reminded her of the time
Dad tried to temporarily repair the coffee table leg with gaf-
fer tape. She teetered forwards and backwards beside the
blade, mimicking its motion.

She didn't notice Frank until he leaned down beside her

and his knees cracked. There were oil stains on his jean shirt. The pale blue truck he'd been driving when Rob tried to hitch a ride with him was parked just behind them, its hood propped up and its guts littered on the grass.

"Y'know what that rock is, kiddo?"

She paused for a moment, remembering Mary's story about the Chinese miners. "Is it jade?"

Frank grinned. "You've seen this before," he said, impressed. She hadn't seen anything like it before but nodded anyway. She couldn't tell the difference in the cut from one motion to the next—the blade didn't appear to be making any progress.

"The water running off the rock is keeping the saw blade cool. Jade is harder than steel. It's very tough to cut through it. You make yourself that tough kid and life will be easy."

Elena drew her eyes away from the motion. Frank had been watching her as she'd been watching the blade. Even as she stared back at him now, he didn't look away.

"Eventually, the rock will split into two and we'll see the face of the jade. Unlike people's faces, if you polish it up enough, you'll always get a stunner." Frank winked.

"Where did you get the jade from?" she asked.

He pointed to the foothills. They looked blue because they were so far away. Frank leaned forward, cupped his hands at the base of his back and stumbled around as if he was lugging something incredibly heavy. "I carried it down here myself," he said in a deep voice. "I had to fight off five grizzlies, and I almost dropped it when I tried to scratch my ass." The kids laughed and Logan had to jump out of the way before Frank lurched into him.

Frank fumbled in his pockets and produced two tiny jade turtles. "Got something for you. Made them myself. They're good luck."

Logan stuffed his turtle straight into his pocket, but Elena studied hers, the lines of the turtle's shell; its four stumpy legs. It must've taken ages to carve a perfect little turtle out of such a hard rock.

She turned it over and examined its belly. The tiny print read: MADE IN CHINA. She looked up at Frank.

"You're welcome," he said.

She read the little letters again. It didn't really matter, did it? He was just trying to do something nice. She wrapped the turtle carefully in a tissue before tucking it into the pocket of her jean cut-offs.

"Uncle Frank," Logan announced in a serious tone, "we're going to find out if there are ghosts in the Chinese Cemetery."

"Awesome!"

"Can you help us?"

"Sure! What do you need?"

Frank was very enthusiastic about being their ghost tour guide, but Elena knew sooner or later he'd ask if Mamma was okay with it. "She already said yes," Elena mumbled as soon as he brought it up. It was her turn to be dishonest. Frank pulled a surprised look but he accepted it and moved on.

"The Inn is haunted y'know. By two restless souls. People like to say Stapleton is a quiet town, but it was different when my great-great grandfather established this inn. Back then you had to be tough to survive."

Logan bounced on the spot in his black sneakers. "Tell her about the ghosts."

"Two brothers were murdered in their beds. They haven't left that room since."

Frank pointed at an upstairs window. The ghosts didn't appear behind the glass to wave or stare back, but Logan pointed too and muttered: "I heard them once, making the floorboards creak when no one else was in the room." Elena could picture them in the darkness beyond the window— long ghostly faces shadowed by their broad-rimmed hats.

Stapleton would have been a row of wooden shacks back then, surrounded by miners' tents. Elena had seen photos in the museum. The Inn stood out with its name painted large in capital letters above the long veranda. Whenever Frank talked about the Stapleton Inn, his face lit up and he pulled his shoulders back and Elena thought about how grand it must have been.

"The brothers were looking for their uncle when they arrived in Stapleton," Frank said. "Some miners told them typhoid killed him on the journey up, but those boys didn't buy it. Their uncle was bringing up supplies to build Stapleton's first general store. The brothers got close enough to the truth of what happened to him to end up dead themselves. The general store was built and the owner made more money than most of the miners. Those brothers are so angry about it, they still won't leave the Inn."

"Uncle Frank even had a priest in there who couldn't chase them out," Logan said proudly because he knew his uncle had all the best stories.

Elena thought about the hanging tree that still stood by the river, a short walk from the Stapleton Cemetery. Local legend held that the bodies of criminals and a few rebellious Natives swung from that tree during the Gold Rush. Elena thought it was the spookiest thing around and always hurried past its gnarled old limbs.

"Did the murderers get caught?"

Frank shook his head. "The brothers didn't have people out here who knew them, who would fight for them. That's how life was in those days." Frank looked at their rapt faces. "Sometimes it still is."

❧ "Can I hang out with Logan tomorrow?"

"Where? What time?"

"At the park." Elena hesitated. "At night."

Mamma put down the salad spinner. Rob always complained about having to eat lettuce and Elena would pick out the croutons, but Caesar salad remained a summer staple in Mamma's kitchen.

"Why do you two want to go to the park at night?"

"To look at the stars."

"Be back by 7 pm."

"But it won't be dark …"

"7 pm. That's my best offer."

Elena nodded and slipped around the corner into the living room before Mamma changed her mind.

"Stop blocking the TV."

Dad didn't even turn his head. She hopped onto the sofa next to him as orange chests and tight white legs sprinted down the field and crashed into their opponents. The football commentary came out of the walls in surround sound.

Dad had bought the big screen and fancy speakers a few months ago. He and Ken spent half a day setting it all up, Ken smoking, Dad drinking and the pair of them taking it in turns to decipher the manual. When they'd finished, Elena, Rob and Mamma were allowed to come in and admire their handiwork. Dad said the BC Lions were going to take home the cup this year; that's why they needed the big TV. Mamma said it made the room look smaller.

When Ken left, Mamma and Dad fought about money. You could hear everything in their little home. Elena hated hearing them fight.

The commentator announced a touchdown. Dad rose from his chair and roared at the screen. He sank down into the sofa again, his face split in a grin.

When the ads rolled in, he turned to Elena, finger pointing. "I told you. This is our year." He kissed her head and asked her to get him a cold can.

∽ Frank pulled out a flashlight but not to help them see. He put it under his chin and made a wavering "ooooooh" sound that was supposed to be creepy. Enough daylight remained as the sun gradually sank towards the horizon. Logan had been disappointed when Elena told him about her curfew, but he agreed 7 pm was better than nothing.

Broken branches marked the path Ken and Rob had carved out a few days earlier. The dry summer had turned the grasses and leafy plants brittle and brown. The sagebrush smelled sweet and comforting.

"There's a lot of strange happenings in these parts," Frank murmured ominously from behind them. "The Natives got a lot of stories to tell. But I want to know what you two found out about these ghosts." He cast the flashlight around chaotically, to no effect, before switching it off.

"They're called hungry ghosts, and they come out from hell at this time of year," Elena explained.

"Why's that?"

"Because nobody's been feeding them."

"Is that right? Is there no food in hell?"

"There is, but it's gross food."

"Gross like human brains?"

"Yeah."

The bushes grew thicker on both sides of the path and sewed them into single file. Elena wore the most inconspicuous clothes she owned; a dark purple t-shirt and black leggings. Logan marched ahead in a bright red Chicago Bulls shirt. It wasn't as if they would actually see anything worth hiding from, but the anticipation gripped her just the same. Something scuttled through the leaves. Frank wailed faintly but he didn't scare her.

The trail opened up again by the headstones. The markers stood in silent rows, casting long shadows. Elena and Logan approached the first graves together, cautiously. Logan touched one stone very delicately, as though a firm push might tip it over and wake the dead.

They looked across the empty cemetery, neither of them wanting to rush ahead in case there was any truth to Mary's tale. The river rumbled through the quiet. No sign of ghosts.

Logan turned to her. "Where were you when you saw something?"

An eerie cry, higher than the river's noise, echoed across the cemetery. Logan giggled, then spun around to see if Frank was responsible. Frank was behind them, plucking sagebrush leaves and inhaling the scent.

Something was out there, in the gloom that cloaked the far side of the cemetery. Elena took a few steps forward because they were supposed to be investigating but she didn't really want to find out what had made the sound. Logan matched her move, crunching gravel and long grass.

They both saw it. Creeping through the bushes that blocked the river. White eyes, tiny at first, glowing brighter as a shadowy body emerged. The creature hissed, deep and low. Logan's body slipped backwards out of the corner of Elena's eye, but she couldn't move. Fear gripped her so tightly she couldn't even turn her head. It slunk closer. It looked like a large person, except for its long neck. Elena's entire body went cold, as if she'd jumped in an icy lake and her toes couldn't find the bottom.

"Whatcha lookin at?" Frank bellowed behind them.

The figure shrank back before vanishing into the foliage. Frank pushed Logan further forward, but he grabbed Frank's sleeve and spun himself around so his uncle was between him and the gravestones.

"We saw something ... over there." Logan pointed at the bushes by the river's edge.

"Probably just a coyote."

The children looked at each other nervously.

Frank leaned towards his nephew. "D'you think it was a ghost?"

"Mary said if the ghosts see you, they'll put a curse on you," Logan whispered.

Frank chuckled. "That's nothing. I heard a story about this one guy who saw a ghost out by Emmet Lake ..."

"... We should go," Logan said, interrupting. "Elena has to be home by seven."

"We've got a few minutes." Frank checked his watch. "But I guess if you guys are too chicken ..."

"... We're not chicken! We're here, aren't we?" Logan said.

Frank shrugged. "I gotta get going anyway. If I leave the regulars to run the Inn for too long, it'll be a lot scarier than this place when I get back."

The kids rushed back to the truck as though the path was too hot for their feet to touch the ground. The truck's engine roaring to life was a welcome sound but Elena couldn't begin to relax until her mom opened the front door.

"How was the park?" she asked. Elena stuttered: "Fine."

Dad wasn't home. The house wasn't properly warm until he came home. After her experience at the cemetery, she couldn't wait to see him. He would crack open a can, relax on the couch and remind her that ghosts only existed in movies. She waited for the sound of his key in the lock and the stomp of his boots on the doorstep as he kicked off the dirt. Mamma hated dirt in the house. She could see dirt where no one else could.

~ They all heard the bang. It felt close and yet sounded distant, like thunder. They peered out of the windows but there was nothing to see except shadowy houses in the twilight.

Others heard it and stepped out onto the street. The adults waved at each other. Nodded. Crossed the road and chatted. No one knew what it was or where it had come from. After a couple of minutes, they headed back inside and closed their doors. Rob returned to his shoot-em-up game and Elena curled up beside Mamma, who was watching her favourite cop show. Elena couldn't follow the drama. Her heart was pounding. She couldn't stop thinking about the curse.

~ There was a sudden burst of knocking on the door. Maybe Dad lost his keys. Elena dashed into the hallway, opened the door, ready to propel herself into his big arms.

A heavy young man filled the doorway. The whites of his pupils popped eerily against his skin, powdered with ash that also covered his clothes. He coughed violently, and with each gasp his body began to droop slowly in on itself. The stench of burning filled Elena's nostrils.

She knew the man. He had come to the house before, although he never came inside. He lived on the reserve and drove Dad home from work once when the truck broke down. Elena had opened the door on that occasion too. He'd smiled at her then from his truck, a warm smile that spread across his face. His name was Brandon.

"Brandon," she squeaked. He didn't seem to hear her.

He unfurled his fingers. They were burnt and blistering. She followed the march of his receded jacket sleeve with her eyes. It was charred up to his elbow, the skin beneath it seared red. He opened his mouth to speak, then closed it again. She watched a tear slip away from him, unattached, as if he wasn't aware that it had left his eye. Another tear followed and she realized her own eyes were stinging.

Elena touched his wrist very gently; the red, raw skin. She wanted to see if he could feel anything. He didn't even flinch. She took his good arm and led him into the kitchen. The water from the kitchen faucet ran ice cold; that would be good for him, she thought, but he wouldn't drink. She pulled a bag of ice out of the freezer, wrapped it in a tea towel and tried to present it to him.

"Elena, what are you doing ...?" Mamma was in the doorway. Her words emptied out when she saw Brandon. "Go see your brother."

"But ..."

"... Now! And tell him to get off the phone."

Rob threw his dirty socks at Elena. He didn't like to be interrupted when he was talking to Ashley, his girlfriend. Even the sound of Elena's voice in the background embarrassed him when he was talking to Ashley. Elena tried to tell him about the burnt man, but he wouldn't listen. Then they heard the chop-chop of helicopter blades passing over their thin roof. Rob raced through the hallway and into the kitchen. Elena scuttled after him. She could hear Brandon coughing.

Brandon was speaking very softly when they entered. "Curtis was ahead of me and then he disappeared ..."

Elena felt certain as she watched them, Brandon in shock and Mamma trying to reach out to him, that it was the curse. It was real. It had torn through the mill, and now Dad was missing.

"What do you mean he disappeared?" Mamma panicked. Brandon started coughing again and Mamma looked desperate enough to grab hold of him and try to shake the words out. Then she spotted Elena in the doorway and picked up the phone to call an ambulance.

Loud voices disturbed the quiet road. Sirens grew until they pierced their paper-thin walls. Elena put her windbreaker and sneakers on. She had to find him. It was all her fault.

Elena slipped out while Mamma helped Brandon drink some water. A few neighbours were standing on the street again, listening to the little planes coming in overhead, the kind that dump water on forest fires. No one seemed to notice as she ran past them and headed up the steep adjoining street.

Logan's house was the second in a row of blue-grey townhouses. His bedroom window faced the street; it had a skateboard decal in the bottom corner. She knocked on the front door, and then again, louder. Logan opened the door enough for her to see his frightened face. He was thinking it too. The curse. She opened her mouth to speak, but he slammed the door shut before any words came out.

She didn't want to cry on his doorstep, so she ran up the hill and past the houses. Mary would know what to do, but she didn't know where Mary lived. She didn't have the courage to return to the cemetery and face the ghost alone.

Her name echoed from the bottom of the hill; Rob yelling, his voice scraping. He'd seen her. She couldn't go back, not until she'd figured out a solution. Mamma and Rob wouldn't understand about the curse. She caught her leggings on barbed wire as she disappeared into the long grass.

Clouds hid the moon and there were no lights in the fields. Darkness was descending quickly. The ground was uneven and it forced her to move slowly. She stepped in something soft; fresh cow dung, she guessed. Cows grazed up here sometimes but there was no sign of them now. Maybe they had somewhere else to go at night. She was supposed to be at home. Facing Mamma's anger was better than being alone out here. The stillness was starting to frighten her. She looked around and could no longer see the lights of her community. Behind her had to be the way back; that was the way she had come.

After a few minutes, she reached an old barn where a barn should not have been. There were no structures of any kind when she walked into the fields. The walls of the barn were made of wooden boards that supported a v-shaped, thin metal roof. Elena had played at the top of Logan's hill before but she'd never come this far. She doubled back, certain this time that home had to be behind her.

She took small steps to make sure she was travelling in a straight line. The grass was longer in some areas, short in others; shaved thin by animals. It smelled like manure. The lights on Douglas Street did not emerge from the darkness.

Stars appeared and disappeared as the clouds shifted. The night got cooler. She zipped her jacket up to her chin. Her legs grew tired, her eyelids heavy. It felt as though hours had slipped away as she stumbled onwards through the cold air.

In the distance was a barn. The same barn.

There had to be a way back; why couldn't she find it? In the blackness that surrounded her she imagined the white eyes she'd seen at the cemetery. She was in the semi-wild now; the space between the community and the wilderness, and she didn't know this place. The night was hiding her home, and it could have been hiding other things, cursed things.

The wind picked up and howled through the eaves of the barn as soon as she shut the door behind her. Hay was packed up at the back but she couldn't curl up on it for fear of discovering a rats' nest. Dad had told her once that vermin liked to make their homes in hay. He should have come home with Brandon.

Had Dad heard the bang? Had the flames licked at his arms and peeled away the skin? She found a corner near the door and tried not to think too much. She brought her knees up to her chest and rested her head against the wooden wall, eyes half open until they had to close.

It was a long night. Her neck ached and it gripped her shoulders like long fingers digging under her skin. Every time she drifted off, the wind broke through the quiet and startled her awake. Distant noises drew closer. Ferocious creatures disturbed her erratic dreams. Bears, cougars, hungry ghosts. She worried her breathing was too loud. She tried to breathe more softly. If she moved an inch she'd give herself away; her presence would be revealed to whatever might be lying in wait outside.

Scraps of dreams and the sounds of the night were hard to separate. Elena thought she'd heard voices too, and vehicle engines, planes, tires rolling over dirt, but she couldn't be sure. Dad said ranchers were hard-working but he never said they were kind. They had guns; she knew that. Dad had told her stories about hunters shooting other people by accident. They could mistake her for an animal in the darkness. She was too afraid to do anything but wait for morning to come.

◇ The hanging tree had a distinctive twist. There was a knot in one of the upper limbs where the dying left their sins in an attempt to get closer to heaven. That's what people used to think, according to the little plaque positioned in front of it for the tourists that never came. The tree was down by the river, near the new cemetery, but at that moment it was also outside the barn door. She could hear the knotted limb creaking in the wind. If it broke, all the rottenness that was inside it would fall down on her and the curse would never be lifted.

Her neck was in the noose and many people came to judge. The people of this town. They all knew what she had done. She had released the curse. She had ruined everything. The rope tightened and the tree creaked and her little legs kicked around in the weightless air and nobody came to rescue her.

~ Daylight broke through the barn door. Elena woke with her head resting on the floor where the rats could crawl over her and chew her long hair. She sprang up and brushed her hands against her head, swatting away imagined vermin.

Fog spooled across the fields like lost clouds. She pulled her cold hands up inside her jacket sleeves and moved quickly through the dew.

There was a small log house nearby with a green roof. She hadn't spotted it was when she stumbled into the barn the night before. The front door was open a crack and it was dark inside. She didn't know whom she might find, out here in the semi-wild. She sprinted to the nearest fence and spun around to make sure she wasn't being watched.

With the sunlight to guide her, it didn't take long to reach the top of Logan's street. She was so relieved to see it that she propelled herself out of the wildness and onto the top of the road in one quick burst. She half-walked, half-skipped down the asphalt, but there was a strange kind of quiet around her; the kind of stillness she sometimes sensed when she'd fallen behind on hikes in the forest. It was exactly how she felt when she was completely alone.

By the time she laid eyes on their little house, it hardly

mattered that Mamma would be furious. Elena opened the front door and tiptoed inside, readying herself for Mamma's tirade and the joy of seeing them all again. Dad would be home, too. They would've found him by now.

"Mamma?" she called out. "Rob? Dad?"

The house was quiet. No one was in the living room or the kitchen. The bathroom door was open and the light was off. She peeked into her parents' bedroom. Empty. Rob was not at his desk armed with his game controller. The emptiness rattled her but she knew they were out looking for her, worried sick.

Her stomach was so empty it hurt. Two strawberry yoghurts and a leftover slice of Hawaiian pizza helped. She splashed water on her face, changed her clothes, brushed her teeth and hair so at least she would look presentable when Mamma saw her. She intended to go straight to Ken's café because he would know where they were, but she sat down on the sofa for a second, curled up and fell asleep.

When she woke she checked the clock on the mantelpiece—11 am. Everyone would be awake now, and the café would be open. Ken was probably worried, too, but he would be kind. Maybe he'd help her explain things, make Mamma understand that she ran away because she was scared.

Elena pulled her bicycle out of the shed and sped to Main Street. The wind had picked up again and it pummelled her so badly that it felt like she was merely steadying herself against it instead of moving forward. Not a single car drove past her. No one strolled by and said, "Mornin'," the way people in Stapleton always did.

She tried the handle on Ken's café door three times, but it wouldn't budge. Through the window the interior was dark, the tables empty. She hammered on the glass, but there was no answer. The wind barrelled down the street and it carried a smell that made Elena shudder. Smoke.

Fear of the curse filtered back into her mind and the more she tried to ignore it the bigger it got. The supermarket was closed. So was the pharmacy and the restaurant. The lights were off in the salon and the doors were locked. Sunlight touched the curved metal of the machines behind the large windows, but nobody occupied the chairs beneath them. Elena looked closer and caught what might have been a shadow pass by a doorway in the back. She struck her knuckles against the glass, but no one was there.

She began knocking on doors: politely at first, and only houses of school friends or family acquaintances. Then, more frantically at the homes of strangers. THUMP. A fat tabby descended from a fence and crept across someone's yard.

"Hello!" she shouted down a deserted street. "Hello! Is anyone there?"

A historic house stood on the corner with beautiful hanging baskets on the veranda, and beside it was a row of newer homes with tan sidings and cedar hedges. Every window and door was closed. Her calls echoed down the lanes that shot off Main Street in neat rows.

She circled back and rolled her bike down the middle of Main Street, waiting for a car to honk. Then, because it was better than crying, she sat on the white dotted line, stretched out her legs and pushed her feet into a large pothole. If anyone saw her sitting in the middle of the road, even a Stapleton road, they'd come and yell at her.

It was the worst kind of nightmare because there was no one to go to for help. They were all gone. She wiped her arm against her eyes. The hungry ghost was supposed to take her, but instead it took everyone else.

"Grow up, Elena," Rob would tell her. "Stop crying."

She stood up and threw her bike against the tarmac just to hear it clatter against the quiet. She wanted the ground to rumble, faintly at first and then louder. The rumble would bulge into the squeals and hisses of the freight trains that crawled past Stapleton at regular intervals, day and night. She hadn't heard them all morning.

⁓ The low rumble of a vehicle approaching should have been a happy sound. A relief. But who would travel through a cursed town?

Elena slipped behind the church fence and sent up a quick prayer. "Dear God. I'm sorry. Amen." He already knew the rest. Rob and Dad didn't think prayers worked but Mamma did. She hoped Mamma was right.

Through the cracks in the fence she could see a truck approaching, not the kind of truck that usually rolled through Stapleton. It was muddy green and rugged. She expected it to rumble past her down the street but it stopped right there in front of the church. She slipped along the fence and into the bushes beside the church.

Doors opened. Boots hit the ground. Footsteps coming closer. A clatter; the spinning of her bike tire. That's why they stopped. They had seen her bike from the road. Movement by the fence. The church gate opened with a rusty squeak.

"Elena?"

They knew her name.

"There's nothing to be afraid of. You're not in any trouble. We just want to get you back to your mom. She's very worried."

She could've seen his face if she'd dared to look. A snap of a twig and they would hear her. Footsteps entered the neighbour's yard. "Elena," another voice called out. She was surrounded. Two more men lingered on the sidewalk while the others moved around the grounds. One went inside the church and repeated her name as he scoured the space between the pews.

The men on the sidewalk were close enough that she could have reached out and touched their heavy boots.

"Do you think he took her?" one asked in a hushed voice.

"Guys on the run don't take their kids with them. She's just scared. She'll show up."

She fought the urge to abandon her hiding spot and demand to know what they were talking about. They wouldn't tell her anything. Adults never did. They must have been referring to Dad, which meant he was hiding from them, too. She wished there was a way she could reach him.

The soldier in the church came back out again and stretched her name out in a long, low call from the front steps. "Eleeeeeenaaaaaa." She wanted to tell him to stop using it. He didn't know her. Another soldier picked up her bike and threw it in their big truck. Then they all left, as suddenly as they came.

Elena stayed in the hedge for a while, scrunched up with her legs cramped. When it hurt too much to remain there any longer, she crawled out cautiously. She hadn't counted them. One could easily have stayed behind, lying in wait like a hunter tracking a deer through the forest. She stood up to full height. No one charged at her. No trucks flew down the street towards her. She didn't trust those men, but they knew where Mamma was. She had no choice. She had to go where they had gone.

CHAPTER 4

2 0 1 8

Stapleton used to be a much more vibrant place. Sometimes Vivian forgets just how much they have lost, and she chalks it up to old age when she asks Todd if he'd like to go for dinner at the restaurant or to a show at the tiny theatre that hasn't been lit up since she was a girl.

On days when everything appears clear, she knows just as well as everybody else that daily social interactions can now only be found at the post office, the gas station and the Inn. Vivian hasn't stepped inside the Inn for 25 years (for reasons she keeps to herself) but she still makes frequent stops at the gas station.

The coffee is brown water with a mild chemical bite to it and the aisles are stacked full of shiny, colourful junk. Bread that lasts forever and cans of chunky soup, instant oatmeal and piles of chips and candy. She knows a few old bachelors who do all their shopping at the gas station. She's quite sure none of them use their ovens, except perhaps to store their tax returns.

Rhonda is at her post behind the counter in her usual attire: old jeans and a sweatshirt swathed in dog fur. She has the voice of a chain smoker and the grace of a long-distance trucker but Vivian likes her. Rhonda doesn't pretend to be anyone else. She just is. That makes her an easy sort of person to understand.

Vivian picks up a packet of individually foil-wrapped chocolates and two scratch cards and places them on the counter. "How are you today, Rhonda?"

"Oh, you know …" Rhonda grumbles about her lazy husband who spends hours at the Inn drinking away his newly-acquired pension. Up until a couple of months ago, Rhonda's husband was one of the few people still employed in Stapleton. He was the village's maintenance manager, and they had struggled to find someone to replace him. No one is looking for work in Stapleton these days. Those people left long ago.

Vivian pushes a scratch card in Rhonda's direction. "If you win, don't give him a cent." Rhonda takes a good look at the gold-lettered promise. JACKPOT. Relationships with people who see things are invaluable in a small town.

Their exchange is interrupted by the sound of a car pulling up out front. Not an unusual sound at a gas station, but they both instinctively do the Stapleton turn-and-stare. Vivian hmms in surprise. It's a new car. An Audi? She can't quite see the logo and she doesn't want to gawk like some country bumpkin. The vehicle is sleek and black and businesslike. Or at least it would be, if it hadn't just been driven through the dust of the semi-desert.

A young man gets out. Well, he's probably in his forties, but that's a good couple of generations younger than most in this town. Black shirt, sleeves rolled up for fashion not work, and tight beige pants. He must be lost. Probably took a wrong turn on the highway while he was tapping away on his phone.

Vivian pulls her shoulders back and straightens the amber beads resting on her olive silk blouse. She steps away from the counter as if to leave, though that's the last thing on her mind. He pulls the door marked PUSH. She forgives him. He's probably tired after all that driving. Black hair left long enough on the top to be tousled. Sharp green eyes, clean shaven at his slender jaw. Average height; defined upper body muscles suggest he works out but he remains on the slim side. Leather shoes. Italian perhaps? Custom-made certainly. Details that would be lost on Rhonda.

"Long drive?" Vivian asks casually.

"Not too far."

There's a warm resonance to his voice, friendly and self-assured, and a familiarity in his expression.

"Are you visiting or just passing through?"

"I'm visiting."

"Welcome to our community."

"Thank you." He smiles politely as he makes his way over to the counter.

Vivian takes another step towards the door, but she picks up a local paper and examines the front cover. GEARING UP FOR A GIANT FALL FAIR. "Giant," as everyone knows, refers to the anticipated size of the locally grown vegetable entries.

"This is the most expensive gas I've seen outside Vancouver," she hears him remark. Vivian can't help shooting a glance in his direction.

"It's 50 kilometres till the next pump." Rhonda replies flatly, and Vivian is grateful that she didn't add, as she has before: "Go ahead. See how far you get." Rhonda could never comprehend the potential value of this presumably wealthy stranger who appears to be in some way connected to their one-foot-in-the-grave town.

The young man asks about coffee, and Rhonda directs him to the corner of the store, where there are a couple of little tables, a coffee machine and a basket of plastic-wrapped muffins. A wall-mounted lottery screen flashes life-changing numbers.

"Did you win?" Vivian hears him ask somebody. She lowers her paper and peeks between the metal racks. Pam, Frank's sister, heaves herself out of a chair, and the stranger's jaw drops.

"Pam?"

He knows Pam, of all people! He didn't recognize her at first. She has changed.

As a young woman, Pam was one of those adrenaline junkies. All the women who lived in Stapleton in the '80s and early '90s attended at least one of her Jazzercise or aerobics classes at some point. Then came the incident at the mill and like the town, Pam hit a slump. But as the town contracted, she expanded. Vivian has absolutely no sympathy for such acts of self-neglect, and as a rule avoids Pam. But now, she moves closer.

Vivian looks on with fascination as Pam gives the young man a damning stare. "That property's been in my family for generations. You better look after it."

The man with the flashy car has no words for Pam. She throws down her useless lottery slip and reaches for her purse.

Vivian adopts a passive expression and slips out before anyone mistakes her for a common snoop. It's time she got home to feed her French bulldog, Cherie, because Todd never cooks Cherie's meals properly, and there are some things that man just can't seem to learn no matter how many times he is corrected.

～ Todd does most of the cooking now because he doesn't think she's capable. That's fine. She is tired of cooking for him. She cooks dinner when she feels like it and only left the gas on once just for a minute.

Todd can't roast a piece of meat without using a thermometer to guarantee it's done to perfection. Cooking was one of the things he took an interest in when he hit middle age, along with fine wine. The money was really coming in back then. They jetted off to upmarket destinations and kept company with a better sort of person. It was clear he felt like a small-town hick, even though it was he who had been born and raised in a Vancouver suburb and Vivian who had grown up in a coal mining backwater. His father managed a car dealership that did well enough. Vivian's father did infinitely better. She came from Stapleton's most prominent family and was sent off to private schools from a young age. She knew everything there was to know about life's finer things.

Only recently has Vivian begun to understand her husband's fear of appearing inadequate. Along with the frailties of age come the judgments of others than can erode one's confidence. She knows she has little slips—a consequence of being old. She also knows it's more than that; more confusing and frustrating and terrifying than she lets on. There are only so many times she can put off doctors' visits before Todd will drag her there.

"What do you think of the beef?" he asks her.

He's marinated it in something. He wants her to guess what. She lets a smile slip across her mouth as she chews. "Excellent," she says, because after all, he has gone to the effort of cooking it. She has never derived the same degree of joy from eating that other people seem to experience. There is a specific spice she can identify, but what is it called? Its name has escaped her. She changes the subject before he has a chance to engage her in a guess-the-spice game.

"Have you spoken to the ..." What's the word? She fumbles for it and finds something. "The reference people."

"Who?"

"The reference people, Todd!"

He looks at her blankly. She huffs at him. Then it comes to her, the word.

"Refuse. You know what I meant. Have you spoken to the refuse people?"

"You asked me that before we sat down."

She doesn't remember. She wonders if he's lying; if he's begun to use her little slips as a way to control and belittle her. "Do we have a deal with them or not?"

"Not yet, Vivian. As you know, these things take time."

"There's always a way to speed things along."

"It doesn't work like that these days. We have to be patient. They'll come through. We need to give them time."

"We don't have time, and I sure as hell don't trust the rest of the council to push this through without us. This could be Stapleton's last chance and who knows how long you and I have got left?"

She puts her fork down and pouts at the French bulldog, who grunts loudly in her sleep from her spot on the sofa. Sometimes Vivian feels that dog is her closest companion in this world. Cherie is old, too, but that allows her the dignity of sleeping most of the time, a luxury Vivian doesn't have.

"I'm not hungry," Vivian declares, leaving most of her meal on her plate. She hobbles over to the sofa. Cherie shuffles out of sleep and onto Vivian's lap before nodding off again.

Vivian picks up her knitting. She hates knitting. Always

has. The mayor's wife, Carol, who is excruciatingly enthusiastic about everything, is running a campaign to send knitted blankets to refugees. Vivian tried to explain that a blanket she purchased would do a much better job of keeping someone warm, but Carol found her an extra set of needles and some wool so she could "take part."

Vivian is just about ready to stab Carol with her knitting needles. She has made so many mistakes she could have knitted ten blankets in the time it has taken to undo stitches and start again. If Vivian takes something on, though, she sees it through. This blanket will be perfect, eventually. She picks up the shamefully small beginnings and the rhythmic clicks become slower and slower until she, too, falls asleep.

~~> Vivian rifles through old mail stuffed into the narrow drawers of the hallway table. Todd has hidden the car keys again. He says there's a problem with the engine and he's going to get it fixed. He's always been a terrible liar but he's getting sly in his old age. It's all she can do to leave the house without him.

Abandoning the key search, she grabs her beige jacket to guard against the early morning chill. Todd hears her from the kitchen. "Wait. I'll come with you."

"I can manage a walk to the post office on my own."

She slams the door behind her before he can respond.

The route to her planned destination sometimes eludes her. The network of little roads connects in unexpected ways. The grinding of metal on metal grows louder as a freight train passes and she knows she can't be that far off course.

The quiet residential street is a mix of cared for older homes and a string of others that have been boarded up. She turns a corner and stops abruptly. The stranger she met at the

gas station is standing in front of Pam's house and he's holding something in his hand. Dressed handsomely again in
jeans and a pressed white shirt, he hasn't noticed her.

He seems captivated by the house and Vivian wonders if
there's someone inside looking out at him. She checks her
watch: 11:30 am. It's bingo day. Pam will be at the community hall with the other gamblers. She can't think of anyone
else who would be inside the home. Pam's son Logan hasn't
been seen in Stapleton for many years.

It is a rock, in his hand. He turns it over a couple of times
before rolling his arm back and pitching it through the front
window. An explosion of glass, then a dull thud as the rock
drops into the room.

Vivian clacks her cane on the tarmac. The stranger stumbles backwards and spins around, as if her presence is more
shocking than his mischief.

"Vandalising our town already?" she calls out to him as
she approaches.

He looks at her, mouth half-open. "I'm sorry ... I don't
know what I was thinking."

"You might want to come up with a better explanation
before you talk to Pam."

"Pam?"

"Yes, that's Pam's window. Pam's house."

The man stares back at the house in disbelief. "No. This
was the Petersons' house, and it's obviously been abandoned."

"Oh yes, it was the Petersons' house, but that was a long
time ago. Before the incident at the mill. Now it's Pam's
house."

"It can't be. It looks ..."

His eyes scan the buckling roof shingles and the sloping
front entrance with the rotting steps. The homes on either

side are boarded up. The yard is a dense mat of weeds, dead and living, slowly choking each other.

Vivian pokes her stick at the foliage. "Pam has never been a particularly talented gardener." She turns to the young man, waiting for a better explanation, but he's fixated on the jagged hole he just created in Pam's living room window.

Vivian changes tack. "Everybody knows Mr. Peterson was a ... difficult ... person."

The man steps back a couple of feet, running one hand through his thick black hair. He finally faces Vivian. "It's not an excuse, but I went to school with Kyle, his oldest boy, and it was hell. Kyle shot me with a pellet gun out of that window once. Old Man Peterson was there beside him laughing and there was nothing I could do except run."

Vivian shakes her head. "Nobody ever was able to put Mr. Peterson in his place."

"I heard he died." No pity in the stranger's voice.

"Yes, he did." She stalls. It's a topic she doesn't like to discuss. "I'm Vivian Lennox."

She puts out a hand which he shakes firmly.

"Dean Masset."

Masset. She tries to place the name. It doesn't ring any bells, but names don't stick the way they used to.

"Tell Pam you were driving by and you saw two kids causing trouble. You feel responsible because if you had been paying more attention you might've been able to stop them. Offer to pay for the damage. She'll refuse at first but if you offer again, she'll let you pay for it. She doesn't have much."

"Thank you. Not everyone would be so understanding."

Vivian waves her hand airily. "I'm old. I live vicariously through the mistakes of others. And in small communities, we have to help each other out when we can."

She's thrilled to have him feeling indebted to her so quickly. That's the secret to success in business and in life. Making others believe they owe you.

Dean hesitates. "Can I buy you lunch? To say thank you."

She smiles. "Where would we go? The gas station?"

"No. The Inn."

Vivian's smile flattens. "I should be on my way, and the Inn isn't my sort of place."

"It isn't my kind of place either, but I just inherited it. I'm Frank's son."

She blinks. There is familiarity, in the hair and the eyes, sharp features and slender build. He even shares some of his father's expressions. Aside from his youth and vastly superior manner and dress sense, he looks just like Frank.

"I didn't know he had a son."

"It's a long story. I really would like to buy you lunch. I could do with more of your advice."

He is charming, like Frank, but in a very different way. A few moments later, she's in his car (it is an Audi) and wondering at her compliance. She is allowing her curiosity to break the rules she laid down for herself with good reason, and there's no way to back out now.

⁓ The mustiness in the bar is overwhelming. Stale smoke in the walls even though cigarettes have been banned for years. It is so dark that she has to pause in the doorway to let her eyes adjust and her heartrate slow. There is no sign of that woman, the one who brings it all back like it was yesterday. Where is she lurking? And where is Frank? He isn't here, she reminds herself. He's gone.

Gently, Dean takes her arm in his and guides her to a table. Frank kept the old tables, heavy dark wood, scratched and stained. Not much has changed; a couple of newer TVs, a board with neatly chalked daily specials and fake miniature sunflower centrepieces in tiny ceramic vases. Did that woman add those touches?

They're alone except for an older couple slurping soup and a village maintenance worker who nods at Vivian from the bar. A girl with purple streaks in her hair comes over to take their order. Vivian relaxes a little. Perhaps that woman isn't here after all.

Dean insists on ordering her a drink because he says he needs one. He tries the wine and then scrunches his face a little melodramatically.

Vivian sips her whiskey. "Frank wasn't a wine connoisseur, but he always had a decent rye."

"It's that sort of information I need more of," he says with a smile. "It's strange to talk to people who knew him so much better than I did."

"But you lived in Stapleton as a boy?"

"I did. With my mom and my stepdad. When I was 12 my mom decided she'd had enough of my stepdad and this town, so the two of us moved to the Lower Mainland. Stapleton was a different place back then."

"Did you see much of Frank?"

Dean stares at his glass of vinegary wine. He pauses long enough for Vivian to wonder whether he'll answer.

"A lawyer contacted me a few weeks ago to tell me this eccentric guy I barely knew from my hometown had written me into his will. I called my mom and she finally told me that Frank was my dad."

Dean traces a scratch on the table with his index finger, then taps it repeatedly, a hint of tension in his attractive face. Vivian finds it hard to match it to the angry man who lobbed a rock through a window.

"What will you do with the Inn?" she asks.

"Burn it down."

He laughs.

"I imagine profit margins are slim."

"It barely pays for itself. But Frank had a live-in manager who has been running the show since he got sick, and she seems capable enough. She can handle things until I decide what to do next."

The manager. He must be referring to that woman. Vivian craves fresh air. There's no reason to panic, she reminds herself. She hasn't even seen her yet. Perhaps she won't. Perhaps she's out.

"So, you're considering running it yourself?"

Dean shrugs. "The lawyer said Frank gave it to me because he wanted it to stay a family business. His sister can't handle taking care of it herself and his nephew didn't want it. He hoped if I came here and saw the place, I might take an interest in running it. But I have a life and a successful career in Vancouver."

Vivian has spent the past twenty odd years trying to make Stapleton attractive again. It frustrates her that others struggle to see the potential here but he is not to blame for the sad realities of this town.

"What line of work are you in?"

"I'm a management consultant."

Vivian raises her eyebrows. "I'm sure Frank would've been very impressed."

Dean takes a large swig of wine. Apparently, the taste has improved. He taps the table again. "Was he such a bad person?"

"What do you mean?"

"My mom thought it would be less damaging for me to think that my dad was a stranger she had a one-night stand with."

Vivian considers his question and forms a delicate response. "Small towns shrink to the size of fishbowls when it comes to gossip. She might have been trying to protect you by keeping Frank out of it."

He finishes his glass and orders a rye. Vivian declines another. The atmosphere in here is making her fuzzy-headed enough.

"You won't hear this from many people because it isn't widely known yet, but Stapleton is on the cusp of a revival."

He grins, and she is reminded of Frank. He thinks she's joking. She doesn't blame him.

"I'm quite serious, Dean, and in all my years here I'd say this opportunity could be the one to turn Stapleton's fortunes around. You'd be wise to hang onto your investment a little longer. It could be worth a lot more in a year or two, even if you do decide to sell."

That catches his interest. She knows it's not just about the money. Business excites him. He is exactly the sort of person this town needs.

"What kind of revival should I be expecting?" he asks.

"We're in the middle of negotiations with the company at the moment so I can't disclose any specifics, but it's an enterprise that will bring jobs to our community by providing a valuable service to other residents of our beautiful province."

He seems impressed. He should be. She gives a good sales pitch but the plan is brilliant on its own merits. All she needs is a bit more time to bring the company on board officially. The town will follow.

Their food arrives and Dean removes the limp lettuce from his burger before taking a bite. "How is it?" she asks.

"The bun's freezer burnt, but apart from that, not bad." Dean is much more straightforward than his dad. Frank could never give a clear answer, even to the most mundane question. That's what made him useful. If there ever came a time when Vivian needed to make excuses, she could argue that she never really knew what he was up to, and people would believe her.

Vivian spies her husband hobbling in through the side entrance, thin strands of white hair dishevelled by the breeze. He gasps when he sets eyes on her.

"Vivian! I had no idea where you were! What are you doing in here?"

"Oh, please. Stop fretting." She turns to Dean. "You'll have to excuse my husband, Todd. He's become quite a worrier in his old age."

Vivian rolls out the usual polite introductions, with Dean issuing an unnecessary apology to Todd for whisking her away to lunch.

Despite her husband's annoying protectiveness, it is freeing to step outside into the warm air and see the sunlight again. Todd drives her home and sits her down at the kitchen table, placing two yellow pills and a glass of water in front of her. She looks at him incredulously. What is he trying to do now? Sedate her?

"I'm not taking those!"

"Your doctor prescribed them. You need to take them."

"For what?"

He loses his patience. "Why, for once, can't you just take them when I ask you to? Why do we always have to fight about it first?"

"What do you mean, 'for once?' I've never seen these before."

"You have, Vivian. You just don't remember."

CHAPTER 5

1 9 9 4

Elena had seen it in a documentary once; an entire city rising up out of the desert, surrounded by nothing but sand. It seemed impossible. That's how the school looked in that moment. It was hard to comprehend.

Army vehicles fronted the entrance and soldiers stood scanning the area like hungry eagles watching the river. Metal fencing enclosed the playing fields. Inside, groups of people sat, paced or just stood and stared. Overnight, the military must have scooped the townspeople up and dumped them in clumps behind the high fence while guarding the only exit. Were they all captured by the curse, or protected from it? In that moment, she didn't care. She just wanted to see her family.

Elena took up her own perch on the grassy slope overlooking the school. She lay beside a dead ponderosa pine and watched the soldiers coming and going. She fidgeted with the tree bark that fell like puzzle pieces around its trunk, trying to figure out how everything had fallen apart so quickly since the night before.

She needed to get closer. She couldn't see whether her family were behind the fence. She scrambled down the slope on hands and knees hoping the tall clumps of grass would disguise her. Sagebrush roots, rocks and clusters of prickly pear cactus tore at her palms and shins.

Familiar faces came into view. The grocery store manager was chatting animatedly with one of Elena's former teachers. She recognized some of the little kids chasing each other around the perimeter, colliding and giggling. She inched closer. Her elderly neighbour, Mrs. Dubov, sat alone on a bench. Chief John's son Terry towered above the other boys at the basketball hoop. Terry was one of Rob's teammates and the best player in the school but Elena couldn't spot her brother on the court. She slammed her knee into a rock and bit her lip to stop herself from screaming.

Some families were clustered together. The Clarks and the Toews, who were good friends, and the Wrights, Nadeaus and Powells who were neighbours on Logan's street. There were a couple of large groups of Native families, too, but Elena didn't know their surnames.

Finally, she saw them. Their figures were unmistakable; Rob taller even with his shoulders hunched, wearing the blue plaid shirt she'd seen him in the night before, and Mamma with her big shades shielding her eyes, holding his arm as they stood. Elena wanted to jump up and run to them and wave and hug them all at once. But it was just Mamma and Rob. No sign of Dad. Elena swallowed the lump in her throat and tried not to think of Brandon's burnt skin.

She shuffled a little closer, then a little more, and two big hands scooped her out of the dirt like she weighed nothing. She let out a little scream.

"It's alright, Elena. You're safe with me."

The soldier didn't look scary. He was young with very short hair and bright white teeth like the actors on TV, and he had a dimple in the middle of his chin. He took her by the hand and led her away from Mamma and Rob. They hadn't seen her; no one had, but she didn't try and shout for their attention. It happened so quickly she didn't know what to do except go with him.

As they approached the entrance to the school, he bent down to talk to her. "We've been looking everywhere for you. Where have you been?"

Elena kept her mouth shut. She didn't know anything about him, not even his name, and yet somehow he knew hers.

"Your family is safe. They're inside. I'll take you to them."

He pulled forward, but she dug her heels in.

"Why are you here?" she asked.

"To keep you all safe."

"From what?"

"The curse," she imagined him whispering cruelly. She wanted to take back her question in case it really was all her fault.

"Let's talk about that inside."

"How did you get here so fast?"

"We're the army. It's our job to get places quickly in an emergency."

"What's the emergency?"

The soldier gently tugged her hand.

"Come on. Let's get you back to your mom. She's going to be so relieved to see you."

She wanted to see Mamma more than anything. The soldier opened the main doors. Reluctantly, she stepped inside and followed him down the long hallways.

Yapping and barking echoed through the back of the building; a few people were walking their leashed dogs beyond the open fire escape. The soldier gave her a reassuring smile and told her he had a pug named Sam. Then he thumped on a door marked Principal's Office and Elena panicked. She was in trouble. They were going to ask her about what she'd done. She would have to tell them about the curse.

An older, uniformed man opened the door. His red cheeks popped out of his big round face and words came out of his mouth with such force Elena couldn't imagine him trying to whisper.

"Come in, Elena. My name's David. I'm in charge of the evacuation."

"Where's my mom?" she asked timidly.

"We're going to have a quick chat and then we'll take you to her."

Elena heard him but was busy trying to puzzle out why the principal's office seemed so small. She sensed the big man with the big voice was taking up extra space. She turned around, but the young soldier filled the space behind her. "David" took the principal's leather chair and told Elena to sit opposite him. The young soldier closed the door and crossed his arms.

"Where did you go last night, Elena?" David asked.

She hesitated. She didn't know them but they had little red Maple Leaf flags on their shoulders. Soldiers were supposed to help people.

"I got lost so I slept in a barn."

David looked puzzled.

"How did you get lost?"

"I was scared. I ran away and my mom will be really mad so can I see her now?"

"You can very soon. Where is this barn?"

"At the top of Douglas Street, where the houses end."

David glanced at the other soldier in a way that meant something, but Elena didn't know what.

"Who looked after you all night?" he said.

"No one."

"But you weren't out there on your own all night, were you? Someone must have been there with you."

Elena shook her head.

"What about your dad?" he boomed.

"I don't know where he is."

David leaned forward. "Are you sure?"

"Do you know where he is?" Elena asked.

David shot the soldier a look and then refocused on Elena. "If you see him, or if you have any idea where he might have gone, it's very important that you tell us."

"Did he get hurt at the mill?"

"That is a possibility. He might need medical treatment. Where do you think he would have gone if he was in trouble?"

"He would've come home," Elena said earnestly. "Mamma would've helped him."

David and the other soldier exchanged glances again. They had a secret language of looks.

"What happened at the mill?" she asked.

"There was an explosion. We're keeping everyone at the school as a precaution because the fire's still active."

David stared silently at Elena as if that would persuade her to tell him more. She didn't have anything else to say. She just wanted to see Mamma. Finally, David stood.

"Alright. Let's get you to your mom."

⁓ Mamma rushed across the room and smothered her, tears dropping on her head, and Elena was glad until it was too much and she needed to breathe. She apologized and promised never to do anything like that again. Mamma said she would never be given the opportunity.

Rob pushed in and hugged her. "I wasn't worried. I knew you'd come back."

She didn't believe him. He worried about things almost as much as Mamma did; he was just better at pretending otherwise.

They walked across the shiny gym floor to the spot Mamma and Rob had established for themselves near the stage. The air was sweaty and stale, and there were even more people in here than there had been outside. Tables had been set up along one wall with blankets and water and boxes of supplies.

"Your dad's missing," Mamma told her gently, "but they'll find him, so try not to worry. He probably just got disoriented, like you did."

"Why are there soldiers here?".

"Sometimes they help out in emergencies."

That explanation seemed to be good enough for Mamma.

Ken smiled at Elena from a corner of the stage where he sat with his girlfriend, but he didn't come up and hug her like he normally would. Maybe he was feeling sad because Dad wasn't with them.

She went up to him and gave him a hug and said: "It's okay. He'll be home soon." Ken's eyes watered and he said he needed to go outside to get some air.

∼ It was loud in the gym. Sounds echoed and people had to speak up to talk over each other. Classroom chairs scraped across the floor. Babies wailed. A few kids had managed to evacuate with their Game Boys, colourful slap bracelets, bouncy balls or collectable POGs and Elena watched them enviously. Mamma wouldn't let her wander, not even to find friends, so she settled beside her and did her best to discreetly tap into other conversations, leaning this way and that as voices caught her attention.

Most of the chatter revolved around what had gone on the night before: the thoughts that had rushed through their minds when they first heard the bang; how they'd tried to contact people who worked at the mill; gossip about people absent from the school.

It became clear to Elena that her dad wasn't the only one missing. Others were also worried about family members and friends. But Dad's story was different. These people were afraid that their loved ones had been trapped inside the mill. If the soldier she'd overheard was right, Dad had gone missing after getting out.

When Elena complained of hunger, Mamma led her to a row of tables at the far side of the gym laden with juice boxes, coffee, cookies and fruit, and a sign that said the items had been donated by the grocery store. Beside them were strips of dried salmon bagged in plastic with another sign that read "Donated by the Sampson family." Elena grabbed a cookie and rushed back towards the stage, trying not to think of the salmon she'd seen jump out of the water by the cemetery, or everything that had gone wrong since then.

As the minutes and hours ticked by, people approached Mamma and whispered kind words about Dad. They already knew he was one of the missing workers. Everybody knew everyone's business in Stapleton.

"I'm Brandon's mom." She had his broad face and kind eyes and her voice shook as she spoke. "I just wanted to thank you for helping him."

Mamma invited her to join them on the floor and they sat together for a few minutes, the two moms with their heads together talking too closely and quietly for Elena to hear, but she saw their tears before they swept them away. Elena refused to be sad. Brandon was getting his arm fixed at the hospital and Dad would be home soon.

When Mary approached, Elena assumed she wanted to talk to Mamma, too, but she lowered herself gently beside Elena while complaining she'd never be able to get up again. Mary looked as though she'd been awake all night. Most people probably had been.

"I came to apologize to you, Elena."

"For what?"

"Frank told me about your ghost hunt. I thought you and Logan were going to turn the Chinese cemetery into a playground, so I asked Frank to scare you away."

Elena tried to process what Mary had said. The eerie wail that had lifted the hairs on her arm, white eyes bursting out of the shadows. The body with the long neck. Frank had tricked them. There was no ghost in the cemetery. No curse.

"But the mill ..."

"... Just bad timing," Mary muttered. "I heard you ran away after the explosion."

Elena didn't confirm or deny it. It was too embarrassing.

"Hungry ghosts aren't real. They're just a myth."

Elena glared at her defiantly. "I know. I'm not stupid."

"No, you're not."

Just a big stupid joke. Logan probably wouldn't ever speak to her again. She hadn't seen him at the school yet but she was forbidden to wander through the throngs to look for him. She hoped he'd understand. He needed to know it wasn't her fault.

∾ By nightfall, everyone was sent home. The young soldier who had lifted her out of the long grass and escorted her to the principal's office wheeled her bike over and told her in a serious voice not to wander off again.

The fire was contained, they heard, but the road in and

out of town, the one that ran by the mill, was still blocked and strictly off limits to anyone who might be thinking about investigating the damage for themselves. No one could leave town until the firefighters and the military said it was safe.

"They're looking for Dad," Elena said.

Mamma had made dinner for the three of them. Rob pushed a strip of beef around his plate, sulking. Mamma patted Elena's hand. "Of course they are. Don't worry. They'll find him."

That wasn't what Elena meant. She meant they're looking for him. In a bad way, like they did on Mamma's cop shows.

"Did he do something wrong?"

Rob glowered at her. Mamma put her fork down. "What do you mean?"

"Nothing."

"Do you know something, Elena?"

Elena shook her head. Mamma didn't eat anything else.

⤳ Mamma went outside after dinner. She stood under the willow tree and stared out across the river. Mamma never just stood there like that, arms crossed, for such a long time. Once in a while, her arms would let go of her body so she could dry her eyes.

Elena kept an eye on her from the kitchen window and whispered to God. "Bring Dad home quickly please. We need him. Amen."

God didn't whisper back.

CHAPTER 6

2 0 1 8

"Cherie! Cherie! Come!"

It turns her stomach, the thought of her all alone out here. Poor Cherie, lost as the sun begins to drop. The coyotes prey on roaming pets. Soon she'll hear their distant, eerie calls in the darkness.

"Cherie!" she cries down the street. Barking erupts from a neighbouring home. She's hopeful for a second, even though it is the deep bark of a much larger breed. She curses her weary legs for not being able to carry her as far as she wants to go and her cloudy eyes for not seeing as well as they should.

There's a drop of blood on the sidewalk, just one drop, but it rattles her. Cherie is hurt. She cut herself on something and now she's limping and frightened. Vivian touches her nose. It's bleeding. She's bleeding. It's her blood on the sidewalk. She pulls out a tissue and dabs at it until it stops. It isn't serious. Must be the dry air.

A flashy black car pulls up alongside her. A young man gets out. She recognizes him, but she can't place him. What was his name? She smiles out of politeness and calls out for her dog again.

"Cherie!"

He approaches. "Did you lose someone?"

She stares at his sharp features and then looks down the street again. "My dog, Cherie."

"What kind of dog is she?"

"She's a ..." She brushes the lost thought away with her hand. "My husband must've left the gate open."

He follows her down the road a short way, semi-scanning the front yards as she does.

"Thanks again for your help with Pam. She believed the story about kids breaking her window. She let me take care of the damage. I don't think she'd ever forgive me if she knew the truth."

Vivian looks at him as though he might be soft in the head. He doesn't appear to notice.

"I have to run. I'm supposed to be meeting Frank's lawyer and I'm already late. Is anyone helping you look for your dog?"

"My husband," Vivian mutters.

"I hope you find her. I'll keep an eye out."

Vivian stretches to look over a neighbour's hedge. "Cherie?" She releases a long, shrill whistle.

"I owe you one," he says, but he leaves too quickly to catch her response: "Everyone in this town owes me one."

Shortly after the young man drive off, Tim pulls up and tells her to get in. He's taking her home. Not Tim. Tony. Todd. He says he's found Cherie. Vivian peers into the car. No sign of Cherie.

"She's at home," Todd says, not very convincingly.

Vivian squints at him, trying to focus on his little lying eyes. He's always playing tricks on her, and he isn't as gentle as he used to be. If she doesn't get in the damn car, he'll probably drag her in. He's so much stronger than she is now. Was he always? She's suddenly too tired to argue.

⁓ Stuart is sitting in their living room, a glass of whiskey in one hand and one of Todd's fat books in the other, his grey curls ruffled because he plays with his hair when he concentrates. No doubt it's about a great battle. Stuart and his father share an interest in books about great battles, even though the pair of them would have been shot for cowardice if they'd actually been in one.

"Life is full of battles," she remarks as she approaches. "Why do you need ... these?"

Stuart looks across at his father. The pair of them, with their sneaky little looks just because she forgets the odd word.

"When did you get here?" she asks her son.

He hesitates and glances at his father again. "Last night. Don't you remember?"

One of their traps. Trying to trick her into being confused. "Of course, I remember. There's nothing ..."

She trails off because the words have gone. Fizzled out like her interest in the useless people surrounding her.

She turns to Todd. "Have you spoken to the reference people yet?"

He quietly corrects her. "The refuse people."

"Have you?"

Todd doesn't say anything. Stuart looks at him. "What's she talking about?"

She keeps her voice raised. She isn't afraid of them. "Do it, Todd. Make sure it happens."

"I am, and it will," Todd says meekly. "But for now I need you to rest, Vivian. You're very tired."

He's right, she realizes, tired again, and that in itself annoys her. He passes her two little pills and a glass of water and she asks what they are for. "The doctor wants you to take them." Lacking the energy to argue, she swallows them in one gulp.

Todd leads her to the living room sofa. In front of her is the mantelpiece and the wall of family portraits, old and new. The largest photograph in the most lavish frame takes centre spot. The man in the photograph is her father, there for appearances. She stares at his image as her drowsy eyes try to fight the exhaustion that washes over her.

In the photograph, Father has the appearance of a man other men looked up to, and he was. Suited and clean-shaven with neat blonde hair. He was only middle-aged then, when Vivian was a girl, and already at the helm of the Stapleton Coalmine. Mother hung that photograph above the mantelpiece in Vivian's childhood home and it remained there until her death. Todd had put it in the "keep" pile when he and Vivian sorted through Mother's things. Vivian thought about transferring it to the trash pile, but Todd would have asked questions she didn't want to answer. So, now Father sits above her mantelpiece in the spot that Todd arranged for him. Father's eyes are smiling, almost smirking. At her.

~> Summer vacations are long and thick in the Stapleton heat. Vivian attends school in Vancouver, but she returns home during every break. The local kids are strangers and Father is always away. Mother busies herself with housework and only really focuses her attention on Vivian when she yanks a comb through her unruly brown curls. Vivian's closest companion is Ruby, the horse Father bought for her 12th birthday.

Ruby is a beautiful horse. She's an Appaloosa with a chestnut head and a white back flecked with chestnut spots. Vivian feeds her carrots in the paddock and gently strokes her long snout.

"Vivian!"

Father's bellowing voice. She turns excitedly to see his

figure at the front steps of their grand house. Pale skin and pale hair; a little heavier on every visit but the way he carries the weight only makes him look stronger. These are the best days; the days he comes home. He works so hard, Mother says. He travels a lot. He attends very important meetings in Vancouver, Mother has explained, but he never visits Vivian while she's at school there. Vivian doesn't think anything of it. Parents don't visit their children at school, not unless there's some sort of family emergency.

It had started during the war, Father's gradual disappearance from their home, or at least that was the first excuse for his absence that Vivian could remember. He didn't fight overseas but he was very involved in the war effort, Mother said, though neither of her parents ever went into detail about his work. It must have been important. He was an important man. But when the war finally ended, he continued to keep his distance.

Father holds his suit jacket and dimpled hat over one arm and his fat leather briefcase in his other hand. Vivian scrambles over the fence and runs towards him as he waits. "Father!" she shouts happily. He is unmoved. Father says too much fussing ruins children. It makes them weak. Vivian will run into him anyway and throw her arms around his broad chest. He'll let her do that once. Then he'll straighten his tie and clear his throat, which means "back to business," and he will do the talking and she will listen as well as she can and Mother will make sure they have a very pleasant dinner so he will come back sooner.

Vivian can't resist one question, just one. "Can we go for ice cream?"

She loves ice cream, but more than that, she loves the feeling of striding around Stapleton with him at her side. Some men tip their hats at him when he marches by. Others make space for him as though he is the boss, even out there on the sidewalk. Father runs the coalmine, and that makes him King of Stapleton. It's a powerful feeling, to walk beside him. It isn't the same when she walks around town with Mother, who is so meek people barely notice she's there.

Father ignores her request, and when she stretches her arms around him, he pushes her back firmly. "Come inside."

Nothing feels particularly odd to Vivian until she skips into the dining room. Mother is seated in her usual spot as though she is about to have dinner, but it is mid-afternoon. Mother's eyes are wet and she is dabbing them delicately with a handkerchief. Vivian looks at her father but he offers no explanation. "Sit down," he says. She sits in her chair opposite Mother but Father doesn't join them. He stands at the foot of the table and looks down on them. Mother is a petite woman and Father's shadow seems to swallow them both.

"Your mother and I are separating."

Mother weeps a little more forcefully, then covers her mouth with her handkerchief to stifle the sound.

"Why?" Vivian asks, more confused than traumatised at that moment.

"That is not your concern," he says.

Mother lets out a few more sniffles.

Father sighs impatiently. "There's no need to make a fuss. You can continue to live here, at least until you are an adult or until your mother remarries."

"I'll never remarry," Mother says, sobbing. "What an awful thing to say."

She and Mother are being abandoned. They have no choice in it. He decides everything. He always has. They are lost in his shadow and Vivian has to get away from him, into the light. She leaves the table without asking his permission. He walks out.

Mother cries for days afterwards. She calls her sisters but they won't talk to her. A divorced woman. In their family. One evening, sherry on her breath, she sits Vivian in front of her and drags a comb through her hair. She pulls at the knots so hard Vivian's scalp burns.

"I lost the boy. He was stillborn."

A heavy silence falls between them. Mother tugs at another tangle.

"Then you came along, and you were a girl. Your father couldn't forgive us. It's my fault."

That was the first and last time Mother mentioned Vivian's brother. Vivian never asked why Mother thought his death was her fault, or if they had decided on a name, or where they buried him. But she thought of him sometimes; the tiny being who never took a breath and left a great big scar across her childhood.

Vivian decides if she wants to be happy, she ought to be more like Father. She must be the one making the decisions. If not, she'll be the person things just happen to. She's not like Mother.

"Where's Father?"

Todd blinks at her a couple of times and Vivian registers this other place, this real place, with the mantelpiece and the dead people trapped inside photographs.

"I mean … never mind."

He pulls out a tissue and starts dabbing at her face. She shoves his hand away.

"What are you doing?"

"Your nose is bleeding. Must be the dry air."

She grabs the red dotted tissue from him and dabs her own nose. She hates being treated like a child.

CHAPTER 7

1 9 9 4

Elena would find Dad herself. She would find him before
the soldiers did. She had to. If he was hiding from them,
maybe he needed her help.

She packed water and snacks and went to tell Mamma
where she was going. Mamma was in the yard, settled into
one of their cracked plastic chairs, and she was trying to appear normal even though her eyes looked sore and her hair
was messy and she hadn't put her makeup on today.

"I'm going for a bike ride."

"You're not going anywhere that I can't see you."

"But Mom!"

"Your dad's missing. I almost lost you. I'm not letting you
wander off on your own again."

"I'll go with her."

Rob had just come outside, his basketball tucked under
one arm. It wasn't like him to be helpful.

"I'll make sure she doesn't get into any more trouble."

"No," Mamma said. "I want you both where I can see you."

Elena stamped her foot but Rob, for once, remained calm.

"Mom, there are soldiers everywhere. We're not going to
go missing. We can bike over to Ken's and see how he's doing.

And I finished the bread and milk. We can pick those up on our way home."

"I should go see Ken myself," Mamma said quietly.

"But someone needs to stay here in case there's any news about Dad," Rob said.

Mamma thought about it for way too long, looking at them and then at her watch and then back at the two of them.

"Fine," she said. "But be back by 4, no excuses. And, Elena, I mean no excuses."

Mamma gave Rob some money for the groceries. They got straight on their bikes and rode out together, like they were heading on a real adventure. Elena expected Rob to pedal away from her as soon as they were out of sight of the house but he didn't.

"Where are we going?" he asked.

"As close as we can get to the mill."

"Why?"

"Something isn't right."

"You know something, don't you? Something you didn't want to tell Mom."

That's why he wanted to come with her. He wanted to find out what she knew. Elena was glad, actually, to be able to discuss it with him. Mamma would freak out but not Rob.

"I overheard some soldiers talking. They said Dad was on the run."

"Why would he be on the run?"

"I don't know."

"Who is he running from? The army?"

"Maybe."

Rob went quiet. "This whole situation is weird," he said finally. "They won't let us anywhere near the mill."

"But maybe we'll see something they missed on the way. A clue."

He didn't have any better ideas, so they went with her plan. Biking through town was easy enough; they'd both done it a thousand times. But as they crossed the bridge and slowly wound their way up the reserve hill, the sweat piled up on Elena's back and her hairline became sticky. Rob got a little further ahead of her with each push, while she puffed and struggled and wondered if her lungs would burn up.

Eventually the winding road levelled out and the reserve houses popped up on either side of them. Rob hung back until she'd caught up but he didn't wait for her to catch her breath. They didn't have a lot of time. There was no way they'd be able to make it to Ken's. They'd just have to hope Mamma never thought to ask him about their visit.

The reserve was quiet; nobody around. But a couple of black and brown dogs followed them briefly, jogging up beside them to say hello with their tongues lolling out.

"Maybe he's hiding out here," Elena said.

The houses were set back from the main road, spaced further apart than the houses downtown. No fences separated the grass into square lawns; often the wild sagebrush and grasses grew right up to the steps.

Elena slowed down as they passed a derelict church with a crooked roof and faded wooden tiles. Next to the church was a small home with a neat path to the door. An old woman sat on a wooden bench, enjoying the blue sky and early autumn warmth.

Elena braked. She hopped off her bike and walked it up the path. Rob turned and pedalled back towards her. "Elena!" he half-whispered, but she ignored him. The cops on Mamma's shows had to talk to people to find things out, and the old woman was the only person they'd seen so far.

"Hi."

Elena introduced herself from the middle of the old woman's yard. She looked fragile; thin and crinkly like hand-made paper and she had a blanket wrapped around her shoulders. She didn't respond. Elena tried again.

"My name's Elena. I'm looking for my dad. He went missing in the mill fire."

The old woman focused on her.

"Have you seen him?" Elena asked.

"What does he look like?"

"Tall, kinda big." She gestured outwardly from her ribs with her hands. "His hair is shaved but it's brown. His name's Curtis Reid."

"That your brother over there?"

Elena nodded. "Yeah."

"Helping you look?"

"Yeah."

"You're good kids. I got eight grandkids. They're all grown up now. Youngest is 21. Oldest is 37. Most of 'em got kids of their own."

"My brother is 14. I'm 10."

"If I see your dad, I'll tell him you're looking for him."

Elena turned around and saw Rob, off his bike, kicking the dirt. She couldn't go back to him with nothing. The old lady was probably out here all the time, watching. She had to know something. She turned back.

"Did you get evacuated too?"

"No. I'm too old for all that. They knocked on the door but I pretended I wasn't home. When they left, I came out front here and sat on my bench and watched everyone hurrying around."

"What did you see?"

"Well, I saw everybody leave. One of my granddaughters gave me the evil eye as she put her kids in the car. She couldn't see me in the darkness, but she knew I was out here and she knew I wasn't coming."

The old woman let out a little chuckle.

"Let me see now ... there were army trucks and a couple airplanes and I saw a few guys driving away from the mill in their vehicles."

Elena perked up. "Did you see an old blue Ford truck? With a lot of mud on it?"

The old lady looked around, as though someone might be hiding in the grass, listening.

"I heard something about a truck like that."

Elena's heart jumped. "What?"

"My daughter's husband. He's been looking around to see what went on. He said he found a truck that had been driven off the road into the forest. He said somebody drove it in there recently, and they got as far in as they could go and then abandoned it. He looked around for a while to see if anyone needed help, but he never found nothing."

"Where was it?"

"Not far from the mill. He figured someone was headed towards town before they took off into the forest. They went off on that side of the road." She pointed helpfully.

"Thanks!"

Elena wheeled down the path back to Rob. She explained everything to him as quickly as she could get the words out, and they both agreed that they had to find that truck. Elena looked back as they pedalled away. The old lady remained on her bench, watching.

The road that led from the reserve to the mill wasn't as steep as the first stretch but it wasn't flat either. Elena was jealous of her big brother, peddling with ease, so much stronger.

"You could cycle to Stony Creek if you want to leave home," she said.

Rob glanced back at her guiltily. "I'm not leaving. I was just angry. Mom's so annoying sometimes."

Elena turned to smile at him and her front tire hit a rock. She steadied herself just before she slipped over the verge.

"Watch where you're going!" he said.

Elena thought about Mamma. "Do you think Dad wanted to leave us?"

"No," Rob said firmly.

"Maybe he got sick of Mamma."

Another thought came to her. Maybe he got sick of all of them. A small tear dropped from her eye, but she rubbed it away before Rob saw. She hated being called a baby.

Just beyond the reserve, pine trees littered the sagebrush until it was mostly trees, and eventually there was no more brush. They were entering the forest. "We're getting close," Rob shouted back to her.

The further they went, the more determined Rob seemed to get, and a couple of times she lost sight of him as he pushed ahead. Then, suddenly, he stopped.

The trees had opened up a little, as though they had once given way to a side road or an old driveway. Something had crashed through there recently. Branches were broken and leaves were flattened against the dry ground.

"He came in this way!" Elena said excitedly, already certain that the truck they were looking for was Dad's.

"It's here!" Rob shouted, a short distance ahead of her.

Elena burst forward. There it was, just below them, where the land sloped downwards. At first she thought it had smashed into the trees in front, but it was perfectly parked so it was hidden by the ridge. It was Dad's truck. Old Beat-Up, he called it, on account of all the rust and dirt and dents and scratches. It was unlocked. Elena opened the driver's door and jumped inside. The keys were still in the ignition. They jangled as she turned to see Rob hopping in from the passenger side. He opened up the glovebox. Tissues and insurance documents and an AC/DC cassette tape. Why would Dad have left the truck all the way out here?

Rob flinched as though he'd heard someone. He pressed one finger to his lips and gestured for her to duck down in the seat. She disappeared into the well below the steering wheel, waiting for the sound of soldiers' heavy boots.

"Did you hear something?" she whispered.

He nodded.

She bobbed her head up as something shifted between the trees. A crow took off towards the open sky.

Rob said they should be careful, but Elena wasn't interested in wasting time. They had found Dad's vehicle. He could still be nearby. She charged into the pine forest before Rob could stop her, hurtling down the slope, skidding over needles and winding around trunks until he grabbed the back of her t-shirt. "We have to find him!" she said as she pushed Rob away.

The hill bottomed out ahead of them and opened up into a meadow where a trapper's cabin stood. Cabins like that were common in the area around Stapleton, although there weren't any trappers anymore. Dad said hunters and hikers sometimes slept in them if they got lost, or teenagers went there to cause trouble.

There was a little creek running along one side of the cabin. Elena saw something in the water and sprinted closer.

A large leaf flopped over bits of a rotting sluice box and followed the water downstream. Elena decided that somebody had discovered gold here a long time ago, and they were so excited they left their equipment behind. It was a good sign. Dad was here, somewhere.

A man's voice came from the cabin; loud, then hushed, interrupted. It didn't sound like Dad's voice. Elena's skin went cold. Rob looked over at her, wide-eyed. She couldn't get back to him. There was no time.

There was a scuffling inside the cabin, men coming out, and Rob's instinct was to run. She saw him dart back up the hill. He said later he had seen someone with a gun pointed in his direction. Elena never saw a gun.

⁓ She was shivering; her wet sweater and jeans chilling her skin as she lay against the slippery rocks of the creek bed. Water crept into her sneakers and turned her toes clammy. The more the cold rattled her, the more tempted she was to look up. She couldn't hear anything. She sensed the men were still there, but she couldn't be sure.

Slowly, she lifted her head to peer through the clumps of grass that lined the edge of the creek. There was the cabin and two men standing out front. They were looking away from her, talking to each other. She couldn't see their faces, but they weren't dressed like army men. They looked like back-country guys, much like a lot of the men in Stapleton. They were wearing camouflage and baseball caps and one of them was tall and stocky and the other one was tall and thin. They could have been hunters, except they weren't carrying rifles.

The skinny man turned and surveyed the hill. Then they

started off in the other direction; deeper into the forest and away from the cabin. In a few more paces they'd disappear. She had to make a decision; to go on and see if they led her to Dad or run back to Rob.

She scrambled along the creek keeping her body low, ready to drop down if the men looked behind them. The big one stopped and the skinny one stood beside him. She got close enough to hear them exchange a few words.

"What if they don't find it?" the skinny one asked.

"… just a backup. There's enough for them to find."

The stocky guy took something out of his pocket. He was wearing gloves, she noticed, which was odd for a warm September day. It was a scrap of something, maybe material. He put it into the creek. Elena wished she could see what it was, but the men diverged from the stream and she had to leave the creek and creep through the trees to keep up with them.

Elena followed the men until the forest was broken by a narrow dirt road. The skinny one put something to his ear and she could hear the crackle of a radio. Elena waited patiently, curled into the coarse branches of a sprawling juniper, trying to control her shivering.

A few minutes later, she heard a vehicle approaching. It wasn't like the military trucks she'd seen outside the school. It was just an old banger and it barely stopped long enough for the two men to jump in. After a U-turn it headed her way with its nose pushing into the forest. She saw the driver. It was Frank.

~⁓ Elena found Rob hiding in the trees near Dad's truck. She almost screamed when he popped out in front of her but she could tell he didn't mean to make her jump. He didn't ask where she'd been, or what she'd seen. He grabbed her arm and dragged her back to their bikes.

The way home was quicker. They flew down the hill and over the bridge and Elena pedalled hard to keep up with Rob.

At the house, Elena was red-faced and breathless. Her clothes had dried a bit, but Mamma still wanted to know why she was wet and what happened to the groceries. Rob sat Mamma down in the living room and started to explain but he got it all wrong.

"What were you thinking?" Mamma snapped at him when he admitted where they went. Her mouth opened and her eyes watered when he told her about the truck. "Are you sure it was our truck?" she said. Both kids nodded. The two of them agreed on everything until Rob mentioned what happened once they reached the trapper's cabin.

"We heard voices coming from the cabin. We didn't know who they were so we came straight back."

Elena shot a glance at him, "No ..."

"... that's what happened."

He didn't want to tell Mamma the truth. Sometimes he had a good reason for it but not this time. He just didn't want Mamma to know what a coward he was.

Elena piped up again. "No. Two men came out of the cabin and Rob ran off ..."

"I didn't! She's lying ..."

"Let her finish."

Rob let out a massive sigh but Elena kept going.

"I hid in the creek and followed them." She spoke quickly as she explained the rest, keen to deprive Rob of an opportunity to interrupt.

Rob rolled his eyes. Elena glared at him. "He just doesn't want to admit he was too scared to come with me."

Rob tried to object, but Mamma shushed them both by raising her hand.

"Enough fighting!" She turned to Elena. "Did you see who they were?"

"I didn't know the two men but I saw the driver. It was Frank."

Rob threw up his hands, "Mom, she's obviously making this up!"

Mamma stared at him. "How would you know?"

"Okay, but ..."

"So she did go off without you?"

Rob realized too late that Mamma had caught him in his own lie. She was good at that.

"I didn't run off. One of them had a gun!"

Mamma gasped. "Who had a gun?"

"No they didn't!"

"They did!"

Mamma hushed them. "Tell me the truth, Elena. You won't be in trouble."

"I just told you the truth."

Mamma got up and went into the kitchen and stared out of the window for a while. Elena heard her pick up the phone, her voice cracking.

"Ken? The kids found something."

Ken arrived about 20 minutes later. He barely looked at Elena when he came in the door, but she saw the dark circles under his eyes. The thin hair he usually tied back was hanging loose and greasy around his shoulders. His breath reeked, and Elena could tell Mamma had noticed too, although she didn't say anything. Mamma led him into the kitchen and they had a hushed discussion that Elena only caught pieces of: "Rob said they had guns ... wouldn't the police want to talk to them ... I'm worried about the kids."

Once Mamma and Ken reached an agreement, it was

Ken who came to speak to them while Mamma hung back, hugging herself nervously. His voice was slow and his hands shook.

"I called the cops before I came over. They said they're looking into it. They told us to stay away because they don't want any evidence disturbed."

"Did you tell them about the men who put something in the creek?"

Ken looked at the floor as though he hadn't heard. Elena was about to ask again but Rob interjected.

"Are they going to talk to Elena and me?"

Ken coughed. "They might, but I gave them a good account of what you saw, so hopefully that will be enough for now."

"What about Frank? Are they going to talk to Frank?" Elena asked.

"I'm sure they will," Ken said.

He left quickly and didn't hug them. Maybe he knew how bad he smelled. Ken wasn't himself and Elena wondered why he was so different around them.

As soon as Ken left, Elena began working on Mamma. If they couldn't go back to Dad's truck, they at least needed to speak to Frank. Maybe he could explain the whole thing so they wouldn't have to sit around and wait for the cops. Maybe he knew what happened to Dad.

Mamma pretended the whole thing was a bad idea, but Elena sensed she wanted to be persuaded. She wanted to know what had happened to Dad just as badly as they did. And though she'd hate to admit it, Frank was the kind of guy who knew things, especially things other people weren't supposed to know.

"Elena's just making up stories again, Mom." Mamma didn't even look at Rob so he went to his room and slammed the door.

"Elena, if we go to the Inn, you can't get your hopes up, alright? Frank might not have anything to tell us."

Elena shot out of her chair and dashed to the front door. Before they left, she stuffed the little jade turtle Frank gave her into her pocket for luck.

As they approached the Inn, Elena scoured the parked vehicles on Main Street for any sign of the truck she'd seen Frank driving. Whatever those other men were doing she wanted to believe Frank was on their side.

Mamma said they should go in through the reception area because kids weren't allowed in the bar. The foyer was a mess. An old armchair sagged next to a table cluttered with leaflets. Flyers and newspaper clippings pinned to the walls fluttered in the draft from the door closing behind them. No one was around. Elena rushed ahead and slammed her hand down on the little bell so hard that Mamma flinched.

Nothing, for a minute or so. Then they heard creaking floorboards and the bar door opened. Frank was calm and casual as always. Elena's mouth burst open as he neared.

"I saw you this afternoon."

Frank's brow crinkled. "I don't think so, kid. I've been here all day."

"No, you were on a back road near the mill and you were driving a truck and you picked up two men."

Frank's frown deepened and he shook his head, miming puzzlement.

"But I saw you! You were wearing a green t-shirt just like that one!"

"I got a few green shirts. Your mom probably doesn't wanna hear this, but I've been wearing this one for the last couple days!"

Frank put his nose to his armpit and pulled a face like it was all a big joke. It wasn't funny. None of it was funny. Dad was missing. She thought again that maybe the curse was real. It was like a bad dream. People were flat-out lying.

"But I saw you!" she said again, exasperated. He had to tell the truth. They needed to know what happened to Dad.

"I don't know what else to tell you, kid. Maybe I got a look-alike."

"If you can think of anything at all that could help us, Frank ..."

Mamma tried, but he shook his head. "I'm sorry. I really am."

Mamma took Elena's arm and tried to lead her away gently, but Elena shook her off. She pulled the turtle out of her pocket and slammed it down on the reception desk. She rolled the turtle on its back so he could see the "MADE IN CHINA" imprint.

"I don't want it anymore. You lie about everything!"

Mamma apologized to him. "Elena's very tired," she said. "We've been through a lot in the last couple of days." Elena scowled as Mamma led her out. She turned around as they left and caught a glimpse of him through the crack of the closing door. He had collapsed into the old armchair and buried his head in his hands.

The Inn was a big part of Stapleton. It was one of those buildings people referred to when they were giving directions to out-of-towners. It was where people went for "Ribz Nite" and "Wingz Nite" and to watch the game.

The Inn had always been at the core of the town, and at

the heart of the Inn was Frank's family. Elena imagined they all had the same quirky smile, and every time they smiled, things that were there a moment ago vanished, and new things appeared. They could create anything or make anything disappear with their stories and their smiles. Like the murdered brothers and the men Frank picked up in the forest.

Maybe Frank had some kind of power over Stapleton. He was always busy doing something that Elena didn't quite understand. Did he want her dad to disappear, or was he trying to help bring him home? If she could understand that, the mystery surrounding the mill explosion might start to make sense.

CHAPTER 8

2 0 1 8

Celeste describes herself as an energy healer. Vivian releases a long, withering sigh. The 20-something year-old recently moved to Stapleton with her boyfriend, who took Rhonda's husband's job as the village maintenance manager. Had Vivian been younger and faster, she would have sped past Celeste's Fall Fair poster board with its bizarre symbols and healing hands, but spritely Celeste cornered her easily.

"What I do is I channel energy to relieve emotional stress, which I see you carry a lot of."

Celeste's beads jangle as she opens her silver-ringed fingers, inviting Vivian to take her hands. Vivian takes a half step back while Todd quietly slips his hands into his cardigan pockets, a bemused expression on his face.

"A past trauma, or a family conflict?" Celeste asks gently, as though Vivian would willingly divulge such a thing in the middle of the Community Hall. "It is never too late in life to clear those energy channels."

"At which fine medical establishment did you qualify?"

"I trained with a master energy healer. Those who open their minds to experience their life force flowing through them can achieve true happiness."

"Do you have a business licence?"

That shuts her up.

Vivian wastes little time thinking about "higher powers" but sometimes it feels as if the forces that be, whatever they may be, are working against this town. "Perhaps you could use your special abilities to improve Stapleton's fortunes," she suggests to Celeste as she continues on through the decorated hall.

Last week, a mudslide swept across the highway and cut them off from the rest of the world for an entire day. Mudslides are a new problem, a consequence of the previous summer's wildfire. The blackened vegetation does a poor job of holding back the earth beside the highway. The road has since re-opened but with more heavy rain in the forecast, the handful of people who usually travel from Stony Creek to catch a glimpse of life in the ghost town have chosen not to attend the Stapleton Fall Fair this year.

The mood inside the Community Hall is subdued. Vivian recognizes the disappointment on the faces of the old-timers. There used to be enough people participating to add a bit of intrigue in every category, and there was a category for everything from quilting to braided garlic. Back when the schools were still open, a local ranching family would set up a miniature petting zoo in the empty lot beside the hall. Even Lloyd Bryant's table-breaking pumpkin fails to cause much of a stir this year. Their hearts aren't in it anymore.

They'd had a hot, dry spell when the plumes of smoke erupted from the hills. Then the plumes became the sky itself, dark and threatening by midday. Ash dropped on their heads; pieces of dead matter a warning that the fire was coming. The flames advanced with enough speed to risk cutting them off at the highway and there was only one way out of town. It was the first time since the Gold Rush that there had been a line of traffic moving in or out of Stapleton.

Todd drove. Vivian stared out of the passenger window, eyes and throat stinging. The flames were out of view but rushing towards them eating up leaves and blackening thick trunks. As they wound up the hill, more vehicles joined the highway from the reserve. Only the houses right beside the road were visible, the land behind them greyed out. The old mill site was completely shrouded in smoke, but she felt it, like an old scar. Land that had burned before.

Then the wind changed, and the threat was gone. As if someone had snapped their fingers and decided that the little town at the end of the highway deserved one more chance.

"Would you like to see an ancient knife blade?"

A middle-aged man, long black hair tied back beneath his baseball cap, points at a chiselled rock on the table in front of him. "That's approximately two thousand years old."

Vivian hums politely.

"We've found a lot of artefacts where the fires burned through the forest last year."

The table is filled with small stone objects that could be a collection of pebbles for all Vivian cares. The man has dark brown eyes, thin wrinkles creeping in around them. She can't make out the logo on his lanyard. She doesn't recognize him from the reserve but she heard they've taken an interest in digging up bits of history. He could be from the university.

An unmistakable figure stares at her from the far side of the table. Mary Jones in a shapeless black sweater; flat white hair, thick lenses and wobbly pink lipstick.

"Mary told me there's no council support for heritage funding," the man who might be from the university bemoans. "That's a real shame. There are so many stories that could be told about this area, enough to support a small visitor attraction …"

"… I look to the future, not to the past," Vivian says dismissively as she spots her neighbour, Liz, and waves. "We already have an economic plan for our town."

She refuses to make eye contact with Mary or the archaeologist as she moves towards the safety of her sensible neighbour, whose conversation points rarely extend beyond the day's weather. Mary can complain to whoever she wants. This is Vivian's town.

CHAPTER 9

1 9 9 4

"WHY DO BUILDINGS burn down?"

St. Margaret's was a white church, inside and out. White siding, white walls, white cushions on the hard pews. Even the roof was off-white. It had been around a long time, but in other incarnations. It had burnt down twice since the gold miners first built it.

"I told you to behave." Mamma's hissing aggravated Elena's eardrum. "Nobody wants to hear about burning buildings right now."

Today was a serious day, and Mamma's face was solemn, her hair pinned neatly to the back of her head. She patted down the butterfly collar on Elena's cotton dress and the three of them sat uneasily in their pew. Mamma made Rob wear a tie. He kept tugging at it. Elena wondered if it was horribly uncomfortable, like an itchy sweater. She nudged him, but he wouldn't look at her. She knew he was thinking about Dad.

Elena sensed eyes settling on her. She turned around and stared back. They were pitying her because her dad was missing. They didn't know him like she did, so they didn't know he was fine. Her nights were restless as she fought off the horrors her mind conjured up, but during the day it was easier to convince herself they weren't true.

The pews were hard even with the thin white cushions on top of them. Elena wriggled. Mamma reached out and held her hand firmly. Her hand was cold, so Elena wrapped both of her own around it to warm it up. Mamma almost smiled.

Elena hadn't wanted to attend the memorial service. The explosion was everywhere. Every conversation, every news report was littered with reminders that Dad wasn't there to hold her or explain things. That morning she'd complained of having a headache but Mamma ignored her whining.

No one knew yet exactly what had caused the explosion, or they weren't telling. A group of older kids who were hanging out at the park said some people's skin came off like layers of clothing, and one man lost his sight and another died when a wall crushed him. With each new rumour, she wondered if her dad was part of that. Had he felt it? Had he seen it? Two died; then four, then five, until Dad was the only one still missing. They'd found the remains of all the others in the mill. She'd heard the teenagers talking about one guy had to be identified by his teeth because his whole body had burnt up. Maybe Dad's teeth were in there too and the firefighters hadn't found them yet. Elena tried to push her mind away from the awful thoughts. Anyway, he must've got out. They'd found his truck.

Elena looked back at her brother. He was rubbing his eyes with his sleeve, casually, but his eyes were red. He had barely eaten or slept since the explosion. Elena never lost her appetite and wondered if that meant she was a bad person.

"Such a terrible tragedy," an old lady murmured to them as she squeezed in at the end of their pew. Mamma um-hummed politely as she shuffled closer to Elena, who was jammed into

Rob. Elena looked back at the stuffed pews and the line of people still trying to make their way in. The whole community was inside the church or waiting to enter. Their bodies dripped sweat and service cards fanned glistening skin and puffy eyes.

Gathering in the pews at the very front were the families of the men that had died. It was hard for Elena to understand the weight of their sadness. One woman was crying so hard she was hiccupping. The woman beside her took the baby out of her arms to help calm its wailing.

When the church got so crammed that people were clogging up the aisle and there was still a queue trailing out of the door, somebody important decided they needed to find a bigger space. The swollen congregation emptied into the neighbouring park. Out there, a light breeze touched their faces and gently nudged clouds across the sky. It dispersed the sounds of movement and chatter and sadness so that the gathering seemed more peaceful. Elena spotted Logan with his mother and tried to rush over to him, but Mamma held her arm. "Not now," she said softly.

Men talked. Religious men, chiefs, a politician, the brother of one of the deceased. A silver-haired man from the mill company told them all he wasn't going to rest until the disaster was fully investigated. Elena saw his car heading out of town minutes after his speech.

The mayor and the local councillors were all there. A blonde-haired woman locked eyes on Elena. She wore a sharp black suit and was Stapleton's only female councillor but Elena didn't know her name. She came into the café sometimes and ordered a coffee with something sweet, which Ken served with a miniature fork. Everyone else just used their fingers. The councillor kept staring at her, not in a particularly friendly or even pitying way. Elena felt awkward so she slipped around the other side of Mamma.

Brandon was standing nearby, one hand wrapped in a bandage that disappeared up his long-sleeved shirt. He was calm now, not like the night he'd knocked on their door, smothered by ash and shock. He was holding a young woman's hand. Elena thought about asking Mamma if she was his girlfriend but Mamma probably didn't know or care and she'd just get shushed again.

Brandon looked directly into Elena's inquiring eyes. He'd caught her staring at him and she smiled awkwardly and looked away. When she glanced back the grief on his face made her look away for good.

Elena didn't know who Peter Bernier was, not when Mamma had softly mentioned his death earlier in the week, and not when the mayor read out the names of the dead men. She didn't make the connection between Peter Bernier and Pete, Logan's dad, until the mayor talked about Peter Bernier, loving father and loyal friend and she saw Logan's mom flee the crowd on unsteady legs.

Elena couldn't remember a time when Logan was a Bernier. He was a Kerr now, like his stepdad. Logan leaned into Mr. Kerr's arm. His step-brother Taylor stood on the other side of him. Logan spotted Elena and he stared right through her. No one held her back this time or told her not to go to him, she didn't move. She couldn't.

The first day of the school year was delayed until after the memorial service. Mamma snapped a couple of barrettes onto Elena's hair and kissed her forehead. When she stepped out of the door, Mamma grabbed hold of her hand as if she wasn't going to let go.

Elena's class had a new teacher, Miss Meyer, who wore long cardigans and skirts that fluttered around her ankles. Her frizzy curls bounced when she moved and she spoke softly about finding peace and love even during times of crisis. She was very young and she wasn't from the area, and if the explosion had never happened, that would have been enough to make her the talk of the café.

"We don't always get a chance to say goodbye," Miss Meyer murmured when Elena asked where Logan was. He wasn't in her class and she couldn't find him in the playground at break time. Elena was sure her new teacher had misunderstood. Logan had been her friend since kindergarten. He'd be back as soon as he was feeling better.

～ "Curtis? Are you home?"

Mamma called for him every time they returned to the empty house. Elena wanted her to stop. She made it sound like he'd just nipped out to get something, as if they'd see his shaved head pop around the kitchen doorway and he'd say: "I'm back now! I'm fine." As if his absence didn't hurt. The only reply was from the humming refrigerator.

Mamma used to be the first one up in the morning but now she often stayed in bed until almost midday. Rob said she wasn't sleeping at night so they should be quiet in the mornings.

Mamma used to make them a special breakfast on Saturdays. French toast or eggs and bacon. Rob scowled as he scraped the burnt bits off his toast. Then he slathered blueberry jam onto the salvaged remnants. Elena tiptoed around him and made her own breakfast, smearing her bread with peanut butter and honey. He snapped at her for using his knife. She sat opposite him and quietly ate her toast while he stared at his.

"Why won't he just come home?" Rob said.

"Maybe he can't."

"What do you mean?"

Elena didn't have an answer but knew he'd come home if he could. Something was stopping him. Or maybe someone. A dangerous someone. Or someone that Frank knew. Or Frank himself.

CHAPTER 10

2 0 1 8

THE AIR HAS a bite to it and the sky is darkening for a storm. Vivian wraps her cardigan tightly around her chest as she deadheads clusters of marigolds, pansies and geraniums. They might get a few more flowers if the frost holds off.

Dean sits on the garden bench. He did offer to help. Todd jokingly suggested he could mow the lawn. "Are you able to get assistance around the house?" Dean asked. Todd shuffled inside to make tea. He doesn't like being made to feel old, either.

"Frank didn't want a funeral. He asked for his ashes to be scattered at a viewpoint in the mountains," Dean tells Vivian. She examines the limp brown petals in her gloved hand. "He also wanted everyone to come to the Inn and have a good time but not call it a celebration of life, because that makes it sound like a funeral."

She sighs as she looks up at the clouds. Even in death, Frank has failed to keep things simple. Gathering above her are the black beginnings of another almighty downpour, another highway slide, another mess to clean up.

"It's on Friday. Will you come?"

"No. Frank never liked funerals."

"But it's not …"

"His lawyer no doubt told him if he didn't provide any instructions, people would organize a funeral. He'd have been perfectly happy simply blowing away on the breeze."

"You knew him better than I did but it's important to say goodbye to old friends. And it's an opportunity for me to introduce myself to the community and let them know what's happening with the Inn."

"What is happening with the Inn?"

"Nothing. For now. But they should know it has changed hands. I'm waiting to hear more about the business development you mentioned."

Vivian points her pruning shears at him. "You will be the first to know. It is worth the wait, I promise."

She leaves the shears on the wrought iron table and sits beside Dean. He leans away from her, very slightly.

"I wanted your advice on another matter."

The first drops of rain fall and Dean looks anxiously at the sky. He's in short sleeves, hairs raised on his exposed forearms.

"I didn't make the connection before, that Frank's manager, Giulia Reid, is Curtis Reid's wife. One of the regulars mentioned it to me and then I remembered his name from all the media coverage of the mill explosion."

Vivian bristles at the sound of their names. Her home is her sanctuary. Todd should have told Dean she was busy when he showed up on their doorstep.

"Why did Frank hire her? You'd think she'd drive business away after what her husband did."

"Beauty blinds a lot of men."

Dean frowns. "Were Frank and Giulia … a thing?"

Vivian shrugs. "Technically she's still married."

"Is she bad for business?"

"I have no idea, Dean. I haven't seen Frank's books."

The drops fall more heavily. Dean stands and hovers beside the bench, waiting for an invitation to enter the house, but Vivian has no intention of continuing this particular stroll down Memory Lane.

"So, will you come to Frank's send off?" The raindrops collect on Dean's shirt, forming dark patches.

"I appreciate the invitation, but I don't think it's what Frank would've wanted."

Vivian's wool cardigan offers more protection than Dean's shirt. It isn't long before Dean makes his excuses and exits through the side gate.

"What are you doing? Come inside!" Todd yells through the rain as he approaches her. "Where's Dean? I made tea."

~ Cars are parked all along Main Street. Vivian hasn't seen it so busy in years. She inspects them as she walks by: Kirk George's F150, Pam's red Corolla, dinged on the passenger door, Len Sampson's classic blue Chevy pickup, Liz's Rav4 with a sticker on the bumper. "If you can read this, you're TOO CLOSE!"

She looks up and finds herself under the shadow of the Inn's veranda that stretches across the sidewalk.

"Vivian, you came!"

Dean strolls out of the main entrance, both doors wide open letting out the noise of the gathering inside. He's wearing a black shirt and pants, black leather shoes. She remembers; Frank's non-funeral.

She pushes her palm forwards defensively before he can

take her arm and lead her anywhere. "I'm not going in. I just wanted to …"

Dean rests his hand against one of the veranda's thick supporting beams. "I understand. It's hard, losing people."

He doesn't understand at all. Silence lingers awkwardly between them, both looking for a way out. Beyond the open doorway, a loud voice rises above the rest and a peal of laughter follows.

"I should get back inside. You're more than welcome to join us if you change your mind. Thanks for coming."

He disappears into the dark building that holds the town's secrets. She had been proud of the Inn once. However run down, it remained a central piece of Stapleton's history. Now it makes her sick.

She turns away from it and walks right into another piece of the past she would rather forget. Mary is blocking the sidewalk in her mobility scooter.

"Surely you haven't come to say farewell to Frank?" Vivian asks incredulously. Mary knows too much and hasn't forgiven either of them.

"I heard the Inn was under new ownership. I thought I would introduce myself."

Vivian steps delicately off the sidewalk and squeezes between two parked vehicles. Mary's words follow her.

"Did you know it's the seventh month in the lunar calendar?"

"No, I didn't."

"In the seventh month, the dead come to visit the living."

"Fascinating," Vivian mutters. She's relieved when she hears the whizzing of Mary's scooter, but it stops almost as soon as it has started.

"It's the end of your era, Vivian. Frank is gone. You're not doing so great yourself from what I hear."

Vivian turns and glowers at Mary, then regrets giving her the attention when she sees the smirk on her face.

"Out with the old. In with the new. Maybe it's time you made peace with the past, while you still can."

Vivian ignores her, tightening her grip around the top of her cane. She resumes her slow march down the street. She looks back only once, when she hears Dean introducing himself and welcoming Mary inside.

CHAPTER 11

1 9 9 4

"WHAT GRADE ARE you in, Elena?"

"Five."

"Do you enjoy school?"

Logan hadn't come back. Miss Meyer was still offering them sympathy at every opportunity and Elena's classmates couldn't stop talking about the explosion, which made it really hard to stop thinking about Dad.

She stared at the female officer's shoes. Flat and black with laces. Very plain. Not the kind of shoes Mamma would ever wear.

"What do you remember about the day of the explosion?"

"It was hot."

The woman made a note. The officers wanted to speak to each of them individually. They sat down with Elena first. Mamma and Rob lingered nervously in the kitchen.

The female officer was older than the man, but they both had the same way about them. They spoke as though they were reading from a script.

"Is there anything else you can tell me about that day?"

Elena shrugged. She wasn't feeling very talkative. The questions kept coming whether she answered them or not.

"Did you see anyone else at your house? Have you ever seen anyone threaten your dad? Or give him money? Or ask him to do something he seemed uncomfortable with? Who are his friends? Is he close friends with Brandon? Where does Brandon live?"

"The reserve," Elena answered, and the policewoman paused, just for a second, long enough for Elena to hope it would stop. It didn't. "Did you see your dad drinking that day?"

"He had coffee at breakfast," Elena told her. "And he also had toast with peanut butter." That was the only question she could answer comfortably.

"Did he ever talk about leaving? How was he feeling? Was he angry? Was he sad?"

Was he? Wasn't he? Was Elena supposed to know? She prayed for some emergency that would whisk the police away. But God didn't work like that. Elena wasn't sure exactly how God worked. It was becoming less and less clear how He could help.

The officers smiled in unison, as though they had timed it. It didn't mean they were pleased with her—Elena knew they weren't. All she'd really been able to tell them was about Dad's breakfast, and the only thing she gathered from their questions was that Dad was in trouble in a way she still didn't understand.

"Did you find my dad's truck?"

"Yes we did," the man said calmly. "How do you know about that?"

"Me and my brother found it. What about the men by the cabin? Did you find them?"

"Which men are you referring to?"

"Ken called you to tell you we found the truck and we

saw them. One of them dropped something in the creek and then Frank came by and picked them up in another truck and drove away."

The woman frowned this time and scrawled something on her notepad. "Who is Ken?" she asked.

"He didn't call you, did he?"

The officers looked at each other but didn't give her a proper answer. They said something about how he may have spoken to another officer and that they would look into it. It didn't make any sense. The police shared their information; she'd seen it on Mamma's cop shows. They had meetings in front of big boards patterned with photos and pieces of string. She didn't have a chance to press them any further on it. Mamma came in and gently pushed her out by her shoulders. "Come on, Elena, it's Rob's turn now."

~ Elena was never left alone, not for a moment. When Mamma had things to do, somebody else was responsible for her. Ken was looking after her today, a Saturday, and she was restless. She watched him for a while and concluded that something still wasn't right about him. The Ken she knew was particular about cleanliness, especially at the café, but his plaid shirt looked as though he'd picked it up off the floor this morning. His skin sagged underneath his eyes and he didn't hum along when Alan Jackson came on the radio.

"Did you really call the cops?" she finally asked him.

"Pay attention or you'll drop it."

Ken was referring to the pastry she'd pulled out from behind the glass with a pair of tongs. Mrs. Ellsworth had ordered it, one of the regulars. Ken showed Elena how to select the right-sized plate and then he entrusted her with the tongs. She thought about dropping it just to make him listen to her. She let the pastry hang over the floor long enough that Ken grabbed the tongs and shoved it onto the plate a little too violently. The icing went all wonky and Mrs. Ellsworth's smile froze. She peered across the counter.

"Don't worry, dear. Those things can be tricky. I can't use them at all now, what with my arthritis."

Mrs. Ellsworth was always nice but she also liked to remind everyone of her old-person ailments. She had a different one every time Elena saw her in the café. Ken finished pouring Mrs. Ellsworth's tea and the two of them stood in silence as the old woman hobbled over to a two-seater. Elena turned back to Ken. She wasn't going to let it go that easily.

"You never called the cops, did you?"

"Of course, I did."

"When I asked them, they didn't know what I was talking about."

Ken's voice had begun to falter. She knew it was because she'd caught him. "There are a lot of cops working on the case. I must've spoken to somebody else."

"But the cops that came to talk to us knew everything about us except that, because you didn't tell them!"

"I'm not going to stand here and argue with you. I've got a café to run."

Ken made her a hot chocolate and told her to go enjoy it. She sat down but she didn't enjoy it, and he didn't look like he was enjoying himself much either. He was hunched up, frowning at the counter as he scrubbed it with a cloth. He caught her staring at him and that seemed to agitate him even more. She knew if he could send her home, he would, but he'd already told Mamma he would look after her for the whole morning.

Sitting beside Elena were two really old guys that came to

Stapleton to work in the coalmine that no longer existed. They were regulars at the café, and they often talked loudly about the old days so everyone could hear about how things were when they were young. Elena liked their stories, but no one else ever seemed very interested. Dad called them windbags.

One of the old men straightened up and took an interest in a mill worker who came in with his family. The old guy's throat rasped as he cleared it. "You lookin' for work then?"

"No. I got a job."

The mill worker turned to his wife, but the old man kept going.

"You better start lookin'. Everyone's gonna be leaving town trying to find those same jobs somewhere else. You gotta get ahead of the competition. How many guys worked at the mill? A few hundred?"

The mill worker ignored him. Ken came over and took their order. The old men kept staring at the young family. Ken brought over coffees and glasses of coke.

It was clear the mill worker hoped the conversation was over but the old man continued. "All I'm sayin' is they won't rebuild. Whatever the company tells you is bullshit. This whole thing is bullshit. It stinks. But no one's talking about that, are they?"

Elena's eyes widened. She wanted to ask the old man what he meant, but the mill worker raised his voice. "I'm here with my kids, as you can see. Why don't you keep your opinions to yourself?"

"Just trying to give you some friendly advice."

"You don't know what you're talking about."

Ken banged a cup on the counter and squared his shoulders. He was much bigger than the other men.

"It's alright, Ken. We're leaving anyway." The old men got

up and scraped their chairs back from the table. Elena desperately wanted to follow them and enquire about their suspicions but she could see that it was not a good time to ask questions.

Mary came in as the two old guys left. Elena could tell she'd picked up on something by the way her gaze drifted casually from the old men to the mill worker. But Mary didn't deviate from her routine; she dropped money on the table and Ken brought her a coffee. She pulled open her newspaper and began examining it. Elena brought her hot chocolate over to Mary's table, sat down on the chair next to Mary and stared at her until she put the paper down.

"We're not leaving town," Elena said. "They're going to rebuild the sawmill."

"Things change, Elena."

She glared at Mary. She was supposed to be on her side. Mary shuffled her paper.

"Why did they send the army in?"

Mary shrugged. "All I know about the military is that they don't answer to you and me."

Ken reappeared with Mary's change. He didn't look at Elena.

"Ken lied about ..."

"... Didn't your mom tell you to behave?" he said.

Ken never spoke to her like that. Even Mary looked surprised. He cleared his throat quietly as if his words had just been part of regular conversation. He retreated behind the counter, his barricade. With a snap of her newspaper, Mary put hers up, too. Elena was shut out.

In a bit, Ken came back, this time with two cinnamon buns. "On the house," he said. Elena loved cinnamon buns. Mary eyed her bun but didn't touch it.

"What do you want?" she asked cautiously.

Ken laughed uncomfortably. "Elena's been stuck inside all morning. If you have time, maybe the two of you could go for a short walk."

Elena looked at Mary excitedly. She knew Ken was trying to get rid of her, but she didn't mind. She didn't want to be around him either, not now that he was on her list, along with Frank, of people who could no longer be trusted.

"Where do you want to go then?" Mary asked. "The park?"

Elena shook her head. "The park's boring. I go there all the time." She thought about it. "Did you live in Stapleton as a kid?"

"Yeah."

"I want to see where you lived."

"Alright then. But it's too far to walk." Mary folded her paper and got up. Ken boxed the buns and a few minutes later Mary was driving the two of them out of town along a bumpy forestry road. Her old car jolted violently, sending crumbs flying from Elena's sticky bun. With every bump she felt a little more nauseous. As they climbed, more and more trees crowded the sagebrush until the forest was a wall of green.

Not far from town, they pulled in hard against a grassy verge. It didn't seem like the kind of place kids grew up. No homes or cars or basketball hoops in driveways. Maybe Mary had forgotten where she lived. That happened to people when they got older, but Elena wasn't sure Mary had lived quite long enough for her memories to get jumbled up.

Mary turned the engine off but didn't move. Elena unclipped her seatbelt and waited. "I've never brought anyone here before," Mary mumbled as she stared out of the window.

Elena followed Mary through the pine trees into a clearing taken up mostly by tall grass and clusters of sagebrush. Mary hovered over the charred stumps of a building frame.

"What is this place?"

"The Deer Creek Camp."

"What kind of camp was it?" Elena asked. There were no spots to pitch tents. She couldn't see any fire pits or swimming holes or a place to pay fees and pick up firewood.

"It was a prison kinda camp."

Elena found the two words difficult to put together in her head. "What's a prison camp?"

"It's a place to put people you don't like without having to go to the expense of building an actual building to house them."

"So the tents were like jail cells and no one could leave their tent?"

"We didn't have tents. We had huts and we could leave our huts. But we couldn't leave the camp without special permission."

We, we, we. Elena had to process it for a moment before she spoke. "They put you in the prison camp?"

Before Mary could answer, Elena had to ask another question. "Did you do something bad?"

"No worse than what you get up to. I was four years old when they brought me and my parents here. My parents were farmers who kept to themselves mostly, but we were Canadians with Japanese ancestors, and there was a war on. The Japanese were the enemy. The government decided we were a danger to society. So they took our home and everything we owned and sent us here."

Elena couldn't make sense of it, and Mary appeared to have said all she wanted to say, so Elena stayed quiet. She knew there were two of them, world wars, and people from Stapleton who died in them had their names written on a big piece of rock in front of the Village Hall and they put a wreath in front of it on Remembrance Day and old people showed up wearing colourful medals.

The sky clouded over and the wind tugged at the sagebrush and the prickly grasses. Miss Meyer had said sagebrush was a healing plant. She'd brought bound sprigs into the classroom that her students passed around and put to their noses to smell the outdoors inside. Then she announced that Logan and his stepbrother Taylor had switched schools and their family was moving to Stony Creek.

Elena ran to his house after school and tried to say goodbye. She knocked on the door a few times but no one answered. She wanted to know if Logan was still angry with her for the cemetery trip and if he blamed her for what happened to his dad. Maybe he didn't think it was all just a coincidence. Maybe he still believed in the curse. It was too late to find out. There was no longer a sticker on the upstairs window. The blinds were drawn downstairs but she could see bare walls through the cracks. He had already gone.

Elena stooped down and pulled at a piece of sage. She inhaled the sweetness that stuck to her fingers. "Sagebrush has a taproot," she found herself telling Mary. "That's how it gets water when it doesn't rain for a long time. The taproot goes deep down to the water underground. Miss Meyer says Stapleton is like the sagebrush. Things have changed so we have to adapt."

Mary let out a peculiar sound, a strangled laugh, the kind that meant it wasn't funny.

"Stapleton is going to grow a taproot, is it? Is that what your teacher told you?"

Elena went quiet. She didn't want to hear any more about what Mary thought. This was her home. It would get better again. It had to.

She circled the scorched wood and then poked it so that it powdered the tips of her fingers black. There had been a fire here, probably a big one, a long time ago. Fire seemed to destroy everything in Stapleton sooner or later.

Elena scuffed her shoes against the dirt as she explored the clearing. Leaves were coming off the aspens by the creek. The water was shallow; the banks were too big for the thin stream that burbled over the stones. A rotten board had sunk into the side of one bank, wedged in by larger stones. She pulled it out of the stream. It was long enough to make a bridge over the creek, but she wasn't strong enough to man-oeuvre it across to the other side. She latched onto one end of the board and dragged it into the clearing, stumbling over the rough tangle of shrubs and roots. Mud stains marked her t-shirt and the bottoms of her jeans. She looked up at Mary guiltily. It was now Mary's job to look after her, and Mamma would surely have something to say about the state of her clothes. But Mary didn't seem to care. She watched as Elena leaned the board against the cremated remains of a shelter.

"We used to play in that creek." Mary's voice was quiet, as though she was speaking to herself. Elena wiped the creek dirt from her hands onto her jeans. If Mary didn't care, she wasn't going to.

"I was younger than you then. Skinny as a whip."

It was hard to imagine Mary young and thin, splashing in streams. Elena teetered along old scars underfoot; a rotting wooden frame hidden beneath the sagebrush. She scuffled around in the undergrowth looking for more clues. Maybe a rescued picture frame, a pair of old-fashioned spectacles or those funny metal baths people used to wash in.

She didn't find anything but she could imagine the place as Mary described it. Rows of makeshift huts and in one was a little schoolhouse. That came later, Mary explained. For a while they didn't go to school at all. The huts didn't have toilets; they had to use the communal outhouses which stank. Mary was afraid to go in them at night, especially in the winter when they had to trudge through snow to reach them.

Though the day was dull, the earth was still warm and when Elena took Mary's hand she felt that warmth flowing through her. Mary looked surprised, but Elena didn't let go. She led Mary to the creek, to the place she said she used to play. They didn't go too close. Mary couldn't manage the slippery rocks anymore, but Elena knew she could hear the water washing the stones because a smile slipped over her lips. Fragments of dazzling light bounced off the shifting surface.

"Did you have friends at the camp?"

Mary didn't answer at first and Elena thought maybe she wouldn't, but then she said: "I had a friend named Kazuko. She was like a big sister. She was a year older than me. Our families lived in the same hut."

Elena wanted to know what Mary and Kazuko's hut looked like exactly, and if they got to bring anything with them, and if they had their own bedrooms, but Mary was already talking about another place.

"Before the war, we had a farm in the Lower Mainland. I loved it there. I always thought we'd go back. We never did."

"I'd like to live on a farm."

Elena wouldn't exchange her own home though. She'd rather stay exactly where she was than live anywhere else. She hadn't been to a lot of places, but she was pretty sure there wasn't anywhere else better to live. Rob thought Stapleton was boring, but he thought everything was boring except basketball and computer games and his girlfriend.

"Did Kazuko live on a farm too?"

"No. Her family came from Ucluelet. That's about as far west as you can be and still be in Canada," Mary explained. "Kazuko used to say her dad could see all the way to Japan from his fishing boat."

"Could he?" Elena asked curiously.

"No."

Elena thought about how intensely Mamma could look at a single photograph from her cluttered box of Italian mementoes. "Places don't leave you," she'd said once when Elena had asked her about it. They weren't going to leave Stapleton. Dad was coming home. The mill would be rebuilt.

Mary told Elena how cold it used to get in the winter. They weren't used to it, coming from the Lower Mainland where there wasn't much snow, and the shacks weren't built for keeping the cold out. Her back drooped as she sank deeper into her memories.

"My dad left us for a while in the beginning. He was taken to a different camp. But he came back. Kazuko's dad was sent east. They didn't see him for years."

"Because of the war?" Elena asked. Mary seemed not to hear her as she carefully navigated the rough ground.

It was hard not to think about Dad. When her heart hurt so much that she felt sick, she reminded herself that he would come home. Maybe it had been the same for Mary and Kazuko.

Mary tried to show Elena where their shack had stood, though she couldn't be sure of the exact location. It looked so different back then, she said. Elena examined the evidence beneath her feet, but there was only earth. She pulled a stick from the ground, the perfect height for a walking stick, and she used it to poke between the shrubs.

Mary checked her watch. "It's time we got back."

Elena wanted to stay longer, but she wouldn't argue with Mary. She trailed her across the clearing towards the road.

"Why did everyone leave the camp?" Elena asked.

"The war ended. Kazuko and her family went to join her dad in Ontario. None of us got our homes back so people dispersed across the country. But our family didn't have to go far. My dad found a job at a local ranch. He was a hard worker and he knew about farming. The rancher had a trailer on his property and we lived there for a while."

"My dad's coming home soon. He'll find another job too. We won't have to leave Stapleton either. We like it here."

Mary was quiet. Elena drew her stick against the spiny pads of a little prickly pear cactus, pretending not to care about Mary's response, which didn't come.

"Why does everything burn down?" Elena asked.

"It's nature's way of getting rid of the old wood. Fire makes way for new life." Mary interrupted her own thought. "I don't mean the mill. When there are people involved it's different, but in nature, that's what fire does. It cleans house."

Elena liked that idea. Fire wasn't always bad. Fire could clean things. Mary seemed to know a lot about a lot of things. Elena decided to tell her how she'd found Dad's truck and then spotted Frank nearby. Maybe Mary could explain what Frank was doing out there on a lonely backroad.

"No one believes me because Frank said it wasn't him but I know it was."

Elena examined Mary's expression to try and figure out if she believed her. Mary didn't seem surprised by what Elena said, but then Mary never did. Whatever she was thinking, she was keeping it to herself.

They were interrupted by a crack in the trees. A figure moving through the bush a short distance away. Mary grabbed her hand.

"Let's go."

"Who is it?"

"I don't know."

"Then why do we have to leave?"

"Because I don't know who it is and we're out here on our own."

Elena didn't know why they had to be scared of one other person, but Mary was insistent. She kept a tight hold of Elena's arm all the way back to the car.

When they got to the road, Mary yanked Elena's hand. There was a man in black pants and bomber jacket leaning against Mary's car, casually, like it was normal for him to be there, out on the forestry road alone.

"Stay close to me," Mary whispered.

This man was young with hair that was almost curly and almost red, eyes almost blue, almost green. He didn't smile. His face was blank, just like Mary's. Two hard-edged people staring each other down, waiting for one to crack.

"Are you aware this is private property?" He spoke slowly, deliberately, as if each syllable was a big effort.

"Is it? Where's the sign?"

His stare got meaner. "What exactly are you doing out here?"

"We're getting some fresh air. Who are you?"

"I work for a private security firm. It's my job to keep out trespassers."

"Maybe your employers should invest in a big fence and some signs. Like they used to have up here."

"So you do know this is private property?"

The two of them glared at each other, Elena wondering who would break their gaze first. The man bent down in front of Elena; his breath on her face.

"Do you come up here often for fresh air?"

Elena was too afraid to answer. She looked at Mary and decided to imitate her. She gave the man the coldest stare she could.

He got up slowly. "Don't come back."

Mary pulled Elena's hand and they walked towards the car. Elena thought about turning around but Mary yanked her arm again and they hurried as quickly as Mary could hurry to her vehicle. As soon as they opened the doors and got in, Elena looked back to where the man had been standing, but he wasn't there anymore. Mary had noticed too.

"Where the hell did he go?" she muttered under her breath.

Mary started the engine. She spun the car around and they bounced over the potholes back down the logging road. Her eyes kept flitting back and forth between the road and the rear-view mirror. Elena spun around in her seat, half expecting to see a black sedan with tinted windows speeding towards them, the kind she'd seen hurtling through Mamma's cop shows, but they were the only vehicle on the road. Mary clunked into a different gear and Elena scanned the trees for signs of people. Neither of them spoke for a minute.

"He's part of the curse."

"No, Elena."

"He could be. That's how he just appeared and disappeared."

Elena sat back and thought about it. The trees raced past the windows, more quickly as the road surface improved.

"Listen to me," Mary said firmly. "Your dad's caught up in something. Whatever it is, you need to stay out of it."

"But he didn't say anything about my dad."

Mary just looked at her and Elena knew then she was right. The mill was in this area, too; it had a proper road leading up to it, not a raggedy forestry one, and it was nearby. As the car lumbered into town, Elena was more convinced than ever that something much bigger had happened than anyone was talking about, and somehow Dad was tangled up right in the middle.

CHAPTER 12

2 0 1 8

Todd insists on driving her to the post office. He says he
wants to come, but that's a lie. He helps her put on her shoes
and he buttons up her jacket. She's having trouble with her
hands at the moment, but it will pass.

A man stands beside the towers of little metal mailboxes.
He is flipping through envelopes, his mailbox door still hanging open with the key in it.

"What's his name again?" Vivian whispers to her husband.

"Dean. Frank's son."

"Good morning, Dean," she says with a smile.

Dean starts at the sound of her voice. "Oh ... hi Vivian.
How are you?"

"Very well. How's business?"

Dean glances at the envelopes. "We'll see. I should be
going."

He locks his mailbox and barely acknowledges them as
he leaves. Vivian stares through the glass until she sees his
black Audi roll by.

She turns and looks at her husband. "You should find
out what that's about."

He rolls his eyes, but he'll do it.

⤳ Vivian sits on the bench and admires a Steller's jay as he struts across the lawn in his fine black crest and deep blue coat. Their house is modest compared to her childhood home but it suits two seniors. The garden backs onto fields and the street is always quiet, so she can imagine she is part of the countryside.

She click-clicks her knitting needles and examines the lumpy blanket. She rests her messy handiwork on her lap and closes her eyes so her eyelids can soak up the sun's warmth.

Todd lowers himself gently beside her, folding his reading glasses into his shirt pocket. "I think it would be best if you don't spend any more time getting to know Dean."

"Who?"

"Frank's son."

"Yes. Why? What about him?"

"Mary Jones has been talking to him. About the mill."

Out of the corner of her eye she catches the jay spread its vibrant wings, escaping with its beauty.

"Are you sure?"

Todd interlocks his fingers and looks down at his knees. "Mary has found a new audience for her theories. Apparently he's listening. He's been asking around."

"There's no ... existence. There's no ..."

"Evidence. Proof. Maybe not. But Mary's started something and Dean's been talking to the right people. They're trying to dig it up again. I just want you to be prepared for that."

Prepared. Half the time he talks to her like she's a child, and now he wants her to be prepared.

He rattles on but his words are coming apart as they fall

out of his mouth. She can only collect fragments and wonder at their meaning. She deciphers a name. Pam. He is saying something about Pam. She taps her forehead, but she can't place Pam at the mill. She didn't work there, did she?

"What could Pam have told him?"

"She might have mentioned Pete."

"Who?"

"Pete Bernier. Her ex-husband."

Yes, she remembers now. Pete Bernier was supposed to be dependable, but he couldn't hold his nerve. Frank said trust him, but Vivian didn't. He spent too much time propping up the bar at the Inn. She should've trusted her instinct, but who else could she rely on to take care of that sort of thing, if not Frank?

Todd unlocks and relocks his fingers again. "If you remember, Pam did make a bit of a fuss when Pete … about the timing of everything."

"I don't. Remind me."

"The explosion happened about 20 minutes before the shift change. Pete was scheduled to work on the next shift, which meant he was inside the mill at least 20 minutes early. Pam told the police he wouldn't be on the job a second before he had to be. She also told them he'd been working for Frank on the side, and that he mentioned he was expecting a big payday, although Pete never told Pam what they were up to. That was just before the explosion happened. The cops never followed up on it, of course, because you saw to it that they wouldn't."

That sounds about right, although she has no memory of the specifics. She tries hard to remember Pete. A well-built man with centre parted hair that stopped around his ears and the hint of a moustache. He had an accent, didn't he?

Todd continues to churn up things that were and things that are and things that could be. She doesn't catch any of it until he repeats her name: Mary Jones.

The young man has been talking to Mary Jones.

Vivian rubs her temples. It's too much. This can't happen now. Todd is looking at her again in that odd way, as if down a microscope, pitying how small she's become. She tries to come up with some clever remark, but the words shuffle uncomfortably in her brain and she needs to shut him out. Shut it all out. Why is she so exhausted? Is he giving her those pills again? She can't ask him. She can't fit the words together.

～ The year is 1976. A frost arrives much earlier than usual and kills her tomato plants but it doesn't keep the residents of Stapleton from attending the most important council meeting of the decade. She's wearing a midnight blue skirt suit with gold buttons, her feathered blonde hair revitalized earlier in the day at a Stony Creek salon. Todd says she looks like a business executive in a Hollywood movie. She touches her pearls, straightens her back, lifts her chin and marches into the council chamber.

The village hall is as busy as she has ever seen it. The welcoming nods and pleasantries from the residents remind her of strolling down Main Street holding Father's hand, except this success is her own. These people respect her and they have come today to support her proposal. They voted for her because they trusted her to get this town back on track after the closure of her father's coalmine some years before. They know she won't let them down.

Vivian can barely concentrate as the mayor rumbles through the banal discussions that clog up every session. By the time he clanks his gavel and moves the meeting forward to the only important matter on the agenda, bodies have become restless and yawns indiscreet.

Alan Watford, their aging CAO, brings no colour to Vivian's proposal as he reads her words aloud. Nonetheless, there are excited murmurs in the public seating area. This is the turning point and they have come to witness it: the end of Stapleton's slump.

One person stands opposed. A short, unbecoming figure in flared pants and a knit sweater. Muddy green and brown. Hair flat against her head and large glasses that take up half of her round face. She stands at the head of the full room with the kind of awkwardness that makes other people wish the ground would swallow her up for her own sake.

"For those of you who don't know me, my name is Mary Jones. My maiden name is Ishida. I was born in Canada to Japanese Canadian parents. We were forcibly relocated to Stapleton during the war."

Vivian casts a discreet glance at a couple of the old timers; expressions steeled by their wartime hatred of the "Japs." Mary's voice wobbles and then levels off into a steady monotone.

"I was 4 years old when we arrived in 1942. That was 30 years ago, but it was a traumatic period in my life and some of the memories I have of that time remain very clear to me."

A wary murmur creeps around the room as Mary pauses to check her speaking notes. They're all wondering what this has to do with the proposed sawmill. Mary is up against a town that is hungry, a town that longs for what they had. It will take a powerful speech to turn them around and Mary Ishida Jones is not the one to deliver it. Vivian looks her opponent directly in the eye as she lifts her head to continue.

"Many of you have lived here long enough to remember that the internment camp was located on the land adjacent to the proposed mill site. During the war, all of us at the camp knew there was a military installation next door to us. We could see the buildings from the camp but none were visible from the town and most people assumed the military's activities on that site were associated with the camp. I believe that's why the military chose that location; the internment camp was the perfect cover for their secret operations. After the war, they pulled all the buildings down and made the whole area off-limits. For a long time, there were huge No Trespassing signs and a fence blocking access from the road. We heard that the military had been doing chemical testing in the area and that's why they didn't want anyone on the land. We don't know what contaminants remain in the ground and what kind of harm they could cause."

Vivian lets out a polite laugh and all eyes are instantly on her. In a charisma contest, she has everything Mary Jones doesn't: poise, dress sense, attitude. She knows how to control a room. She knows Mary, a first-time speaker at council, won't object to her interruption. Nor will anyone else.

"That was a long time ago, Mary. You and I were both children. I remember hearing a lot of wild tales circulating back then too, especially after all the paranoia of wartime life. And I can assure you we have done our due diligence in getting permission to develop the land. If the military had been conducting any dangerous experiments that could pose a risk to our health, we wouldn't have been allowed to proceed this far."

Vivian releases a broad smile, more patronizing than polite. Everybody old enough to remember those days heard the rumours that floated around when the "no trespassing" signs went up. Everyone in the room knows there is nowhere else to develop that would meet the requirements of a busy sawmill. Vivian doesn't even need to say it: We develop there, or there will be no development.

By the time this public forum is held, it's too late, really, for members of the public to get in the way. Pockets have been lined and people who matter have been convinced of the value of the project. The mill corporation is ready to sign up to the promise of dirt-cheap land and low taxes. In return they are offering 500 jobs, a lot for a little town. Quite an achievement. The room agrees with Vivian on that point.

Vivian has been assured there is absolutely nothing to worry about. No health risks to speak of, not after so much time has passed. Yes, they could go after the government for compensation and a proper clean-up, but where would that leave them? Short term handouts after a lengthy legal battle and no long-term jobs. What this town needs is investment. It's in everybody's best interests to redevelop the land.

~ It is all so clear to her at times, how things were back then. Not like now. She gets so easily lost in the present.

In Vivian's lap is a ball of wool and the beginnings of something. She picks up the needles that are supposed to work together and weaves the yarn. She doesn't remember how it is all supposed to fit, so she puts the needles down and holds the soft wool in her hands. It's going to be a scarf, she decides, a beautiful emerald green scarf. She'll work on it another day when she's feeling sharper.

"Do you remember when we moved to Stapleton?"

Todd is asking. He has brought an old photo album out onto the veranda and placed it on his lap. It is one of his games. He is playing with her again. He wants to show her what she doesn't know.

"Yes," she says, although she has no memory of that particular event.

He points to a photo of a boy standing in front of a grand home. It's their son Stuart, of course, but she won't participate in this silly charade.

Stuart looks about 10 or 11 in the photo. He is standing in front of Mother's house, the first place they lived when they arrived in Stapleton. It was Mother who brought them back; Vivian first. When she became terminally ill, Vivian came from Vancouver to care for her for a few weeks. Weeks became months and, as Mother grew weaker, Vivian found herself being drawn back into the town. To her own surprise as much as anyone else's, she suggested to Todd that they leave their busy city life and return to Stapleton. Her expertise would be invaluable in revitalizing the community that had lost so much after the closure of the coalmine. She would do what her father couldn't: keep this town alive. Todd was willing to do the extra travelling in order to manage their business interests. He found city life stressful and had romanticised the idea of a country retreat. Stuart's private school had a boarding option, so his education wouldn't suffer. Yes, she remembers that time very clearly now.

Todd is still pointing at the photograph of young Stuart in front of Vivian's childhood home.

"Well, he can't be yours," she says. "He's far too handsome."

CHAPTER 13

1 9 9 4

"Elena, please. It's important."

"I said I'm busy."

Ken was hovering awkwardly in her bedroom doorway, shirt half untucked and thick stubble around his chin. Elena sat on the edge of her bed painting her toenails. It was a delicate operation, keeping the purple glitter within the boundaries of her littlest nail. She wasn't interested in what he had to say. Whatever he was going to tell them, it wouldn't be true.

"I'll be in the living room with Rob."

Elena watched Ken leave out of the corner of her eye. She blew on her toenails and put her foot carefully onto the carpet; heels down, toes up. She walked as casually as she could, on her heels, into the living room. Much as she didn't want to listen to Ken, she hated the idea of Rob knowing something she didn't.

Ken was standing in front of the TV waiting for her to sit. She flopped down on the sofa beside Rob, close enough that her elbow bumped his ribs and he grunted at her, but he kept watching Ken. Mamma perched on the arm of the couch and put one hand on Elena's shoulder, tapping her fingers nervously.

Ken had a newspaper in his hand. It wasn't the Stapleton Herald—too thick. It was one of the big papers that Dad sometimes bought on Sundays. Ken's mouth started moving —something about preparing themselves for a difficult time —but Elena was craning her neck sideways trying to read the headlines. There was a photo of the smoking ruins on the front cover and thick type next to it: SAWMILL WORKER.

"Elena, are you listening?"

She flicked him a look before scanning back across the type she'd just read. He hid the paper behind his back. She slumped into the depths of the sofa and folded her arms.

"A reporter got hold of some information about your dad."

"What information?" Rob leaned forward anxiously.

"His disappearance is being investigated by the police as suspicious. They're saying the explosion could've been deliberately caused by an angry employee."

Elena looked from Ken to Rob to Mamma and back again to try and understand how serious this was. "You mean, Dad?"

Ken shifted his weight from one foot to the other. "According to the report, the cops think it's strange that his truck was found near the scene, but there's no sign of him. This journalist is making him sound like ... an unstable guy."

"What kind of unstable?" Elena asked.

Ken glanced at Mamma first, but he answered her question. "They're saying he's an alcoholic with anger issues and that he is seriously in debt."

Elena could feel Mamma's fingers sink into her shoulder. Rob got to his feet. "So, they think it was his fault?"

"Well ..." Ken stalled.

"Of course, it wasn't his fault," Mamma said. "It's just a big misunderstanding."

People sometimes got the wrong idea about Dad. He was

a big man and he didn't smile a lot. That was all. Sometimes he got angry with Mamma but they still loved each other. And he drank his tall cans on the lawn chair or the living room sofa but that wasn't hurting anyone, was it? Sometimes Ken came over and they both drank from cans together. No one seemed to be saying bad things about Ken.

"All we know right now is that the police are investigating him, but because of this report, some people in town will come to their own conclusions before the cops do. You kids are going to have to be tough."

Ken offered the newspaper to Rob, but Elena snatched it from his hands. "Hey! Gimme that!" he shouted, but Mamma had already grabbed the paper and was tracing the words with her fingernails.

"Sawmill sabotage. Evidence links troubled worker to deaths." Mamma repeated his name: "Curtis Reid, 37." She picked out the important details: "Married, father of two, missing for 28 days."

"He'll be fine," Mamma said, and then she traced a few more lines. "Police are investigating a possible link between Reid and the sawmill explosion ..." Mamma couldn't read any more. She dropped the paper on the table and walked out.

There were many things that Mamma cared less about since the explosion, like what they had for dinner or how they dressed, or whether they'd done their homework or helped unload the dishwasher. But she still managed to drag them both to church.

Mamma pretended not to notice that the atmosphere in church had changed. The Whitmores shuffled so far along the pew when Elena's family joined them that Elena thought they might fall off the other side. People looked away instead of saying hello and a few old folks scowled at them. Father Craig didn't treat them any differently but he was always standoffish. Church used to be boring. Now it was cold.

Eventually the listening and the singing and the praying ended. The congregation stood up and drifted towards the door. Nobody actually said anything unkind to them as they left, and they never would.

Elena didn't want to hear Mamma's voice calling out for Dad when they returned home, so she walked through the yard and curled up on a lawn chair. Soon came the bounce, bounce, bounce of Rob's basketball. He was probably avoiding Mamma too. It was a cool day and she zipped up the pink collar on her white windbreaker and folded her arms.

Rob lobbed the ball at the hoop and missed eight times out of ten, but he still strode around the yard like he was good at it. Thud, thud, thud. Elena wasn't sure why he was on the school team. Maybe they were short of players. She had suggested that once at the dinner table, and Rob lurched out of his seat towards her before Dad put a hand on his chest and settled him down again. Who would do that now? Mamma couldn't handle him. Mamma couldn't handle much anymore. Rob was constantly hunting for loose change so he could go and buy bread or whatever had run short. Sometimes Mamma stayed in bed all through dinnertime and Rob made the two of them a mish mash of items from the cupboards; mac and cheese, cream of mushroom soup and packets containing bits of meat and vegetables that you could bring back to life by adding hot water.

Elena watched as the ball cracked the edge of the hoop. Ken never came by to help them with anything. He only brought them bad news. Mamma's friends (whose husbands worked at the mill) never visited either. They needed other people, people who were on their side. They needed family.

"Rob?"

"What?" He let the ball roll and came over to her.

"Are all Mamma's family in Italy?"

"Yeah."

Elena paused. She knew that already, but she had still hoped for a different answer. She'd never been to Italy but she knew it was far away; too far for visiting. Mamma's parents immigrated to Canada when Mamma was little. A few years later, after Mamma had grown up, Nonna died and Nonno moved back to Italy to be near his brothers. That's what Mamma said. Mamma stayed in Canada and married Dad.

Elena had asked several times over the years if she could talk to Nonno over the phone, but Mamma always gave the same response. It wasn't possible because Nonno didn't speak any English. Elena thought that was strange for someone who'd lived in Canada, and anyway, she didn't mind. She only wanted to hear his voice, she didn't need to understand his words. But Mamma said no. Mamma didn't even speak to Nonno, and he was her dad. As she got older, Elena realized Mamma could speak to Nonno if she wanted to, but she didn't want to, and Elena never got any closer to figuring out why. It was difficult to speak to Mamma about some things because as soon as the conversation got interesting she would go quiet and leave the room to do something else. In any case, Nonno and the rest of Mamma's family were in Italy and they weren't coming to help.

"Are all Dad's family up north?"

Rob shrugged. "I dunno. Why?"

"Maybe they'll come and help us find Dad."

"If they cared about us, we would've met them by now."

Elena disagreed. They'd come. They had to. Up North wasn't that far away. It wasn't like Italy. They could drive here in probably a day or so, Elena thought. When they came, she'd finally see what they looked like. Grandma or Gran or Nan; Grandpa or Granddad or Gramps, they could choose. Elena wanted a Gramma and Gramps, ideally. She liked the word Gramps. Grumpy Gramps, except he wouldn't be grumpy around her. Old people almost always liked her. Dad called them Jim and Audrey whenever she forced him to tell her something about them (which wasn't often because he said they weren't worth talking about) but she wouldn't call them that because no one called their grandparents by their first names.

At least she had Rob. On their first and only search, they had found dad's truck.

"We have to keep looking for Dad."

Rob frowned. "Mom is never going to let us go out like that again."

"He was at that cabin and Frank knows something."

Rob lost it. "Why do you keep making things up all the time?"

"Why don't you believe me?"

"Because you're always like this. Coming up with stupid stories about things that didn't happen."

"You can't just give up."

"What if he did it?"

Elena couldn't believe those words came out of his mouth. There was no way he could really think that, but he repeated it.

"What if he set the mill on fire?"

"He wouldn't do that."

"How do you know?"

"I just do."

"No, you don't. You're too dumb to understand anything."

Rob picked up his basketball and for once, quietly walked inside.

CHAPTER 14

2 0 1 8

THE COMMUNITY HALL is bare, stripped of the Fall Fair decorations. Vivian hadn't planned on coming in, but the main door had been left wide open and now she's standing on the worn beige linoleum staring at the knots in the wall-to-wall wood panelling they'd installed in the seventies.

In the quiet, she remembers how busy it once was. Local community groups used to fight over time slots in the packed schedule. Club meetings, bingo, exercise classes, performances.

Pam's crop top shows off the tight muscles on her stomach. Her white sneakers and socks over her black leggings flash up and down as she moves. Dance music blasts through the hall and rows of women hop on and off low platforms. "Step, lift! Step, lift! One more time."

Vivian has been invited to speak to the Seniors Club; a chance to network with voters and hear their concerns. She regrets showing up early.

"Switch sides. Lift, lift!"

Vivian stalks around the edge of the hall and stands directly beside the portable stereo system. She looks at her watch. Pam turns and meets her stare, claps her hands twice and shouts: "Great work ladies! Let's cool down."

Pam bounds over and turns off the music as the women reach their arms gently towards the ceiling and back down to their toes. "We've still got five minutes," she says to Vivian.

As the women carry their steps into the storage room, Vivian reminds them not to block the foldable chairs and tables that are about to come out. None of them seem to be in a hurry to leave, even as the seniors start hovering by the entrance.

Pam's class gather around her, chatting as they approach the main doors at snail pace. Her voice sails across the top of the rest: "What?" Vivian instinctively tunes in.

A woman in leggings and a green leotard is speaking. "It's the same type of cancer. Lung cancer, I think Janice said. And they all work at the mill."

The women mutter sympathy. Vivian marches into the storage cupboard. Minutes tick by as she stands and stares at the folding chairs until a white-haired gentleman taps her on the shoulder and offers to help.

꙳ The wood panelling had been a mistake, in hindsight. It makes the hall look so dark and dated now. The storage cupboard doors swing open as the mayor's wife, Carol, pushes through them with chairs under each arm.

"Oh, hello Vivian. I didn't know you were coming to our paint night."

Vivian waves her hand. "No, no. Unfortunately, I have plans. I was just passing by."

"We're painting two cats on a branch under the moonlight. And there's wine. You'd be very welcome. The more the merrier!"

Carol is a beanpole with turquoise glasses. The brightly coloured silk scarf around her neck has been fastened with the knot off-centre, presumably to look artistic, but it makes her look like an ageing flight attendant.

"Maybe some other time," Vivian mutters as she walks towards the door.

"Next month it's Van Gogh's Sunflowers," Carol calls after her.

"Oh no," Vivian answers. "Not my style."

~∾ Three prints by post-impressionist painters do very little to brighten the poorly lit reception area at the clinic. From there, it gets worse; the only colour in the examination rooms are the faded blues of the beds. The doctor's surgery is in a humble heritage building on Main Street, recently purchased from a now-retired physician who never thought beyond the immediate needs of his patients.

"The first heavy rain, the roof started leaking," the prematurely bald young doctor says. He misses his family and hates the summer heat and isn't sure how to fill the shoes of the doctor who spent the last 40 years earning the locals' trust. His girlfriend is dragging her feet about moving to a small town.

He pushes his large glasses onto his nose. "The numbers are unusual," he says. "Much higher than the national average among the mill workers."

His tone is unsentimental, detached from this town and its patients and the faces behind the statistics. For Vivian, that is a relief.

"Please keep this between us for now. I'll have the site tested but for all we know lifestyle factors could be the cause. We don't want to start a panic."

"Of course." He closes his folder of numbers and Vivian takes it out of his hands, his mouth opening to object.

"I have a lot of business connections in the Lower Main-land," Vivian says. "A friend of mine runs a private clinic in North Van and he's looking for a young doctor."

"I did not invite that man over to dinner!"

"Yes, my dear, you did."

"I would never invite someone to dinner on a Monday evening, Todd. We have a council meeting to get to."

Vivian scrutinizes the positioning of the silverware laid out on the dining table before hurrying into the bathroom to put a comb through her layered bob and fumble with her lipstick. She isn't sure why she's holding her handbag or what she's angry about, but she is furious. He makes everything such a challenge. She thinks about it. Who? Who does? Tim. Tab. Todd. TODD. She says it out loud to make it stick and he surfaces in the bathroom doorway like the puppet he is, except that he isn't her puppet anymore.

"Angie says our guest has just pulled into the driveway."

"Who the heck is Angie?"

"She takes care of you."

Yes, Angie. The silverware placer. Useless woman. Vivian would rearrange it, but there's no time. Todd grabs her by the arm and tries to lead her gently out of the bathroom. She shakes him off and marches towards the dining table. Angie hovers by the front doorway; the woman who conspires with him to drug her and confuse her and make her sit when they want her to sit and sleep when they tell her to and get dressed when they say she should.

Angie shows her a ridiculous, oversized grin and says: "It's so nice to be joining you and your friend for dinner."

Why is she joining them? Doesn't she have anything better to do? Vivian stares at the top of Angie's head. She has a dreadful perm; the sort that is falling apart and wouldn't have looked particularly attractive to begin with, puffing out around her scalp and ending abruptly above her shoulders.

The doorbell rings. Todd moves towards it but Vivian pulls him back.

"What about the council meeting? We're going to be late!"

Todd sighs. "We talked about this. We both stepped down from our council positions because of your health."

"I did no such thing."

"Yes, you did."

Vivian shakes her finger at him. "You forced me to, then. You forced me!"

He does what he always does when she gets angry; the most exasperating thing of all. Nothing.

"Who replaced us?"

"It doesn't matter, Vivian. We're out of it now."

"But what about our plans?"

"Someone else will take care of it."

"Hah."

"I'll keep any eye on things."

"Will you?"

"We've been married for more than half a century. You have to start trusting my decisions because you don't have much of a choice anymore."

Vivian is about to object when the doorbell rings again. Vivian looks at Angie and wonders how they're going to introduce Todd's co-conspirator. There's no time to ask. Todd is at the door welcoming their guest.

Vivian looks up at his black hair and thin smile. "Frank!" she says happily.

The young man's expression falters, but only for a second. "I'm Dean. Frank's son."

"Of course. Dean. Come in."

"What a beautiful home you have," he says as he removes his burnished brown leather shoes. He's in a collared shirt and casual blazer and he offers her a very nice-looking bottle of red wine. "Much better than Frank's," he says.

Todd introduces Angie as a family friend, but Vivian can tell by the look Todd gives Dean that their guest already knows what's what. Dean has been fed all this claptrap about Vivian being in "poor health." She would rather have introduced Angie as the cleaner than a family friend but there's nothing she can do about that now.

Dean commends the grilled eggplant and goat cheese salad that Todd has carefully assembled. The two of them have a brief discussion about the availability of locally-grown produce and Vivian zones in and out because the chit-chat is making her sleepy. At some point Todd asks Dean how he's managing to divide his time between Stapleton and his consulting work. "I have a business partner who's helping to fill in while I take care of Frank's affairs," Dean explains. Something seems off about the way he says it: Frank's affairs. Vivian wonders what exactly he means.

The mood disintegrates about halfway through Todd's prized salmon on a bed of asparagus. "My mom said she told Frank about me a few months after the mill explosion," Dean announces out of the blue. Vivian and Todd glance at each other, neither being particularly adept at sensitive conversations. Their guest continues undeterred.

"Stapleton was in the news constantly and my mom thought it was about time she told him."

Another awkward pause.

"It must have been difficult," Vivian offers softly.

Dean doesn't acknowledge her attempt at kindness.

"Frank told my mom he couldn't be a dad because he wasn't a good person, and I was better off not knowing him, so my mom decided not to tell me about him. My mom said he seemed genuinely sad about it, like he wished he'd known about me earlier, when he thought he was good enough to be my dad. It makes me wonder what changed for him."

Vivian hums and Todd reaches for his wine.

Dean turns the conversation and his attention sharply in Vivian's direction. "I heard you were involved in bringing the sawmill to Stapleton."

Todd sees the threat and intervenes before she has a chance to answer. "Vivian was involved in so many projects during her years on council. I think honestly she's quite tired of discussing them."

Dean doesn't take the hint. "Wasn't it built in the late '70s?"

"Yes," Todd answers again, even though the question was clearly directed at Vivian.

Dean nods. "I thought so. I was too young to remember that."

Todd tries to keep the conversation casual since Dean seems intent on continuing, but Vivian can hear the tension rising in his voice.

"Of course, you were. The mill opened in ... let me think ... in 1978."

"Did you work there?" Dean asks him.

"No. We had business interests in the Interior and the Lower Mainland, so I spent quite a bit of time travelling."

"Did you invest in the mill?"

"No. Well ... the group had a few shares in the parent company, but it wasn't one of our primary interests. The fast food franchises always did very well for us."

"Someone was telling me ... I can't remember who ...

that one of your companies provided security services for the mill site after the explosion."

It isn't a question he should be asking, not over dinner, not in their home, and certainly not after his peculiar speculation about Frank's inability to commit to fatherhood. He is beginning to sound accusatorial. Todd stumbles on his answer. "As you know … the key to business is finding opportunities, filling gaps—you know—providing services where needed."

Todd puts a halt to the conversation by asking Angie if she wouldn't mind bringing in the dessert. He has outdone himself with a homemade crème caramel. Vivian's eyes focus on the knife as he slices through the dripping dark caramel and the perfectly soft but firm custard.

Dean scoops up a spoonful and tastes it. His lips lift and he is temporarily pacified. He praises Todd once again on his culinary talents. There's something about Dean's manner that Vivian recognizes in herself. He's a schemer. Didn't Todd say something to that effect? What was it again? Something about being prepared.

"So Vivian," Dean says, "after all your hard work getting the mill built, the explosion must have been particularly devastating for you."

She keeps her mouth closed and watches his sharp green eyes. This is all part of his plan, but she doesn't have an inkling of his intentions. That's alright. She will study his moves until he gives himself away.

Todd fills the awkward pause. "It was a traumatic time. Vivian doesn't like talking about it."

Dean raises a hand apologetically. "Of course. I'm sorry. It's just …"

He looks at her again with those eyes, just like Frank's. "As you know, I'm considering spending more time in this town ... maybe even keeping my investment in it ... so I need to know exactly what, and who, I'm investing in. There appear to be a few anomalies around what actually happened at the mill."

"Anomalies?" Todd repeats.

"Yes. Do you think Curtis Reid was set up?"

Vivian's mind is racing and rambling simultaneously as is now customary. Curtis Reid. She knows the name. She can picture him. Thick set. Thuggish looking. And the girl.

"Elena," she says.

Their guest leans in as though he hasn't heard. "What?"

Todd puts his napkin on the table and stands. "I'm sorry to have to cut this short, Dean, but Vivian is getting tired."

"Of course." Dean pushes his chair back and holds out a hand for Vivian to shake. "It was so nice to see you again."

She doesn't acknowledge him. She's thinking about the girl. Elena. She barely knew her, what with her own son already grown. She stares coldly at the tablecloth. Frank was so upset. But it wasn't their fault. They couldn't have known.

Dean's voice again. She wishes he would just leave. "I keep forgetting to ask you if you found your dog."

Vivian tightens up and glares at him. "She isn't lost."

"Oh, my mistake. Must've been someone else."

She hears the lies Todd tells him as he walks him out, just audible to her not-so-deaf ears. "Vivian's dog, Cherie, passed away a few weeks ago," he tells him quietly. "Vivian doesn't always remember."

∾ Todd is hovering with a cup of water and two little yellow pills. No. She's not taking them. He pushes the cup towards her and she swipes it out of his hand. The water sploshes onto the hardwood, snaking towards his slippers as he steps back, cursing. He clutches his back while he mops his precious floor. He forgets he isn't so young himself.

Father is hanging over the mantelpiece. He shouldn't be here, in her house. Father never visits. A present and a card arrive on her 17th birthday while she is home for the holidays. The card is signed in his name but it isn't his handwriting. The gift is one he'd never have chosen.

She loves the pink sleeveless dress, even though it accentuates things she doesn't have. It is the 1950s; the cars have curves and the women are supposed to, so it fits tightly around her chest and waist and flows out around her non-existent hips. Vivian wonders if it is his secretary who has the duty of selecting her birthday gifts, or his new wife. She does a twirl for Mother, whose only remark is that it makes her look common. It's clear who Mother thinks sent the gift.

Father started a new family soon after he and Mother divorced. Mother insists on making Vivian visit his Vancouver home for at least a few days during each school vacation. Mother says it's good for her and it will prevent Father from forgetting that he also has a daughter to think about.

Two little boys and a wife much younger than Mother. The first time Vivian was sent to stay with them, she felt quite afraid of meeting Mother's replacement. It is bearable though. The boys think only of themselves and her stepmother is hardly the villainous hag depicted in fairy tales.

Unlike Father, Ruth is always very welcoming to Vivian. She's in her twenties (which outrages Mother), and she treats Vivian as more of a friend than a stepdaughter. They chat about fashion and music and movies. Ruth is petite and fine-boned with bright blue eyes that are almost as striking as her wavy auburn hair. It is Ruth who teaches Vivian about the importance of presence, and Ruth who tells her that a woman can be noticed without being spectacularly beautiful if she exudes confidence and learns how to dress well.

Father had been successful in Stapleton but he seems even more so in his grand city home. It's an imposing stone building on a street lined with chestnut trees. A little pathway weaves through the landscaped garden and large lawn, hidden from the street by a low wall and tall, sculpted bushes. The house is so large it has wings and a grand central staircase connecting them.

When Vivian visits, Father works late during the week and golfs all weekend. She hasn't determined if this is his usual habit or he's avoiding her presence. They are rarely alone together. It doesn't hurt her particularly; she's used to his ways, until she sees him with the boys. The youngest one is still toddling, and his big brother is only slightly older. When Father comes home, he grabs them and throws them up and spins them around. She has no recollection of a time when he was ever as enthusiastic about greeting her.

Vivian approaches Ruth when the two of them are alone. "I want to talk to Father privately but I'm not sure when he'll be available."

Ruth treads around the topic as carefully as Vivian. "Oh, I know it's difficult. He's always so busy. But don't worry, I'll make sure you have a chance before you leave."

Ruth keeps her word. Towards the end of the week, the five of them are having dinner and Father seems in a relatively good mood. The boys are fidgeting and he hasn't snapped at either of them. The moment the little one loses interest in his cut-up chunks of food, Ruth yanks them both away from the table. "Come on," she says to their confused little faces. "Let's see if those clothes Grandma sent actually fit you before she calls and asks."

Father barely looks up as the three of them stumble off with minor protests from the boys. He pushes meat and vegetables onto his fork and into his mouth and doesn't acknowledge Vivian. She doesn't know how much longer they'll have alone, so she gets right to the point.

"I've been offered a place at university, to study law," she says, "but I need some help with my student expenses."

He puts down his fork and frowns.

"You don't need a degree. You'll be married soon."

"I can be a married lawyer."

"Your husband will provide for you."

"Please, Father."

"If you're so set on providing for yourself, you can make your own way to university."

She slams her fist on the table and her father frowns at the disturbance, so unbecoming of a young lady. His sons rush back into the room, pushing each other to get through the doorway first. Ruth's voice peals out from another room and they race back out, giggling at each other.

Vivian looks back at Father but he refuses to meet her gaze. "Will you be putting them through university?"

"If they want to go. Someday they'll have their own families to provide for."

He looks over at Charlie, who has darted back in to grab another piece of bread. He is the oldest and chunkiest. Strong for his age, and not stupid, but not brilliant either.

"Charlie will probably do better going straight into business," Father says.

"Why can't I choose?"

"Because you will have a husband and children to take care of."

It is crushing to hear his words but Vivian was expecting

this rejection from him. Mother was right about one thing. Her regular visits to Father's home have made it possible for her to remind him of his duties to his first child.

"I came up with a proposal that might convince you. One that would be mutually beneficial."

Father leans back in his chair and smirks, as though a high school girl couldn't possibly know the meaning of the word "proposal" unless it is related to marriage.

"Go on," he says smugly.

"You cover my university fees and I won't tell Ruth about the woman you visit on Cedar Drive."

⮑ "She's been stealing from me."

"Who?"

Vivian points at the woman who follows her around her home. She wants to say the woman with the terrible hair, but she's forgotten the name of it, that particular form of hair catastrophe. The woman grimaces like she's just been slapped and Todd throws up his hands.

"What have you lost this time?"

"My gold necklace and I didn't lose it. She stole it!"

Vivian is so angry her voice is hoarse. She's right. She knows she is. That woman took it. She's a thief. Perm, that's it. She has a terrible perm.

"Don't talk to Angie like that!" he says. "You probably left it somewhere."

"I'll see if it's in the bedroom," Angie says nervously.

She dashes off. Todd looks around the kitchen as though it might pop out from the fruit bowl or the knife block. He stops, turns. He's holding it in his hand. The gold chain is dangling from his hand.

"You left it by the toaster, Vivian."

"No, I didn't! Why would I leave it there?"

"Why would anyone else?"

He isn't being kind. His tone isn't kind. He walks over to her and opens up her hand and gently drips the gold into her palm. "Here's your precious necklace." Then he walks over to Angie and apologizes to her. Vivian looks down at the gold in her palm. She has nothing to feel guilty about. She worked for it, she tells herself.

~ Father agrees to her terms. He will pay for her university education in exchange for her silence about the woman on Cedar Drive. Vivian is surprised he gives in so easily until she realizes that fighting with her would be more interaction than he could bear. He has only one question for her.

"How did you find out?"

"It wasn't difficult. I pay more attention to you than you do to me."

She doesn't tell him this, but it was Ruth who unintentionally helped her uncover his big secret. Father's study was strictly off-limits, an indication that there was something in there worth finding. Vivian felt sure that if she could gain access to his study, she could dig up something that would cost him more than her tuition fees.

Ruth was her way in, Ruth who seemed to be forever trying to impress her. Vivian chose an afternoon when the boys were being particularly rowdy and asked her for a quiet space with a large desk where she could finish a school project. Ruth flitted around the house and made a few suggestions, but Vivian politely declined all of them for various reasons until they reached the study. Ruth disappeared into the master bedroom and came back with a key. "Don't move anything and don't tell your father!" she said, seemingly excited that she and Vivian were doing something they shouldn't.

As soon as Ruth left the room, Vivian rifled carefully through her father's papers and noticed only one detail that seemed out of place. On the inside cover of one of his notebooks, he'd written in tiny scrawl; 403 Cedar. Wed. 12 pm.

When Wednesday came around, Vivian told Ruth she was going out to meet a school friend. Instead, she made her way over to Cedar Drive. It was a nice house, not as impressive as her father's but still grander than any in Stapleton. She arrived at 11:45, giving herself enough time to find a discreet hiding place. The homes were all large and fenced or walled. There were mature trees with thick trunks spaced at regular intervals along the street, but it would look suspicious if she were spotted lurking behind one of them.

As she was debating where to position herself, she heard a car coming. Dark green and polished, just like Father's. She turned and began walking in the other direction, hoping to slip by unnoticed. The car stopped, a door opened and closed and footsteps crunched gravel. She dared to glance back. There he was on the front steps of 403 Cedar and opening the door for him was a woman.

The scene itself didn't really shock her. What shocked her was how plain the woman looked compared to his current wife. She was almost disappointed that her father didn't have higher standards when it came to his mistresses. The vehicle in the driveway was a sparkling red Cadillac Eldorado. Vivian didn't know a lot about vehicles, but she knew Cadillacs weren't cheap. Vivian slipped away as her father stepped inside the house.

She returned to the house on Cedar Drive the next day. There were no cars parked out front and no sign that anyone was home. Vivian walked confidently up to the front door and knocked as if she had business there. She slid her hand into the mailbox pinned to the wall. Inside was an envelope addressed to Mr. W. Langston. So, there was a husband. She slipped the letter back in the box and knocked again, for the sake of any nosy neighbours. She waited a moment, then walked back down the driveway.

Father was still at work when she returned to his house. Ruth greeted her with a warm smile and drew her into the living room so she could hear her latest record. "Jo Stafford," Ruth said excitedly. "Such a beautiful voice." Ruth had played it enough times already that she could sing along, swinging her hips.

Vivian sat while her stepmother slowly waltzed around the room. Ruth was the type of person who could be completely entranced by the beauty of something, a trait which Vivian both envied and loathed. Vivian waited for the song to end before asking the question.

"Do you know a Mr. Langston?"

Ruth nodded. "Yes. He partnered with your father on a development of some sort, but the two of them couldn't see eye to eye on anything, so they went their separate ways. I suppose they're competitors now."

So that was the attraction of the plain woman.

"Why do you ask?" Ruth asked.

"Oh … a friend at school. He's her uncle. She thought I might know him."

Ruth smiled and picked out another record. Vivian couldn't pity her. She didn't want to know about her father's bad behaviour. She was doing what she had to do. It wasn't fair; it simply … was.

~ "Don't you point the finger at me! I did what was needed!"

A familiar woman rushes over to her bedside and takes her hand. "It's alright Vivian! It was just a bad dream."

Vivian sits up in bed and stares at the woman's bedraggled curls.

"Why don't we get you up now seeing as you're awake?"

The woman puts her hands behind Vivian's shoulders and gently pulls her forward.

"Lift your arms up and we'll put on one of your nice blouses."

Vivian does as she's told. The woman's cold skin brushes against hers as she pulls off her nightshirt, slips a bra around her chest and pulls her weak sagging arms through the sleeves of a crimson blouse. This is what old is. Humiliating.

"What about ..." She can't remember the name. "The girl?"

"Do you mean Elena?"

"Yes. How do you know her?"

"I don't know her. You ask about her from time to time, wanting to know how she is."

"How is she?"

The woman pauses. "Your husband says you don't need to be thinking about her because it gets you all worked up and I agree with him. Leave the past in the past."

"But it isn't in the past. It's ..."

She wants to continue, but she doesn't know what she means. The passage of time is no longer clear to her.

The woman changes the subject. "Your husband told me your granddaughter is starting university. You must be very proud."

Vivian doesn't answer. She has no recollection of having a granddaughter.

CHAPTER 15

1 9 9 4

THE CHILDREN GAGGED at the dead bodies. Their odour crushed all the wonder and anticipation Miss Meyer had been building on the bus ride there. Sand mixed with broken flesh; red and white scales ripped up, partially eaten bodies without heads, heads without bodies, rotting.

Miss Meyer apologized. They had come too late. Most of the salmon had already battled their way upriver, laid their eggs and breathed their last. Riverbanks of dead fish. It wasn't what Elena had imagined when Miss Meyer announced that they would be taking a school trip to see the salmon run. There were no great shoals of fish swimming against the current, breaking through the surface, jumping and splashing. They only saw one or two fish alive; the dawdlers, the late-comers. She wondered if they could sense the dead ones, and if they knew what was coming.

"Who knows what colour a sockeye salmon would be if we saw one in the ocean?"

All the kids had covered their mouths and noses with their sleeves. No one wanted to unmask themselves to speak. Elena had stopped answering questions altogether because for the first time in her life she didn't want any more attention. The kids at school saw her differently now that Dad was suspected of doing something terrible. The longer no one could explain where he was, the guiltier people seemed to think he must be.

"They'd be silvery-blue," Miss Meyer answered cheerfully. "They turn bright red when they return to the rivers to spawn."

Her voice became tinny when she strained it, scraping their ears with her insistence that they listen.

"The wonderful thing about nature is the way it adapts. The salmon have different needs during different stages of their lives and they've learned to change to survive."

This didn't look like survival to Elena. It looked like the exact opposite of survival.

Nathan, the only kid not affected by the stench of death, hopped over to one of the male corpses, identifiable by its humped back and hooked mouth. He bent down to pick it up.

"And we will start to see changes in our own community, as we adapt to our new ... No, Nathan! It's dirty! Put it down!"

Nathan bobbed it up and down as if it were talking. The birds had pecked out its eyes. A couple of the boys laughed hysterically and the girls all jumped back in disgust.

"Put it down, Nathan!" He did, and then he shoved his fishy hands at Kathryn's face. She screamed.

Elena missed Logan. He would've picked up a rotting fish, but he would've thought of something funny to say as he bobbed it up and down. It worried her deeply that he might believe what the others were saying; that it was her dad's fault his dad was dead.

Elena fell asleep on the bus ride home. She had the whole seat to herself because no one would sit next to her. She leaned her head against the window pane, the buzzing glass numbing her thoughts. Her eyelids drooped a few times before they closed.

She woke abruptly, a pungent smell in her nostrils and something tickling her chin and a weight against her chest. A fish tail was poking out of her pink-collared windbreaker, its body bulging under the zip. She shot to her feet and pulled off her jacket. The rotting salmon dropped to the floor. Just the sight of it made her sick. Nathan laughed and kicked it down the bus. Her sweatshirt was damp where the wet, slimy carcass had been. She pulled it off, trying not to feel the dampness against her face.

"Oh my God! That's so gross!" Kathryn squealed while the other kids snickered.

Elena looked down at the smaller dark spot on her t-shirt. She'd have to wear it all the way home. Miss Meyer marched to the back of the bus and told them how appalled she was, but that was all she did.

Elena tried putting her windbreaker back on, but she couldn't do it, so she sat back in her seat, overwhelmed by the smell, and she turned the outside of the jacket over herself like a blanket. Kids up front popped their heads over their seats to gawk at her. She turned away and stared out the window.

~ Mamma threw Elena's fishy clothes in the machine and asked her what Miss Meyer had done about the situation.

"Nothing," Elena told her.

"I should go down there and talk to the principal."

Elena knew she wouldn't. It was alright though. Elena only wanted her to be angry. That was good enough. She had showered and put on fresh clothes and at home at least no one would be mean to her.

Rob stormed in through the front door, threw off his sneakers and went straight into his room. Elena looked over at Mamma for an explanation. "Ashley dumped him last night," she said softly. "He's taken it quite hard. Don't tease him about it, please?" Yesterday, she might have done. Today, she wasn't in the mood.

There was a knock at the door and Elena went to answer it. Brandon. They weren't expecting him. He was one of those people that just appeared.

"Hey Elena. Is your mom home?"

Elena turned around and yelled down the hallway. "Mom! Brandon's here." She stared back at him, lingering in the doorway. He filled the whole space; she couldn't see the world behind him. He hadn't seemed so big last time he was standing there, bent over and coughing his lungs out.

Elena stared at him while they waited for Mamma. "Do you have nightmares? About the fire?"

Brandon lost his smile. "People usually ask me about my arm. Do you have nightmares about it?"

"Sometimes. Do you like peanut butter marshmallow squares?"

Someone had left a box of them on the doorstep. No note. It had cheered Mamma up for the whole morning because it meant at least one person was on their side. Nobody left baking on the doorsteps of people they hated.

Brandon softened his voice like a woman's and brushed his hands delicately against his big stomach. "I love peanut butter marshmallow squares, but I'm watching my figure."

Elena giggled.

"My girlfriend put me on a diet. You think that's funny?"

Elena nodded. She looked at him, seriously.

"Why didn't you stay with my dad?"

Brandon's expression grew heavy. "He needed a tool to fix a piece of equipment. He went to get it, and a minute later, the explosion happened. When I got up, I couldn't see him. I thought he'd got out but by the time I got outside he wasn't there. That's why I came to your place. I was hoping he'd be here."

"When do you think he will come back?" she asked.

Brandon became awkward. Mamma interrupted before he could answer. She was still cheerful. She obviously hadn't heard what they were talking about.

"Hi Brandon. You're looking well. How's your arm?"

"Much better, thanks."

Brandon looked down at Elena and up again at Mamma. He lowered his voice as he spoke. "I just wanted to let you know ... the cops came by to talk to me again."

"Elena, why don't you go outside for a bit?" Her voice was hollow. It made Elena nervous, but she did what she was told. She squeezed by Brandon and stepped into the yard as they went inside and shut her out.

Mamma had just been cleaning, another sign that she was feeling better about things. When Mamma cleaned, she opened up all the windows to get rid of the chemical smells. Elena crept around the house and dropped under the window-sill. She could just about hear them. Brandon was speaking.

"They forced me to say I was confused about my original statement."

"But you're his alibi. He wouldn't have had enough time after he left you to get across the building, set off an explosion and escape."

"They're calling me a liar. They're saying my story doesn't add up, so either he wasn't with me all that time and I got confused because of the trauma or I'm covering for him, and that's a serious criminal offence. So I told them I got confused. I'm sorry, Giulia."

"But now he's got no defence."

"My girlfriend's pregnant. I can't go to jail. No one's going to believe me over the cops."

The room went quiet.

"Thanks for telling me," Mamma says finally. "Congratulations on the baby. That's wonderful news."

"I'm so sorry, Giulia."

There was silence and Elena realized he was leaving. She rushed to the back of the house before she could be seen. Something occurred to her as she ran. It wasn't that everybody hated them; some people were just afraid of being associated with them because of what other people might think. It was like their family had a contagious disease and everyone was staying away in case it spread. Everybody else felt safer that way.

⁓ October girl. She woke up 11 years old. She thought about what it was like to be 11 as she padded to the bathroom, took a shower and picked out her clothes for the day. The skin around her nipples was much fatter than it used to be. Mamma got her a bra a few months back and she still had trouble pulling together the tiny clasp at the back. She was growing, but she'd been doing that since forever and she was still shorter than the other girls. She knew she wasn't going to be beautiful, not like Kathryn. Kathryn was the tallest girl in their class and she had crimped blonde hair. Hannah said Kathryn had her period already. Kathryn's dad was a foreman at the mill. They went to California on vacation. She had a dance party for her last birthday.

Mamma said it was best not to have a birthday party this year, what with everything that was going on. People had a lot "on their plates." Money was tight, that's why Mamma had sold Dad's flashy TV and plugged in the old one he'd left in the shed. The picture wasn't as nice but it still worked. Some of Mamma's jewellery was missing from her dresser, Elena had noticed, and her dark roots were beginning to show where she parted her hair. All of it was temporary. Everything would be back to normal soon. Her twelfth birthday would be extra special.

Elena's tenth birthday had been different. She had a party at the rec centre and Mamma got hot dogs and cakes and cookies. Almost the entire class showed up. Dad put up balloons and banners and played Michael Jackson songs. Mamma said she was getting too old for all that now anyway, wasn't she? Elena looked at herself in the mirror, at her older, 11-year-old face, and thought maybe Mamma was right.

Elena walked down to the park and on to Main Street. Mamma was finally letting her do things on her own again, as long as she knew where she was going. Elena tried to imagine how it looked when Chinatown was there, from the Pharmacy out to the fields where Mary had told her it would've been. A fire came and took it all away. If the fire kept coming, what would be left?

Her thoughts were broken by the familiar sound of giggling. "Was she talking to herself?" she heard one girl whisper. They were much bigger than her, around Rob's age. Three girls.

An older voice called her name from across the street. Mary was making her way slowly across the road. The girls lost interest.

"I'm going for coffee," Mary said. "Are you coming?"

∼ Elena had orange soda. Mary paid for it. They sat in the window and Mary read her paper while Elena stared at all the passers-by.

"It's my birthday today," Elena said.

"Happy Birthday. How old are you?"

"Eleven."

"Did you get any good presents?"

"Not really. But Christmas is coming soon."

"Christmas is two months away."

Mary returned to her newspaper.

"What are you going to do at Christmas?"

Mary ruffled her paper, but she didn't look up. "We usually visit my husband's family in Stony Creek."

Elena didn't see Mr. Mary very often. She didn't even know his name. He liked fishing. Dad would ask him if the fish were biting every time they passed him on the street. He never joined Mary for coffee at Ken's.

"Are you going to have turkey?"

"No. My sister-in-law is vegetarian."

"Why?"

"She likes to ruin Christmas."

Mary turned the page awkwardly, flattening the paper and refolding the seam.

Elena did her best to prolong the conversation. "Why do they make newspapers so big? They could make them like magazines."

"I don't know."

Elena looked at Mary looking at her. Mary was one of the only people in town who didn't try to avoid her. Mary was different. She never worried about what other people thought.

"Were there any kids at the ranch when you lived there?"

"No. It was just Bruce and his wife. Their kids had grown up and moved away. That's why he needed my dad's help."

"Who were you friends with then?"

"I kept to myself mostly. I went to the local school after the war, but it's hard to change people's minds, once they think about you a certain way."

Elena went quiet.

"You'll make other friends, Elena. You don't need ones that are easy to lose."

Mary stared at her again. "I've got a couple of things I need to do at the museum. Do you think you could help me?"

~ Mary unlocked the museum door. It had its own side entrance. Elena peered into the display cases with thin glass panels that moved a fraction when touched. "Last thing I need is to clean your fingerprints off everything," Mary said. Elena took her paws off the glass. Thin strips of printed text with descriptions and dates sat next to every object. There was a set of scales once owned by a Chinese herbalist, berry-picking baskets, a typewriter used by a former editor of the Stapleton Herald and a sluice box that had sieved out tiny chunks of gold from the river sludge. It was in much better shape than the one she'd seen rotting in the creek.

Photographs filled the gaps; rifles and hats and wooden huts and wide-open spaces; men who looked worn like rocks with beards they could carry nests in. They were all doing things; building, mining, fishing and their lives seemed to fit them just fine.

"Was Stapleton better back then?"

"Different. I don't know about better."

Elena followed Mary to her desk at the back of the room.

"Sit down." She moved some papers out of the way, fished a key from her desk drawer and unlocked a display case. She removed a few metal tools and placed them on the desk.

"Be careful. The edges are sharp."

Elena picked up a set of pliers; they looked just like Dad's, but they were heavier and there wasn't any plastic on the handles.

"Would you want to have your teeth pulled out with those?"

Elena squirmed and put the pliers down. "No. Why do you keep them?"

"Everything in this room has a story. It tells us a little bit about who we were and who we are. These tools were donated by the grandchildren of Stapleton's first dentist. He was a black man who came up from California during the gold rush."

Elena watched how carefully Mary put the gruesome tools away, as if those hunks of metal might smash into thousands of tiny pieces. Then their story would be lost.

Mary showed her a lace tablecloth brought over by a German immigrant and a set of silverware from Holland. She pointed at a photograph of a local ranch and told her it was started by a Mexican mule packer. It was the Mexicans who introduced alfalfa to BC, she said, but Elena wasn't sure what alfalfa was. "Cows and hippies eat it," Mary replied. She pulled out a Book of Common Prayer with ivory pages marred by brown age spots and a smell like old curtains. Elena was allowed to touch that one; it wasn't that old or precious. She stopped on a random page and flicked through pieces of Psalm 51: "Wash me through and through from my wickedness and cleanse me from my sin." Church words. They were always difficult.

Elena discovered a large tape recorder perched on a table behind the displays. "We use that sometimes for group visits," Mary explained. Elena inspected it. She pushed down the chunky play button. An old man's voice crackled out; deep as tree roots, old as stone, and his words made more sense than the book of dusty prayers.

> The cow boss sent his boys out
> With the last of the snow.
> He'd seen some wild hosses;
> "Winter-weary," he said, "they'll be slow."
>
> The boys rode through the timbers.
> Quiet as night, they set their trap.
> They rung around those hosses,
> Bein' sure to leave no gap.
>
> Bill Hitchens went and done it.
> He came round much too wide.
> Left a big hole by the timbers
> For them hosses to run and hide.
>
> The cow boss stomped and cussed and spit.
> Not one hoss to break and sell.
> He asked how they'd let 'im down,
> And the boss looked hard at Bill.
>
> Now, Bill he was the youngest.
> Like them broncs, tough to train.
> The boss preferred his brother John;
> Not as strong, but twice his brains.

Bill quivered, "Sorry boss,"
Sweat drippin' from his brow,
And John stepped up beside him,
Brothers, even now:

"Boss you should've seen it.
It really ain't his fault.
Those weren't no reg'lar hosses,
That you can trap before they bolt.

"We set 'em up just perfect,
We thought we had the herd.
But when we rode towards 'em,
They just up and flew, like birds."

Elena liked it. Families stuck together; that's what the old poem meant. She imagined the horses, careering towards the cowboys and then heaving their hooves up and paddling up through the air like it was water. She wanted to be just like the horses in that poem and fly up high where the land looked beautiful and all the people became very, very small. She'd be a bald eagle; so grand that the people would look up and admire her as she soared over their heads. It was then that she saw it; a solution. They could live on a ranch, just like Mary's family had, and Dad could work there too when he came back, so he wouldn't have to deal with the mean people in town. It would be peaceful for them there, just like flying away.

⤳ "They barbeque wild horses round here."
"No, they don't!"
"Yes, they do! The ranchers don't like them scaring their

horses so they shoot them and make burgers and invite their neighbours over for a barbeque."

Rob sat back with an ugly smirk. He wasn't supposed to be that way, not now. She hated the way he put her down when they were supposed to stick together.

～ Stapleton's restaurant reduced its hours to Saturdays and Sundays only. The notice pinned to the door began: To our dear friends and supporters ...

Ken murmured something about having to write a sign like that himself soon. "Problem is, people haven't got any money to spend," he said. Elena told him she didn't care because she knew, now, that he didn't care about her family. Ken did something very strange. He started to go pink. Mamma almost choked on her coffee. "Elena, don't you dare take this out on Ken!" Elena had tried to explain to her that Ken knew something they didn't but Mamma wasn't listening.

The FOR SALE signs began popping up overnight, it seemed. Only one house actually sold and it didn't belong to any of the redundant mill workers. Mrs. Dubov, their next-door neighbour, was the owner. Mamma said her kids forced her to sell it for almost nothing to a retired man from Stony Creek. Their new neighbour didn't seem to like people much. He ignored Elena's frequent greetings.

Mrs. Dubov's kids dumped her into a seniors' home. "Poor woman." Mamma shook her head.

Mrs. Dubov had been proud of her home. The lawn was immaculate. Her roses drew compliments and the miniature hedge around the front was perfectly trimmed. Around the back, facing the river, she had a table and chair set with floral cushion pads and a hummingbird feeder. Elena went over there sometimes to watch the hummingbirds. Mrs. Dubov didn't seem to mind.

Her family gutted her place so the quiet Stony Creek man could move in. Most of it went into a huge container in her driveway. Elena imagined the bears at the dump chewing her grassy green carpet and floral curtains. She hoped they would enjoy Mrs. Dubov's treasures.

CHAPTER 16

1 9 5 6

Father had no intention of housing Vivian while she studied. Vivian complained to Mother that Father's house was too noisy with the boys running around, and Mother suggested that Aunt Faye might appreciate the company and the extra income. Aunt Faye lived in a bungalow not far from the university and Vivian had been there a handful of times with Mother. During their last visit, Aunt Faye had scolded her younger sister for being foolish enough to marry that Irishman, though Father's family had emigrated to British North America at some point during the previous century.

Uncertain what Aunt Faye would make of her decision to pursue higher education, Vivian was relieved when Mother received a letter from her sister agreeing to the arrangement on a trial basis. Mother said it was important never to suggest to Aunt Faye that she benefitted in any way from Vivian's presence in her home. If Vivian could accept that she was no more or less than a burden to her aunt, they'd get along fine.

⤳ "Don't think I don't know what you're doing here, young lady."

Aunt Faye lifts the coffee mug to her lips and takes a sip. Her face sours. "Bring me the sugar. Didn't I say to add sugar?"

Vivian's first instructions were to deposit her bags in a poky bedroom and put the percolator on the stove. Keen to maintain a roof over her head for at least the first semester, Vivian wordlessly obeys her aunt, searching the kitchen cupboards before returning with the sugar, wondering whether the next four years of her life would be like this.

"You want to escape the influence of your sinful father and I admire that. But universities are full of grandiose notions. Don't forget your purpose—to find a husband who will respect you and honour the institution of marriage."

Aunt Faye always dresses in black. She wears her war widow status like a badge of honour. But even black fades. Her clothes were purchased years ago and her grey hair descends to her waist when she releases it from her bun. She wears no makeup and has no telephone. Teabags are reused at least twice. One of her neighbours leaves the previous day's newspaper on the front step every morning.

"As Mr. Lee says, there's no sense in wasting paper," Aunt Faye explains the first time she orders Vivian to fetch it for her. Vivian wonders how many other small acts of charity her aunt accepts from friends and acquaintances.

⮑ The rain pitter-patters on her umbrella and water puddles on the stone beneath her brown heels. Her green bag matches the pencil dress beneath her long trench coat; a simple first-day outfit she spent too much time thinking about.

Black leather Oxfords slap the top step. A freckled man with a red tie tucked into his V-neck sweater races past her to the shelter of the building. A handful of students in sport jackets joke with each other as they hurry up the same steps in unison.

Vivian pauses at the doorway and folds her umbrella. Drops fall onto her curly brown hair, restrained by a green headband. "Law isn't a good fit for a criminal. You should choose a different field of study." Her father's last piece of unsolicited advice. She thinks about her father's condescension, Ruth, his mistress Mrs. Langston, the small amount of money he deposited for her first-year fees and living expenses. Pursuing what she wanted was seen as inappropriate, even wrong. Why?

Someone taps her on the shoulder, and she turns to find a striking woman in a long tweed coat folding her umbrella. Tall with cool blue eyes, blonde hair neatly tucked into a French twist, and a natural elegance that reminds Vivian of Ruth. The woman stretches out her hand. Vivian shakes it.

"Bernice Kingsley."

"Vivian Thompson."

"We're the new world, Vivian. We don't want to be late."

∽ Bernice whispers in Vivian's ear. "Can I borrow a pen?" The grey moustached professor marches over to their seats and chastises the two of them for "colluding." During the next class, a young bushy-browed teacher directs fifty percent of his questions at Bernice; his definition of equal opportunity. Bernice finds ways to exact her revenge. She has a particular talent for making shy, male students blush. "If they can't handle me, they shouldn't have chosen law," she remarks, unrepentant.

On Thursdays, Aunt Faye dons her long black wool trench coat and walks to the seniors' centre to play bridge. Vivian throws herself back onto the threadbare raspberry sofa and puts her feet up on the coffee table, polished to a high sheen.

A few minutes later, Bernice rolls up in her father's Aston Martin. Aunt Faye's is a clean but dull home: old carpet, tired floral wallpaper and mustiness emanating from the curtains. It's so much brighter when Bernice comes to visit.

Bernice brings her usual complaints about having to endure another of her parents' extravagant parties, along with an array of party treats she was able to pilfer unnoticed. Cigars, cognac, glazed shrimp, caviar, meringue, imported cheeses.

While the pair of them work their way through the fancy scraps, Bernice launches into light-hearted impressions of the men who attend these gatherings. She stands by the open kitchen window puffing cigars or swigging whiskey, pushing out her stomach and talking in a booming voice about those stacked pin-up girls. The way she holds herself is uncanny.

"Your father gives you a lot of freedom," Vivian says.

"He calls me a force to be reckoned with," Bernice replies as she thrusts one of Aunt Faye's dull dinner knives into a block of gruyère.

Bernice jokes sometimes that she will cut off her long blonde hair and practice the law in men's suits. Vivian doesn't think much of it until she catches Bernice looking at another woman the way men do, captivating them with her own desire.

Time moves quickly in that first semester. The workload is heavy and Vivian toils ferociously, determined to outperform her male peers. Still, she finds time to socialize despite the inevitable tedium of her dates. It doesn't seem to matter how she behaves or what they do. Uniformly uninspiring: guys who call her "baby," the greasers, the heavy drinkers, the pseudo philosophers, the trophy boys, the wealthy and unambitious, the ambitious and self-centred. She blames her parents' dysfunctional relationship for her resistance to attachment. She hates the idea of being on somebody's arm, being led as if she is incapable of finding her own way.

Yet before she knows it, Bernice is popping over with stolen Christmas party snacks, and the first semester is almost done.

Vivian meets Todd at a Christmas party. He buys her a dry martini and she expects him to be as dull as the others. But he's different. For one thing, he isn't a student. "I work at an office supplies firm," he says and she wants to stop him there, but it is Christmas, so she lets him continue. He tells her about his business goals, his plans for setting up something of his own, and he explains all of it with a quiet confidence that she admires. He inherited some seed money after his father died in the war. Todd stops himself and apologizes for talking about business. "It's refreshing," she tells him, and she means it. He asks her for her opinions.

He has a handsome smile and knows how to dress sharply. Even better, she feels as though she has his full attention and is certain that she'll never have to fight for it. She isn't infatuated. It isn't love at first sight, and yet, there is something about him. They would be good, as partners.

~ Loud knocking on the front door startles Vivian. She pulls back the living room curtain as a cab leaves the curb. Bernice is wobbling on the step. It's 10 pm but it's bridge night and Aunt Faye isn't home.

"These are for you," Bernice manages to say as she passes Vivian a near-empty whiskey bottle and an empty box of chocolates. She lurches into the doorway and Vivian helps her inside. Bernice collapses into a chair, head lolling.

"Daddy's fixed it for me," she says, slurring. "Me and Ralph Locke are engaged. I'm dropping out of law school."

"Who's Ralph Locke?"

"The son of a hotelier. It's because … it's very good for Daddy's business."

"You're a grown woman. You can make your own decisions."

Bernice barks out a laugh and then starts bawling.

The wedding invitation arrives a couple of weeks later. Vivian declines it and all of Bernice's social invitations until Bernice stops asking. It isn't the fraudulence of Bernice's situation that she finds objectionable; it is her weakness, her unwillingness to fight for herself. In the end, Bernice is no better than Mother. Vivian cannot waste her time associating with people like that.

CHAPTER 17

1 9 5 7

FATHER DIES JUST before Vivian finishes her first year. A heart attack. Vivian can't help taking the timing of it personally, especially after a lawyer unveils the contents of his will.

She and Mother attend the funeral near Father's home in Vancouver. Mother doesn't acknowledge Ruth despite Ruth's delicate efforts to introduce herself. Mrs. Langston, Father's mistress, doesn't make an appearance, which disappoints Vivian.

The will provides for all his surviving family members to varying degrees, except Vivian. She gets absolutely nothing. Not even an old teacup. The lawyer is clearly embarrassed. It's a much greater shock to Vivian than Father's death, which was no doubt his intention. Aunt Faye barely scrapes by on her own; she can't afford to house Vivian without a contribution. Then there are the remaining years of tuition fees. In her despair, she considers packing up her things and moving back to the Stapleton family home that he left, fortunately, to Mother. But she thinks about that ugly smirk spreading across his dead face. She will find another way.

Vivian broods for weeks. Todd mistakes her moodiness for grief and she makes no effort to correct him. She cannot tell him that she blackmailed her own father and that consequently she is penniless. Though Todd is a practical man, he never met Father and he would have difficulty understanding her perspective. She will have to rescue herself. Again.

⮑ Unlike Aunt Faye, Aunt Barbara has no problem asking for help. When Aunt Barbara hears about the arrangement between Aunt Faye and Vivian, she asks Mother to send Vivian to her home in Calgary for the summer break. Uncle Edward's health has been deteriorating rapidly since his stroke.

The city is booming; giant cranes hover over the downtown and new suburbs alike. Boxy new malls and movie theatres bristle with crowds and thousands flock to the annual Calgary Stampede. But that is not the city Vivian lives in.

Her aunt and uncle occupy a nondescript suburban home from which Vivian rarely has a chance to escape. She cooks and cleans while Aunt Barbara escorts her husband to hospital appointments and she listens while Aunt Barbara complains about her life and Uncle Edward sleeps.

Meticulous like her sisters, Barbara's sense of propriety leaves little room for humour, but she is more fashionable than the other two. Barbara wears a white sleeveless blouse and black capris, cigarette pinched between two fingers, as she runs Vivian through a day-by-day breakdown of her responsibilities. "Don't cook the ham the way your mother makes it. I'll give you my recipe. The AJAX is under the sink. I drive the car. You can take the bus but don't miss your curfew or you can ride all the way back to Vancouver."

Living under Aunt Barbara's roof comes with one or two benefits. The sheer boredom gives her time to think. Father had many distinguishing characteristics but Vivian realizes that his transgressions were hardly unique. In Calgary alone, she surmises, there must be numerous powerful men engaged in similar activities. Why not capitalize on their weaknesses?

She researches the names of important executives and selects a few: the CEOs of a large brewery and a chain of car dealerships, the president of a financial services company and a partner at a leading law firm, just for starters.

Statistically speaking, only a few men that she writes to will have something to hide, and only a fraction of those will rise to the bait. One or two might go straight to the police but every great venture involves risk. With six weeks left of her summer, she starts small with her first four targets.

The scratchy nib of a borrowed fountain pen (her aunt's) bends her own handwriting out of shape. The wording in each letter is different, but the message is the same: she claims to know about their affairs. The relevant parties will be informed if they aren't willing to part with some cash. She keeps the amount modest, just enough to cover her fees and expenses for the remainder of her studies; an amount a rich man could comfortably afford. They are to deposit the cash at the busy downtown bus depot.

"Your hair looks lovely, Aunt Barbara."

Barbara tilts her head with a girlish smile, showing off her soft bob. The yellow glow from the pendant light above the table bounces off the loose curls that frame her slender face. Vivian tackled all of her chores and offered to take care of Uncle Edward to give her aunt time to go to the salon.

"Could I have a few hours to myself during the week, to see the city?"

Aunt Barbara frowns but Vivian persists.

"Maybe on Friday afternoons? Uncle Edward doesn't have any appointments then."

Aunt Barbara reluctantly agrees. "I suppose I have to let you be young."

Vivian counts down the days anxiously and wavers between deciding to go through with it and being absolutely sure she won't. Meanwhile, her request for occasional time off appears to have reminded Aunt Barbara that her position is not permanent.

"Have you considered studying in Calgary?" Barbara asks with a hint of desperation. "There's an excellent teaching program at the University of Alberta. And plenty of eligible young bachelors."

For a split second, Vivian considers the suggestion. Unlike Aunt Faye, Aunt Barbara offers free room and board in exchange for Vivian's help. Scholarship opportunities could at least partially cover the fees. But teaching is not law. Law is the study of complex power structures. Law is the foundation of her future. Father thought she should abandon the law.

"Calgary is a wonderful city, but law is where my passion lies."

Aunt Barbara blinks. "Does it matter? Pretty young woman like you, you'll be married by the time you graduate."

"Yes, it does matter," Vivian says. "I'm going to do more with my life than be somebody's wife."

Aunt Barbara looks at her husband as if expecting him to rise up out of his wheelchair and put his insolent niece in her place. She wags a finger at Vivian. "This attitude of yours comes of not having a real father when you needed one."

And where are your adult children now that you need help? Vivian wants to ask. She holds her tongue.

 Vivian hasn't slept. She can barely think. She forces down some breakfast to keep up appearances despite her roiling stomach. A blob of jam drips onto her off-white blouse and she rushes to the sink. There's no time to change. Wearing a secretary-style skirt and flats, she should blend in well enough, providing she can get the jam stain out.

Aunt Barbara watches from the front yard, wrenching weeds encircling her hydrangeas as Vivian stands at the bus stop across the street. "Visit the university while you're downtown," Aunt Barbara calls out to her. "There are still a few spaces left in the teaching program."

The bus collects her and rolls through the suburbs into the humming city core, depositing her at the bus terminal 25 minutes later. She hurries inside the ugly concrete building and heads straight for the café. It is just as she had hoped; there's a free table perfect for discreetly scanning the drop location. She orders a coffee and sits quietly, careful to choose a chair facing slightly away from the spot so as to be less conspicuous.

She taps the table nervously, and then silently scolds herself for being obvious. Trying for a natural pose, she rests one hand on her knee and the other on her coffee cup. The wait is so intense she forces herself to focus on something distant to calm her mind. She mentally recites the Latin verbs she learned at boarding school (an expense Father happily paid for to keep her out of sight). Sum, es, est. Habeo, habes, habet. Amo, amas, amat. To be, to have, to love. Amari. Amavisse. To be loved. To have loved. She thinks about her dead brother and imagines what her parents would have called him. Stanley, perhaps, after Father, or William, after his father.

If they catch her, she'll play the grief-stricken young woman who lost her way after the sudden and devastating demise of her father. For a first offence, a kind judge might be lenient. She thinks of Bernice's impersonations of Judge Braithwaite, Blustering Braithwaite, she called him, a frequent attendee at her parents' soirees. According to Bernice, he had at least two mistresses. What would a judge like Braithwaite make of Vivian's attempts to blackmail powerful philanderers? Father has put her in an impossible situation but, if her life is to be derailed, at least it will the result of her own decisions.

Hands tick around the large platform clock. Women in summer dresses and men with suit jackets flopped over their arms move quickly despite the heat. Buses belch exhaust as they come and go. Cigarette smoke blues the air.

A young guy in jeans and a leather jacket approaches the bench carrying a briefcase that doesn't match his style. Vivian holds her breath. He turns and looks straight at her, brown eyes and slicked back hair. She sips her coffee and shifts her gaze towards the platform clock. Video, vides, videt. Cognosco, cognoscis, cognoscit. To see. To know. Casually, she looks back. He has disappeared. His briefcase is beside the bench. The bench.

It's a trap. It has to be, to have happened so fast, for someone to have actually produced the money on her first attempt. There are police officers hiding in plain sight, waiting for her to reveal herself. She glances at the faces around her; wrinkled, young, tall, heavy, sideburns, lipstick, harried, smiling and emotionless, none of them paying any attention to her.

The briefcase won't sit there forever. A good Samaritan will spot it and hand it in, or the courier will circle back and take the cash for himself.

She looks down at her empty coffee cup as though an alternative option might pop out from the speckle of brown grounds. She thinks about her dwindling hopes of getting a fraction of the choices her stepbrothers have. Her legs don't feel quite like her own as she leaves the café. Her heels clip along the platform, but they could be someone else's feet. She would never do something this absurd.

A couple of buses roll to a stop and she gives herself time

to study the destinations. Edmonton. Red Deer. She glances over at the bench. Nobody has approached the briefcase. Her legs take her there. She is close enough to touch it. She does. She bends down and picks it up. It's extremely light. Her future is light.

She walks forward holding the briefcase, one step at a time; gingerly and then with speed. A stranger brushes past her arm. She startles but doesn't stop. She can't now. She's in it, and it is surreal, like a game.

The door to the ladies' scares her as it swings shut. Her whole body is on edge. She locks herself in a stall. The briefcase clasps click open. "DON'T CONTACT ME AGAIN," reads a scrawled message on top. Neat stacks of banknotes courtesy of a financial services executive fill the remaining space. She examines a few; crisp, new. Real and unbelievable. In 30 minutes, it is the car salesman's turn. Would he also bring the money? Would the lawyer, or the brewery owner? Or would they choose to alert the authorities?

As Vivian walks anxiously towards the local buses, the 12 pulls up right in front of her. The bus that travels past the front of Aunt Barbara's house.

The driver examines her return ticket and then looks down at her briefcase. "Busy day at the office?" he asks with a smile. She nods nervously and finds a free window seat. A sweaty man in a thick suit takes the seat beside her and accidentally knocks the case with his foot. She pictures the briefcase popping open and spilling out cash. Questions would be asked, unless the man beside her managed to be discreet enough to seize her future for himself.

The platform is busy but the two black-suited officers weaving rapidly between the passengers capture Vivian's attention. They are making their way directly towards her bus.

Vivian turns away from the window, unable to watch. They can't come on her bus, not hers. They must be heading somewhere else. She rises out of her seat and settles into it again; it is too late. The driver is talking to someone. Shoes hit the metal steps. A broad-shouldered officer climbs on board and begins making his way down the aisle. He stares right at her. He opens his mouth as if to ask her something. Her heart stops.

"Wrong bus!" his colleague shouts from the platform. The officer thumps back down the aisle and down the metal steps. Vivian watches through the scratched glass as a teenaged boy is dragged off the neighbouring coach.

It isn't until a week later, when Vivian dares to deposit her dirty money to pay her tuition fees, that she is able to relax enough to marvel at her efforts. She still can't quite believe she got away with it. The executive who paid her off must have been desperate. He probably has a family, young kids. She doesn't feel guilty. She didn't make his mistakes; she merely found a way to benefit from them. There's nothing wrong with that. She has won and she feels heady for days. The thrill is like none she has ever experienced.

CHAPTER 18

1 9 9 4

Mamma would have been very suspicious of a strange car acting strangely, but she wasn't around when the old station wagon rolled up as Elena walked home from school. Elena had to turn her head fully to see the car that crawled up beside her; her hood was pulled up against the biting wind. It was blueish with wooden panels on its sides and crumbling rust patches along the bottom. Instead of passing, it matched her stride.

Elena picked up her pace, keen to get inside her safe, warm home. As the car crept alongside her, she heard the window being wound down. The driver leaned across the passenger seat and stared at her. The woman looked like a witch; smiling but snarling at the same time.

"I heard you like stories," she growled. Elena struggled to place this unfamiliar person who seemed to know her. The driver smile-snarled again, revealing a mouthful of wandering teeth.

"I got a couple to tell." The woman nodded toward the back of the car. "Get in."

Elena knew better than that. She was only a couple of houses from home. She bolted.

She flew into the driveway and the car pulled in right

behind her. Bursting into the house, she slammed the door shut and locked it.

"Rob! A stranger followed me home." She was out of breath and red-faced when Rob came into the hallway. He looked concerned, but he spoke through a mouthful of sandwich, breadcrumbs dotting his shirtfront. "Is he out there now?" He moved towards the door as if investigating but stuffed another big bite into his mouth so his jaw had to work overtime to get through it all. He was always eating. Mamma said it was his age.

"It's a she. She told me to get in her car."

Rob frowned. A hard rap on the door. They looked at each other. He would have to deal with it since Mamma wasn't home. He shooed Elena behind him and opened the door a crack. Elena stayed close enough to listen.

"What do you want?" he said with a grunt, trying for tough.

"I'm your gramma. Don't leave me standin' out in the cold. Lemme in."

It wasn't Nonna. It couldn't be. Mamma said Nonna had died. Anyway, Nonna was a lady, Elena could tell by the photographs. She wore elegant dresses. She spoke Italian. Her teeth were straight. Rob was suspicious too; he didn't budge.

"What's your name ... gramma?" he asked.

"You think you're a smart one, do ya? Audrey Reid. Let me in before I freeze my ass off."

That was Dad's mom's name. That's about all they knew. Rob looked back at Elena and opened the door, slowly. Audrey stepped inside and looked around the little hallway. Elena kept a safe distance between herself and the stranger. Rob walked ahead into the living room, but Audrey wandered around the house as though she had come to inspect the property. She opened doors and peered into their bedrooms.

She made a small sound as she peeked into their tiny bathroom. Elena couldn't tell whether or not she approved. Audrey marched straight into the kitchen and looked out the window at the river. Elena wanted to ask if she was here about Dad, but it didn't seem like the right moment to ask questions. Rob was shifting his feet uncomfortably. He didn't know what to do either. They'd never had family come to visit.

"Do you want a drink?" he asked Audrey.

"Whaddya got?"

"Water."

"Generous of ya."

Audrey strode to the living room and sat on the sofa. Elena sat in the chair opposite and watched her curiously. Mousy brown hair was pinned back above her ears and the rest hung to her shoulders. She wasn't old old. In fact she looked quite young for a grandma. Her face was tight and serious but fat bulged out around her waist. Dad had light brown hair but a lot of people had brown hair. Audrey was also quite short and Elena wondered if her own shortness came from her grandma and not Mamma. Luckily, she hadn't inherited her teeth.

Rob put a glass of water on the table. Audrey ignored it and he wouldn't sit down. The two of them were engaged in some kind of stand-off. He folded his arms and stared at her as though waiting for an explanation.

"You kids aren't very friendly, are ya? I figured you'd be pleased to meet your gramma."

Elena wanted to try out a smile, but she decided it was safer to follow Rob's lead. They needed to stay united. She might be their grandma, but there was a reason Dad never wanted her around. If she was a normal person, they would've visited, the way other families visited each other.

Rob tried for a stony look as he stared at Audrey. "We don't know anything about you."

"Well, now's your chance."

Elena did want to know about her, even if she was a bit scary. "Dad said you live up north."

"That's right."

Audrey didn't elaborate, which stumped them both. She got up and picked up a photograph from the bookshelf. It was a picture of their family taken a few years earlier. They were camping. Dad had set the camera on a tree stump and then rushed in so he was a blur in the photo and it looked like he was about to bowl them all over. Most people smiled when they saw that photo. From Audrey, nothing. She put it back on the shelf.

Elena opened her mouth and she caught Rob's scowl signalling her to remain silent. She ignored him.

"Why haven't you ever come to visit us before?"

"We live far away."

"You and Dad's dad?"

"That's right."

"But you could've come once."

"Me and Jim run a farm. We don't travel much. We got the animals to look after. And Curtis decided a long time ago that we weren't welcome."

"Why not?"

"Oh, old family drama. Doesn't even matter now."

Rob was growing impatient. "Why are you here?" he asked in his best manly tone.

"The cops got ahold of me," she said. "They thought I might know where my son's been hidin' out."

Rob shot Elena another warning look; one that meant Elena shouldn't get her hopes up.

"My son? I thought to myself, now who do they mean? I got three sons. They said they were after Curtis. I told 'em they must be mistaken. Curtis is a good boy. It must be one of the other two. But then I figured maybe he's changed now he's got himself a wife with a pole up her ass. Maybe he has to find other ways to let off steam."

That got Rob's back up. Redness flooded his cheeks. "You should leave."

Audrey wasn't intimidated by him. She didn't even acknowledge what he said or the way he'd puffed out his chest like he was a tough guy. She just kept talking. "But then they told me it was serious. They told me about this explosion and I told 'em no, none of my boys would ever do a thing like that."

Audrey settled back into the sofa, getting comfortable. Rob didn't do anything. He just kept scowling, and Audrey kept talking.

"I don't know where Curtis is, but I've come here to find him and I will find him, so if there's anything you kids wanna tell me, now would be a good time."

Elena wondered if it was weird to feel so uncertain about your own grandma. Weren't they supposed to love each other? She wasn't sure if that was possible. In any case, it was a relief to finally hear somebody else say it was about time they did something. "How are you going to find him?" she asked.

Rob glared at Elena as though she'd switched sides.

Audrey smiled. "You leave that part to me."

Audrey looked at Elena curiously, and then at Rob. "What did he tell you about me?"

Elena piped in before Rob could stop her. "He said his family were dinks."

"Well ... now you get to decide for yourselves, don't ya?"

"Do you miss him?"

Audrey stared at Elena again and then looked away. Audrey wasn't as tough as she liked to make out. "Course I do. He's my son." She looked out of the window. "But we never had what you'd call a good relationship."

"Did you ever meet my mom?"

"Once. At their wedding."

"Did you meet Nonno?"

"Who?"

Rob sighed. "She means Mom's dad. His name is Massimo."

"No. I didn't meet your mom's folks. Curtis and Giulia got married after …"

Elena desperately wanted Audrey to finish her sentence, but the front door opened. Audrey stood as Mamma came in. Mamma's jaw dropped.

"Giulia, good to see you. It's been a while."

"What are you doing here?"

"I'm concerned about my son. I've come to help," Audrey said gently, much more nicely than she'd spoken to the two of them.

"We don't need your help. Please leave."

Mamma rarely spoke so abruptly, to anyone. Even when she obviously disliked someone, she found a subtler way to get rid of them. Mamma's reaction to Audrey only made "gramma" more mysterious.

"Don't worry kids. I'll find him," Audrey assured them. She moved slowly out of the living room and through the hallway as though she were a fragile old lady, but Elena knew it was an act. She was putting it on for Mamma, just like she put on the niceness. She wanted Mamma to think she was a harmless old woman, but it wasn't working.

Mamma closed the door behind her and leaned against

it. Elena stood in the hallway and watched her recover. "Don't open the door to that woman again!" Mamma said.

When Dad talked about his family, rarely and using few words, they seemed distant and barely real. Mamma treated Audrey, the only other family member Elena and Rob had ever met, as though she was dangerous. Elena decided there and then that she would find a way to speak with Audrey again. At least she would answer questions, unlike Mamma.

Elena went to her room and lay down and thought about it for a while. The more she thought about it, the angrier she got—not with Audrey, but with Mamma. Audrey said she was going to do something. Mamma didn't even pretend she was going to try. Mamma was too scared to try.

～ "Frank offered me a job at the Inn. Part-time." Mamma made the announcement casually as the three of them sat around the table.

"Frank?"

Rob dropped his fork on his plate and Elena leapt out of her chair.

"But you hate Frank!" she said. "And he lied about picking up those guys in the forest."

"I don't hate Frank. We just don't have much in common, that's all," Mamma responded defensively. "You can't keep accusing him, Elena. The police are doing everything they can …"

"The cops think Dad's guilty! But they're wrong and you know they're wrong so why don't you do something about it?"

"Don't talk to me like that!"

"Maybe he's scared! Maybe if we tried to find him …"

"I'm doing my best to keep this family together, Elena.

We have bills to pay. And what exactly do you expect me to do that the police aren't doing?"

"You just have to listen! Nobody is listening."

Elena left her food and ran to her bedroom. There were lots of clues, Elena could see that, so why couldn't Mamma? In the middle of everything that didn't make sense, there was Frank offering Mamma a job when he could've hired anyone in Stapleton. Why did Frank want to help Mamma out? Most people were avoiding them and blaming Dad for the explosion. She still couldn't figure out if Frank was on their side or not.

~ Mamma started her new job on a Tuesday evening. She left them at the house with popcorn and pop. Rob was in charge. It was alright. They watched a movie and he didn't care when Elena went to bed as long as Mamma thought she was asleep when she came home.

Sometimes Mamma allowed Elena to come to the Inn while she worked. The Inn was full of fossils, not like Mary's fossils, but still, everything Frank owned was old. The TV in the breakfast room had a fake wood casing and went snowy a lot. The kitchen microwave was probably one of the first microwaves ever made; a white box with a dial that looked like it belonged on a safe. But Elena didn't get a proper look in there because the cook shooed her out.

She recognized the embroidered armchair occupying the reception area. Frank had sunk into it after she accused him of being in the forest. She settled into it and picked at the faintly smelly fibres but it offered up no clues.

Elena was not successful in uncovering Frank's secrets, but each time she visited he seemed more himself and his place felt more familiar, like Ken's café. Mamma seemed more relaxed about working there too, and she treated Frank differently, not as a friend, but not like someone she'd cross the street to avoid. Rob would usually show up whenever there was a meal on offer and Mamma popped into the breakfast room on her breaks to make sure they weren't causing any trouble. One thing that Elena liked about spending time at the Inn was that everyone seemed content just doing what they were doing. It was harder at home because Dad was supposed to be there and he wasn't.

~~> Father Craig gave the briefest sermon he'd ever given and most of the congregation rushed home without bothering to exchange words over coffee and cookies. Today was Game Day. BC Lions versus Baltimore. Dad's team had reached the Grey Cup Final and someone else would be watching it on his fancy TV.

Elena couldn't stand being in the house. Their little living room overwhelmed her brain with memories of him sitting alone or with Ken, tuned into the games so intently that the world around them didn't exist. Cheering. Cursing. Shouting players' names and criticizing poor decisions.

Mamma agreed to let Elena hang out at the Inn, as long as Rob came by to walk her home after the game ended. The cook switched the TV on for her in the breakfast room but Elena got up and switched it off again. She tried reading a book but the noise from the bar made it hard to focus on the words. She flicked through the images in a fashion magazine that someone had left in the lobby.

The Inn was packed and Elena wondered how Mamma could bear it, surrounded by TVs blaring Dad's game. The roars and disappointment moved in waves through the thin walls.

The Lions won and the excitement turned into a cacophony. Elena laid her head on the table and let her dark hair fall over her face so no one could tell she was crying. Dad said they would win. She wasn't sure why it made her feel so sad.

~ Saturday. Mamma had time off and apparently Frank had some free time too because he drove them into Stony Creek so they could get some shopping done. Rob got very quiet when Mamma mentioned it, but they hadn't had a chance to get out of town since the mill explosion, so he came with them.

The whole trip made Elena think of Dad. It was the first time they had driven past the sawmill since the explosion. Frank sped up as they went by it, but she had time to see the black and broken core of it fly by her window. It looked just like it did on the TV news and nothing like the place she remembered. The main building was a twisted skeleton coated in black.

Some of the surrounding buildings had survived, but even they looked weirdly out of place. They no longer had any purpose. They were as useless as the piles of untouched, stacked timber. Mamma brushed her eyes but no one said anything.

They drove in silence until they reached the scummy little pond by the edge of the highway—another landmark that reminded her of Dad. Crusted white soda deposits edged the pond, and every time they drove by it, he used to threaten to stop the car and throw her in. He said if she touched the white crust trying to climb out she would turn into a Sasquatch. Rob was staring intensely out the window—Dad said the same thing to him when he was younger.

"You're turning into a Sasquatch!" she said, pointing at

the fuzz that was building up around Rob's upper lip and the sides of his face. He batted her hand away angrily. Then he leaned between the front seats.

"When are we getting our truck back?"

Mamma turned and looked at him. "Whenever the police are done with it."

He sat back again and sulked.

As they neared the city, they could see the river winding through the houses below, blue and still. The roads widened and got busier until cars were flying all around Frank's old truck. He pulled into a parking lot.

It was weird, walking around the mall with a man Mamma had always avoided, just like they used to walk around the mall with Dad. Rob hung back, not wanting to be seen with any of them.

Rob needed new shoes because his toes were about to burst out of his Air Jordans. Mamma said she couldn't afford to buy him another pair of those, so they trailed around the budget shoe shop until Rob finally caved. They went back to the sports store and he bought himself a pair of Nikes with a chunk of his paper route savings.

Frank didn't get involved; he just stood around until they were ready to go home, which was exactly what Dad used to do. As they were walking out of the mall, Frank told Rob he was becoming a man now, spending his own hard-earned money. Rob just huffed at him, and then said: "If you didn't want to buy anything, why didn't you stay in the truck?" Mamma told him to stop being so rude.

〜 "Is Mamma dating Frank?"

It took Elena a while to ask him. She was worried Rob might get angry with her just for bringing it up, and she was also worried about what his answer might be. It wasn't that she believed the gossip, it was just that the idea of it, Mamma with someone else, didn't feel right at all. It was a stupid thing to ask. Mamma would never do that. Anyway, Dad was coming home soon.

"Who said that?" Rob said.

She had his attention. They were eating dinner together because Mamma was still at work.

"Some kids at school."

It was Kathryn who'd said it, not directly to Elena but to her girl gang when Elena was close enough to hear. "I heard Frank and Elena's mom are doing it!" The other girls shrieked and chorused "eewww!" and stared at Elena. She pretended not to hear them.

"Don't listen to them," Rob said. "People are pissed because Mom's got a job and they don't."

They heard the key in the front door. Mamma had come home. Rob let his forkful of mac and cheese sit halfway between his plate and his mouth. He put his fork back down and left the table and went into his room and slammed the door.

Mamma came into the kitchen. "What was that all about?"

Elena shrugged.

~ Elena missed the warm weather. Shortly after the explosion, she'd gotten into the habit of wheeling back and forth along their lane, stopping outside their house to imagine Dad was in the living room looking out at her as though he'd been in there all along, hiding from them, and every time they left he'd pop out of the walls with a can in his hand and lie back on the couch.

It was too cold for that now. Her bike had been stored in the shed. There was a thin dusting of snow on the ground, but sometimes she still wanted to be outside because the cold-ness helped to push out bad thoughts, so she walked up and down their lane in her thick winter jacket, hat and gloves, and she imagined he was walking ahead of her. She could see his big silhouette in his black jacket, hat and blue jeans moving almost out of sight. However fast she walked, he was always too far ahead to catch.

She turned back towards their house to see a real person approaching. It was Rob walking home from somewhere, scowling at the pavement with his backpack swinging from one shoulder. He spotted Elena and gestured for her to come with him. Whatever he was up to would be more exciting than what she was doing. It might even involve looking for Dad.

They walked up the hill to where the houses ended and gave way to the tall grass and ranch land where Elena had got lost the night of the explosion. When they were younger they used to come up here to play. Dad got them a kite once, and they tried to run through the knotty roots of the sagebrush with it, waving it this way and that to catch the wind. Elena fell and grazed her knees and chin, and that was the end of that.

Rob pulled an oily rag from one of his baggy pockets.

"Where did you get that?"

"Frank's."

He took out a lighter and lit the rag. It burst into flames that reached up to grab his jacket. He dropped it quickly onto the dirt where it flickered and grasped at the long grass and died in the little scrap of snow. He stomped on it, just to be safe, and they stared at the blackened rag.

Rob lit a cigarette. Elena didn't know he smoked. She tried to look at him casually, like it was no big deal.

"You're not having one," he said.

Elena shrugged. "I don't like smoking anyway. Give me the lighter."

He threw it to her. She lit the ends of the sagebrush and quickly blew them out before they caught properly. She loved being close to that sage smell, but the burning made her think of Brandon collapsing in their doorway and everything going dark.

"What else burns quickly?" she asked Rob.

"Your hair. Don't lean over it like that. Give it back."

Elena threw the lighter back, too short, deliberately, so he had to dig around in the sagebrush and wet snow.

Rob said they were going to get revenge on Frank. "For what?" she asked. But Rob had already moved on to the next phase of his plan. Frank had an ancient record player and a few dusty albums he liked to play, but they skipped and crackled and drove Rob crazy. Rob pulled a few of them out of his backpack and dropped them onto the dirt.

Elena stared at the first album cover; the sun shone bright pinks and oranges above a man with many arms, with people fanned out behind him. The Jimi Hendrix Experience was written on the sun. Rob slipped the record from its sleeve and threw the cover on the ground. "That one's yours," he said, pointing at another album. On the cover was a frizzy-haired woman with round sunglasses sitting on a motorbike.

"The rules are, you have to stand here and see if you can throw the record over the fence. Whoever throws it the furthest wins."

"Won't Frank be angry?"

"He'll never know it was us."

"What did he do?" she asked again.

"He tried to dance with Mamma," Rob said. "I saw them."

"What did Mamma do?"

"She told him she didn't like dancing. But he shouldn't have asked her in the first place."

Elena didn't think it was the worst thing in the world, considering everything else that had happened, but it was more important to be on Rob's side, and anyway, she had to agree with him on one thing. There was no way Frank could ever replace Dad, and she didn't like the idea of him even trying to, if that's what he was doing.

They both knew she had no hope of beating her brother at this game, but she threw Janis as far as she could and she landed in the sagebrush not even close to the fence. "Good try," Rob said kindly, before swinging his arm back and hurling Jimi into the air. He went really high and sailed right through the barbed wire on the way down. It was a great throw—Elena jumped excitedly and clapped her hands. She was happier about Rob's genuine smile than his throw. He pulled out two more records and Elena got the next one a bit further than her first attempt, but Rob really nailed it this time. It went so far over the fence they probably would never find it.

Rob piled up the empty sleeves on a patch of dirt and snow and set them alight. The yellow flame melted the bright colours into a pile of wrinkled, black paper shavings. Eventually the flame ran out of things to eat and it shrank until Rob stamped it out.

➳ Elena didn't have much to do now that she didn't have any friends to hang out with, so she visited the museum most Saturdays and Mary filled her head full of stories about "the olden days." Mary gave her some window cleaner and cloths, and she squirted blue liquid onto smudgy fingerprints and gently rubbed the glass clean. In one display case were Native artefacts: old arrowheads, moccasins with delicate beadwork, a thick beaded belt and a painted drum. On the wall beside them was a blown up black-and white-photograph, and the message beneath identified it as the Stapleton Reserve in 1910. Men—Elena guessed granddads, sons and grandsons—stood outside a wooden hut. To somebody really old, she thought, these photos were like the ones of Mamma's family standing together outside their home. Maybe someone still knew who those people were.

"Are those people related to Brandon?"

Mary was digging a packet of cookies from her desk. She came over and handed one to Elena. Gone in two bites.

"Brandon who?"

"I don't know his last name. He lives on the reserve."

"They might be."

Elena pointed at the photograph. "That old man is his great-great-grandpa." And then she moved on to a couple of arrowheads. "And his great-great-great-great-great-grandpa made those."

"The maker of those arrowheads and the people in that photo probably weren't related."

Elena was annoyed. She liked her theory. "How do you know?" she asked Mary.

"Historical evidence," Mary answered. "There's a ridge just out of town with a meadow on it. You can see depressions in the ground where pit houses sat a long time ago."

"So Brandon's great-great grandpa lived in that meadow?"

"I don't know where Brandon's great-great grandpa lived, but those arrowheads came from that meadow and the people in the photograph didn't. When the gold miners arrived, the people that were here, the ones who built the pit houses, had most of their land taken away from them. They were forced to move to a very small area that became the Stapleton Reserve. Because they lost their fishing and hunting territory, they began to starve. Then a terrible smallpox epidemic wiped them out. They all died. For a few years, nobody lived on the Stapleton Reserve."

Elena wondered how many people had died, and who was last to go, who was there at the very end to see everything and everyone disappear. It made the sawmill explosion sound like a minor incident, like comparing a heart attack to a nosebleed.

"Some years later, a group of people from a neighbouring nation took up residence on the Stapleton Reserve. We know, approximately, when the new group arrived. The men in the photo were most likely part of the later group and were not related directly to the creators of the arrowheads."

Elena looked up at a picture of the family, people that only lived on here, in the village museum.

"There must be a lot of ghosts on the reserve," Elena said.

"You don't need to go chasing any of them."

Elena agreed. This town has been cursed for a long time. Everything that existed now had a before, and sometimes before was so different it was barely recognizable anymore.

She looked over at Mary. "Maybe whatever happened with my dad didn't start with the explosion. Maybe it had a before. Something happened that led to something else that led to the explosion that led to my dad going missing."

Mary nodded. "Makes sense."

"What do you think happened before the explosion happened?"

"I think somebody built on land they should have left well alone."

◁ Mamma stood on the grass by the riverbank, without moving, for a long time. A thick frost and a heavy mist hovered over the water. Mamma must have been cold, especially standing still for so long. Elena peered through the kitchen window and willed her back inside. It scared her when Mamma behaved differently. It meant Mamma was worrying again.

On good days, Mamma told them it would all be okay. The cops would locate Dad and help him, or he would find his own way home. He would be alright on his own for a while, Mamma said. He was a survivor. He knew what to do in any situation. Elena agreed with her completely, except when Mamma behaved strangely. In those times Elena knew Mamma didn't really believe it herself.

"Why did he do it?"

A younger kid in a hockey jersey approached her as she zigzagged aimlessly around the playground. His friends were lingering nearby, waiting to hear the daughter of a murderer's answer. "He didn't," she replied, before drifting away.

The kids at school remained fascinated by the story of the explosion and her dad's supposed connection. They treated her like they didn't know her, in that cautious way that wasn't mean but wasn't friendly. She was learning how to be an outsider and it was getting easier. She kept her head down and tried to put her mind to mysteries that didn't matter, like whose initials were scratched into a heart on the school gatepost, or how Mamma put on her mascara without poking her eyeballs, or why Frank made jokes that Mamma refused to laugh at when he obviously wanted her to like him.

For the last hour of every day, Elena waited for the school bell to sound. She would be ready, one hand clasping her bag strap so she could fling it over her shoulder the second they were allowed to leave. She liked to be first out the door to avoid questions and the sideward glances.

The buzzing sounded freedom. Elena made her move but Miss Meyer put her hand on Elena's bag. "Take a seat, Elena." She wasn't usually so abrupt. She usually said things like: "Why don't we have a quick little chat?" As if it were optional.

The other kids stared at her as they pushed their way out of the classroom. Miss Meyer closed the door. Elena listened to the clock ticking above the blackboard. Her teacher brought a chair over to her desk.

"You haven't seemed like yourself recently, Elena. Is there anything you'd like to talk about?"

Elena shook her head. Miss Meyer studied her face and Elena realized she was going to have to say something if she wanted to leave the classroom.

"I'm worried about what happened to my dad."

"Of course, you are. That's natural."

"The police say they're looking for him, but they haven't found him yet and I want to help look but Mamma says there's nothing we can do."

Miss Meyer hummed gently. Elena waited for a little pearl of wisdom about leaves floating down a river, or winter always leading to spring, or perhaps the fabled sagebrush and its taproot, but her teacher seemed to have run out of advice.

"I shouldn't be telling you this, Elena, so this is just between you and me, but I'm leaving at the end of the year. I've decided to find somewhere that's a better fit for me. There might come a time when you have to do that, with your family. Try to prepare yourself for that."

"But you said things would get better here!"

"Well, none of us really know ..."

Elena wasn't listening to any more of this. There wasn't

anything else to say. She got up and walked out of the classroom. She thought Miss Meyer might try to stop her but she let her go. Elena was grateful.

Outside, she heard the honk of a car horn. Across the street sat the old station wagon, blue-grey with wooden sides, Audrey's face peering out of the window.

"Get in," Audrey barked.

"Why?"

"Jesus Christ, I'm not going to kidnap you. Just get in, will ya?"

Elena glanced around. Mamma had confirmed Audrey's identity but had also made it very clear that she was off limits. No one else was going to help Elena. Maybe Audrey would understand.

Elena yanked open the heavy rear door and climbed in. "Slam it or it won't close properly," Audrey said. Audrey looked at her in the rear view as she put on her seatbelt. "Why are ya sittin' back there anyway? I'm not your frickin' chauffeur. Sit up front."

Mamma said she was still too small for the front seat. Rob teased her about it. He offered to get her a booster seat for his car when he got one. He said he'd be driving before she'd be big enough to sit up front.

Elena hesitated. She glanced around the quiet street and climbed into the front, landing in a heap.

"So where's a good place to eat around here?"

Elena shrugged.

"Where do they sell candy or cookies or whatever you like?"

"Ken's Café. It's on Main Street."

"Seatbelt on. No arguments."

Audrey put her foot down and drove like there was no one else on the road. She didn't bother with turning signals, nor did she stop for pedestrians, not even the old ones. Audrey went where Audrey wanted to go. Elena was amazed they didn't hit anything. They got honked at a couple of times, and Elena shrank down in her seat so no one would recognize her. At least it was only a short distance between the school and the café.

Audrey told Elena to run in and get something while she parked. Audrey didn't offer to pay, so Elena broke the last five-dollar bill of her pocket money. Pocket money had been officially suspended, Mamma said, until things got back to normal. A few hours at the Inn didn't pay what Dad made at the mill. She forgot to ask Audrey what she wanted, so she ordered a chocolate chip muffin and a double chocolate cookie. Ken didn't even try chatting with her. Mamma wasn't around so he didn't have to pretend to care.

Audrey wasn't outside the café. Elena found her at the entrance to the park. Audrey took a cookie without even looking first. She did say "thanks" and Elena thought maybe she could get used to her grandma. Maybe she wasn't all that bad.

They ate their treats as they walked because it was too cold to sit. There wasn't much snow but the cold day had hardened the grass. Elena left a trail of crumbs and Audrey did most of the talking.

"Before all this happened, before the cops got ahold of me about Curtis, I didn't even know you existed. I knew about your brother a'course. Your mom was pregnant at their wedding. I figured that's why she stayed with Curtis."

Elena didn't like a lot of the things that came out of Audrey's mouth. The more Elena thought about it, the more she thought Dad was probably right about his relatives. Still, family was important and this might be Elena's only chance to connect.

"Do you like school?" Audrey asked her.

"It's okay."

"Who's your best friend?"

Elena was too embarrassed to say she didn't have one anymore. "Mary."

"Is she in your class?"

"No."

"Boyfriend?"

"No."

"What about your mom?"

The question confused Elena.

"Does she have someone else? You know, a piece on the side?"

Elena shook her head.

"What about this Frank guy I've been hearin' about?"

Audrey had obviously been doing her research, which wasn't difficult in Stapleton. The whole town had been gossiping about Mamma and Frank since Mamma started working at the Inn.

"I asked you a question."

Elena didn't appreciate Audrey's pushiness, particularly because she didn't like the way this conversation was going. "Why don't you ask Frank what it's all about?" she said.

"Maybe I will. But right now I'm askin' you."

"There's nothing going on."

Audrey relented. "Alright, fine. Whaddya wanna know about me?"

Elena studied her grandma; deep lines around her eyes and a thin mouth. All this time wondering about who her relatives were and now she couldn't think of a single thing she wanted to know about Audrey. She didn't want to be rude though. She had to ask something.

"What's Grandpa like?"

"Jim? I asked what ya wanna know about me."

Elena thought about it. "What kind of things do you like?"

"I like the quiet. Early mornings up on the farm. Sayin' good mornin' to the dogs and the cats and the chickens and the goats."

Quiet moved in between them, neither of them really knowing what to say next, and the silence quickly became uncomfortable.

"What does Jim like to do?"

"Jim likes to come and go whenever he feels like it. But he's gettin' on these days. He doesn't go off so much now there's no kids in the house to look after. He just sits on his ass in front of the TV mostly."

Elena tried to imagine her dad as a kid and wondered what it was like for him growing up with Audrey and Jim. Some of the news reports said Dad had a "troubled upbringing." Did that make the other things they said about him true as well? No. Mamma said journalists exaggerated everything to sell more newspapers.

Audrey stared at her. "You're always listening, aren't ya? I bet you know things other people don't even realize you know." Elena was pleased by Audrey's words but wasn't sure how to respond. Audrey didn't leave her much time. "D'you think you and me can be friends?"

"Yeah," Elena told her, hesitantly.

"Good."

Elena didn't particularly trust her, but Elena wanted friends. She wanted family. She wanted a grandma she could spend time with and tell other people about.

"Why doesn't my mom like you?"

"She thinks I'm a bad person."

"Why?"

"I used to drink a lot. And I said a few things she didn't wanna hear at her wedding. Curtis told me to stay the hell away from them before I wrecked his marriage."

"Why didn't my mom's family go to her wedding?"

Audrey stopped and stretched her back and eyed a bench but it was icy. She turned to Elena.

"If I tell you what I know about her family, we have to make a little deal. I help you out, you help me out, okay?"

"Okay," Elena said, not sure what she was agreeing to.

"I only know what Curtis told me before they got hitched, and he only told me about it because he didn't want me sayin' things that might upset your mom, which I ended up doing anyway ... but it is what it is. Your mom was born in Italy and her family moved to Canada when she was a kid."

Elena nodded. She knew that much.

"Then, when your mom went off to college her dad ... whadd'ya say his name was?"

"Massimo. And her mom's name was Angelica."

"Massimo wanted to move back to Italy and the doctors told him your gramma, Angelica, was too sick to travel. But Massimo decided he was goin' back, so he put his wife on a plane. She died a few days after they arrived in Italy. Your mom never forgave him. That's why they don't talk anymore."

Elena knew Nonna was dead, but Mamma never wanted to talk about it. Just like she didn't want to talk about anything difficult. She was beginning to understand, finally, why her family was so different from everyone else's. They didn't stick together like the cowboy brothers in the poem. They fell apart. That's how Elena, Mamma and Rob came to be so alone.

"I figured that's why your mom married Curtis so quick. He wasn't good enough for her, but suddenly, the people closest to her were all gone, just like that!" Audrey snapped her fingers. "That's gotta change a person. I made a few comments at the wedding ... after a few drinks, y'know. But what's done is done."

Audrey didn't seem very sorry about her past behaviour. She moved right on to the next thing. "And that's all I know, so now it's your turn. You need to tell me everything you know about the explosion."

"It's a big mess. I don't know what happened," she said.

"This is very important, Elena. What you know could help me find him."

"How?"

"Whaddya mean, how?"

"How are you going to find him when the cops can't find him?"

It was Mamma's line but it was relevant. Audrey seemed very confident even though she hadn't seen Dad for years. She didn't know how he spent his time or who his friends were. What made her think she could figure out where he was?

"The cops don't care about finding him. They just sit around all day in their cop cars with their coffee and dough-nuts. It's you and me, the people that know him, we're the ones that will get to the bottom of all this."

"But how?"

"Well, first I gotta know what you know. Howd'ya expect me to come up with a plan when you're keepin' secrets from me?"

Elena went quiet. She watched Audrey move stiffly with the cold breeze. Luckily, Audrey had had enough of waiting around.

"Alright fine. You think about it and tell me the next time we meet. I'm gonna be in town for a few days."

Elena agreed. She waved goodbye to her grandma, who didn't offer to drive her home. It was for the best. Elena didn't want Mamma to know she'd been in Audrey's car.

Elena walked home with a loneliness she couldn't shake. Information-trading wasn't the relationship she'd hoped for and Audrey wasn't the kind of grandma she'd imagined having. But she was family, Elena reminded herself, which was better than nothing.

⤳ Sunday is a day of rest, Elena told Mamma on their way home from church. That's why it wasn't a good day to clean the house. Those were God's rules and they had to be obeyed. Mamma said Elena did not need to remind her of God's rules. Honour Thy Mother was one of God's rules.

They halted their conversation to watch a real estate agent from Stony Creek shove a FOR SALE sign into someone's front lawn. "A bit optimistic," Mamma murmured. Houses weren't selling but people still had to leave, so their homes were being boarded up. Mamma had explained that those houses belonged to the bank now. Before the explosion, Elena didn't know banks took people's houses. Kathryn's big house was boarded up and, when it snowed, the white stuff stayed piled up on the driveway until it warmed enough to melt. On Kathryn's last day at school, she told the class excitedly that they were moving east to be close to her grandparents, but Mamma said the bank had taken their house, too.

"We need to keep our house," Elena explained to Mamma as they approached their front door. "Otherwise, how will Dad know where to find us when he comes home?"

"I'm doing my best." Mamma's voice shook. It could have been the cold.

Elena didn't argue about the chores when she got inside. They all had to do their best until he came home.

⤳ Elena heard the old station wagon belching behind her as she walked home from school. The snow had returned and the wind was stinging her face. It was mostly for the warmth that she got into the car. They didn't drive anywhere.

Audrey didn't waste any time. "Are you ready to tell me what you know?"

Elena shrugged.

"Who's heard from him?"

"No one."

"Are you lying to me? Cuz I'll find out. And we had a deal."

Elena hated being accused of things. She wanted to tell Audrey to go away but she wanted even more for someone to listen. "I haven't seen him. No one's seen him."

Audrey squinted at Elena. "Okay. But you know something. I can tell. I got a sense for these things."

Elena wondered again whether she could trust Audrey. At least she didn't pretend he was going to show up any time soon and surprise them all, like Mamma did. Plus, Audrey was actually looking for him, unlike the cops.

"I overheard Mamma and Brandon talking. The cops told Brandon to change his story about seeing Dad just before the explosion or he'd get into trouble too."

Audrey nodded. "Never trust a cop," she said. "What else?"

"My mom said I shouldn't spend time with you."

"Listen, Elena, your mom thinks she's doing what's best, but she doesn't have the balls for this kinda thing. You know she doesn't. You and me are gonna have to work together to get your dad back."

Audrey was right. It was time to take a risk and tell her everything: how she had seen Dad's truck in the forest, her suspicions about Frank and Ken based on the fact they'd both lied about events following that day, and how a security guard had approached her and Mary at the camp, which Mary said used to be a military base and that seemed to be somehow connected to everything else.

"It's got to be a cover up," Elena said finally, though she didn't fully understand the term. She'd heard it on one of Mamma's cop shows.

When she'd finished Audrey said: "I knew you were holding out on me." But she didn't seem happy about it. It was almost as though Audrey didn't want to hear what she was hearing. Elena wondered if she might have done something wrong by telling her.

The silence became awkward so Elena said goodbye and got out of the car. Audrey barely looked at her before gunning the old car forward.

CHAPTER 19

Vivian is flipping through papers and photographs she discovered in a locked filing cabinet. The house is quiet; Todd is out and his conspirator is doing the laundry. She still doesn't fold things properly though Vivian has explained it numerous times.

It scares her, how little some of these words and pictures mean to her, but as she digs deeper through the albums of photos, press clippings and notes, some things pop out of the darkness inside her head like fireworks. There she is as a child, four or five, sitting on a swing with Mother behind, both of them smiling. She remembers that day quite clearly, a rare occasion when Father was home. He was the one taking the photograph.

The people glued down on the next page are a mystery. She must've known them at one time. Two boys and a German Shepherd, all three of them struggling to stay still; blurry paws and hands. Vivian and the same two boys playing in a park somewhere. Were they cousins, perhaps? Family friends? Does it matter that she has forgotten them entirely?

She picks up another album. Photos, much more recent. She's an adult. Todd is with her. More people she doesn't recognize. She flips through the pages and a newspaper clipping slips out, yellowed with age. The Stapleton Herald. It's about a tragedy at a river. Two names that are so familiar yet still a mystery. She folds the paper carefully and puts it in her cardigan pocket. She will ask Todd about this one. He will remember.

Vivian puts the memories away and decides it's time to go out. She has things to do. She must have; she can't just sit around the house all day. The conspirator is still in the laundry room making a pig's ear out of it. Vivian doesn't bother disturbing her. She slips out of the front door and heads toward the gas station.

⁓ Rhonda gawks like a fish. "Vivian! It's minus 15 out! Where's your jacket?"

"I'm not cold."

Her teeth chatter and her limbs shiver. Perhaps she is a little cold. She hadn't noticed.

"I'm calling Todd."

"Don't! Please! I'm fine."

Rhonda slips into the back. A moment later she returns with a giant puffy jacket. It's grotesque, but Vivian allows her to pull it around her shoulders and guide her to a table. Rhonda pours her a cup of something hot and sets it down in front of her. "That'll warm you up."

Vivian looks around for her purse. It isn't on the back of her chair, or the floor. She's lost it. It's gone.

"Where's my purse?"

"You didn't bring it."

"I did ..."

"You didn't. I would've seen it. Sit down. The coffee's on me. You should eat something, too. How about ..."

Rhonda turns around and inspects the plastic-wrapped baked goods displayed in a wicker basket.

"... a chocolate muffin?"

Vivian doesn't fully register the question. She isn't sure how she got here.

"But the banana bread is fresher," Rhonda mutters.

She puts a piece on a paper plate and leaves it in front of Vivian, who picks at it slowly. "It tastes like dough," she announces after a few bites.

Vivian finishes the sticky bread and looks around for a napkin. Rhonda is back at the counter, on the phone. She can't believe it. Rhonda is betraying her. Rhonda, of all people. At any moment they'll be here to take her away, the people who keep her trapped in her own house. There's nothing she can do about it; no one she can trust.

The doorbell jangles. Someone who looks like Frank—does he have a brother she doesn't know about?—approaches the counter. Rhonda finishes her call and takes money for the gas. He spots Vivian as he's about to leave. He smiles and comes over.

"Hi Vivian."

"Hi Frank."

He hesitates. "I was going to have a coffee. Mind if I join you?"

She gestures for him to sit.

"It's a cold one today."

He's right. She hugs the puffy jacket. He ruffles one hand through his hair. There's something strangely handsome about him. Frank isn't usually so well put-together.

"You dropped something," he says politely and he reaches down to pick up a scrap of yellowed paper from the floor. He opens it up and he sees the tragedy in heavy black print.

Vivian snatches it away and crumples it in her hand. She doesn't know why she doesn't want him to see it because she doesn't remember what it's about, but it feels as though he's reading something very private, like a page from a diary. He inflicts what feels like judgment upon her with a long stare, sips his coffee and changes the subject.

"Giulia's doing a fantastic job of keeping the Inn going."

"Giulia?"

"Yeah. Giulia Reid."

Vivian shakes her head. "You never should've taken her in, Frank. I thought you got rid of her. Why did you take her back?"

"What do you mean?"

"You know."

Frank stares at her, but it's not Frank, is it? Vivian holds her breath. Who is this man sitting at her table trying to read her secrets?

"Do you think she's dangerous because of what her husband did?"

"Who are you?"

"I'm ..."

"You're not Frank. Frank knows exactly what happened."

"I'm Frank's son. Dean."

Vivian is instantly embarrassed. She wants to get out of there, but where would she go? Everywhere is cloudy now. It has all become so difficult to separate and understand.

"I'm sorry if I upset you, Vivian. I didn't mean to confuse you."

"About what?"

Dean smiles and gulps his coffee. Young people carry their drinks around everywhere with them nowadays. It's time he left.

"Did everyone believe what the papers said about Curtis Reid?"

She doesn't want to hear these names. They hurt her and he knows it, doesn't he? That's why he's here. To make her angry. She can't see them completely; their faces, the people they were. She doesn't want to remember them.

"There must have been a few locals, people who knew him, who didn't think Curtis was capable of blowing up the mill."

"Why are you asking me?"

"No reason, except that you seem to know a lot about the town."

"Are you a writer?"

"No. I'm a businessman."

"Then why do you care?"

"I'm interested in the truth."

"Is it her? Is that woman you keep at the Inn telling you lies about her precious husband?"

"Giulia?"

"Yes … Giulia." She hates that name.

"I know there's something else going on here, Vivian, and I know you're at the centre of it."

"Don't be ridiculous."

"My dad, Frank, felt so guilty about something in his past, he didn't want me to know he was my dad. I think you know what he was feeling guilty about. Was he involved?"

"Involved in what?"

"Mary said you were the piece of the puzzle that connected all the dots, and if I could crack you … but you're already cracking, aren't you, Vivian?"

"Enough." Todd's voice, right behind them. He seems bigger than usual, which pleases Vivian for some reason. "The people in this town are old and lonely and they want something to gossip about. My wife is sick. Don't bother her anymore."

Todd helps her up, removes the baggy jacket and puts his own coat around her, carefully doing up the zip. This time she doesn't feel like a child. He's rescuing her from something. Todd thanks Rhonda as they leave and he gently folds Vivian into their car. She rests her hand on his knee as he drives them home.

CHAPTER 20

2 0 1 9

THE SITTING ROOM. Old people sitting. She is old now, isn't she? Is she? Afternoon sun. Heads nod. He is here. Lingering. He waits while the nurse presents her with little yellow pills and the two of them watch her gulp them down with a cup of water. "Well done," the nurse cheers. Vivian ignores her.

The nurse scuttles off with her clipboard and he passes Vivian a box of chocolates. Individually gold-wrapped. "Rhonda at the gas station told me these are your favourites. She said she only stocks them for you."

"Where's Rhonda?"

Vivian looks around, craning her neck around the high-backed armchair.

"She isn't here. She's working."

Vivian nods. Rhonda is always working. Vivian pops a chocolate from its foil and savours the sweetness. She reaches for another.

"The nurse said you can't have too many of those."

Vivian slips the wrapper off and swallows it whole.

"I won't say anything if you don't," he says.

She grabs a third and the nurse reappears to remove the

chocolates, promising to return them later. Vivian glares at the retreating figure, then beckons him closer, whispering: "They won't give them back, you know. They'll eat them. It's terrible here. Can you get me out? I need to go home."

"I might be able to," he says, "if you can help me."

She's listening. The young man leans even closer. "Do you remember my dad, Frank?"

She nods.

The man continues. "I didn't know him very well. I was hoping you could tell me about him."

Vivian riffles through the chocolate wrappers just in case she missed one. Nothing. She stares back at him.

"What do you remember about Frank?" he asks.

"Troublemaker."

"Frank was?"

She nods.

"What about you? Did you get into trouble together?"

She nods again, a sly smile.

"What kind of trouble?"

"Frank helped me. I helped Frank."

He gives her an odd look. Then he points at her face. "You're bleeding," he says, "your nose."

She touches her nose and examines the red drops on her fingertips. He hands her a tissue. She doesn't speak to him after that. There is only redness in her mind. Nothing else. Nothing to talk about.

∼ Busy floral patterns on the carpet, tablecloth and curtains. The cold, white landscape has been locked out by the sealed windows; the inside air is hot and dry. Glazed eyes sit around little tables in a room directed by a woman in a white smock. This is a madhouse. They've locked her in a madhouse.

Vivian lurches to her feet. "Take me home!" she demands of the white smock. "I'm not supposed to be here!"

White Smock snaps right back at her. "Eat your dinner, Vivian."

Vivian stands defiantly but the white smock is distracted by four old ladies who never speak. One of them reaches for the teapot and pours the pale brown water all over her meat as though it were gravy.

White Smock spins around and seizes the teapot. "Mia, I told you not to give this table tea!"

Apologizing, a young girl rushes over and Vivian is forgotten in the fuss. That is what she will become if she stays here, barking mad and ignored. She needs to break free but she can't simply run off into the winter. There must be another way and she will find it, but she must sit down for a moment first. She's suddenly leaden with fatigue.

∽ "You're not Frank."

"No, I'm Frank's son, Dean."

Frank doesn't have a son. She would know if Frank had a son. Wouldn't she? She's well aware how Frank can slip into other skins, other stories. She's always been able to use that to her advantage. Frank fakes it so well it's as though he believes his own lies.

"I brought you some more chocolates," the young man says, passing her a box.

"When have you ever given me chocolates?"

"I brought you some last week."

"I don't even know you."

She clumsily unwraps the foil from one and crams it in her mouth.

"Was Curtis Reid guilty of anything?"

The chocolate sticks in her throat. "Why do you care about Curtis Reid?"

"It's been a challenge to get to the bottom of something that happened over 25 years ago. It would be a lot easier with your help."

She pushes the chocolates back in his direction. She doesn't like them anymore. They look the same as the ones she likes but taste different.

"This is what I've got so far. Feel free to let me know if I'm on the right track."

She stares at him incredulously. Idiot.

"Mary Jones spoke up against your proposed mill development in the '70s. She suspected the military had contaminated the land they occupied during the war but you managed to get your project pushed through anyway. Then, in the '90s, somebody blew the mill up. Now, assuming Mary was right, we have a motive. The contamination was starting to affect people's health and somebody noticed. What was it, Vivian? Skyrocketing cancer rates?"

The man who is not Frank snaps his fingers in front of her face. "Vivian? Are you listening?" She wants to break them almost as much as he wants to break her.

"I tried contacting the doctor who was working in Stapleton in the '90s, but he passed away a few years back. What's interesting, though, is that he left town just a couple of months before the explosion. Somehow landed himself a very cushy gig at a private clinic in Vancouver. Did you help him get that job?"

That isn't the point, Frank. Removing the doctor isn't enough. Others will begin to ask, and eventually they'll start

digging into all the irregularities around the mill development. Fingers pointing at her and the other councillors. They
can't have that. Something more permanent has to be done.

"Frank ..."

"I'm not Frank."

"Talk to Frank."

"Frank's dead."

Vivian shakes her head. She saw him yesterday, wearing
a pale green t-shirt with a hole in it just below his armpit. He
wants the council to buy a large slab of his jade. He's calling
himself an artist now. She grins. The sun feels so warm on
her cheeks, seeping into her wrinkles. She lets her eyes close.

"You can help me solve this puzzle. You can help all those
families get to the truth of what happened."

She glares at him. "I don't do puzzles."

"Do you remember what you did?"

Father likes puzzles. He likes games because he always
wins. Little black and white figures on little black and white
squares. Some are more important than others, aren't they?
Bishops are worth protecting, but not the peasants. They
aren't called peasants though, are they? The little ones with
cone-shaped bodies and perfectly round heads. What are they
called? They don't have any power. That's the point. They
can't do anything useful except stand in the line of fire.

Vivian waves her hands around a bit, speaking without
sound because she can't put the words together to ask Frank
what those pieces are called and she can't remember at this point
what they were discussing. Something to do with her father.

"Just answer me, Vivian. Yes or no. Was the mill deliberately destroyed to hide the fact that people were getting sick?"

She stares at him. She recognizes him. "You're Frank's son."

"Yes," he says, sighing.

"All this …"—she waves her hands again—"won't bring him back."

He is speechless. Good. He's exhausting. She wants him to go away. The room is occupied by nodding grey heads. There is no one here who can help her. It's time she went home. Todd will be wondering where she is. "Can you take me home?" she asks. He doesn't seem to hear her. Her words have become lodged in her head and they won't come out.

"Frank must have been involved in lining pockets or whatever you were doing back in the '70s to make the mill project happen. That's why he helped you destroy it. And there must have been others. Who else was in on it? Other councillors? Your husband?"

She is staring at the chess board and Father is waiting for her to make a move. Mother's suggestion during one of his visits. Father teaches her the rules but he won't let her win. If she doesn't make a move, she realizes, he can't win. She will take her turn, though. Losing is better than not being in the game. She eyes the smallest pieces with their perfectly round heads and squat bodies. Peasants lack ambition. They aren't the ones who make the world turn, who make decisions that change lives. But they're always willing to string up their leaders and watch them swing.

"Do you remember Audrey Reid?" he asks.

A peasant. Can be bought, but like others of her kind, her effectiveness is limited.

"Audrey Reid, Curtis's mother," he repeats. "Mary thought her perspective could be significant, so I tracked her down."

A greedy woman. She took the money but didn't honour their deal.

"She was involved in all this, wasn't she? Did she know what she was doing?"

"They always know," Vivian says, mumbling. Frank lets out a little smile.

"Audrey wouldn't talk to me, but I had a long chat with her ex-husband. Jim told me that after the explosion a man came to their farm and gave Audrey a pile of cash to go visit her grandkids. The man said the money was for some information. Audrey's job was to find out what Elena Reid knew about the mill explosion. He said it was for the family's own protection. Jim told her not to take the money, but she did. You wanted to know how much of a risk this kid really was and you thought she might confide in a family member."

Vivian closes her eyes and turns away, shaking her head. Audrey Reid. Useless woman. Vivian's concern wasn't merely about what Elena knew. She was a girl with a very active imagination and nobody paid much attention to her natural attempts to extricate her dad from blame. Vivian wanted to know exactly how she had gained insights that were, for the most part, very close to the truth, and how many more people might now be in possession of pertinent information, whether they realized it or not.

The young man's hand touches her face, gently turning her head towards his. She opens her eyes and looks at him.

"The more I learn about you, the more I think this is all an act. It's your way of avoiding responsibility for what you've done."

"Who are you?" she asks. "You're not Frank."

The young man sits up slightly and pulls his chair in even closer, as if he and Vivian are the best of friends. A nurse walks by and smiles at them. Vivian is too confused by it all to call out and demand to be rescued from this stranger.

"Jim said Audrey felt so bad about what she'd done that she went to the police maybe a dozen times with Elena's theories. But you're a smart woman. You probably realized Audrey would never be a real threat. The cops only saw a bag lady stinking of booze."

Bad apples. It was very convenient that Curtis came from a long line of them. He was the perfect scapegoat.

"Was it Frank, the man who bribed Audrey?"

She nods slightly at the man who she thinks is Frank but isn't but could be. He knows, anyway, he knows. He grins, a big fierce grin, and it makes her instantly furious.

"Leave me alone!" she screams. Two nurses come rushing over and escort her out of the common living area. She hears them apologize to him. They don't see him for what he is. No more visitors, she mutters. No more.

⌁ The sky is dark. Someone closes the curtains. Vivian touches the books lined neatly against one wall and then slowly settles into a chair. She lifts her knitting out of her bag and examines it under the orange lamplight.

Mary shuffles in, pushing her walker over the wood-like vinyl. She grabs Vivian's knitting. "How is this going to keep refugees warm?" she asks, peering through the holes.

Vivian shrugs. "I told Carol ..."

Mary tuts and lowers herself into the chair beside her. The stitches come apart easily as Mary unravels the rows. "What a mess," she mutters. "Most of this needs to be redone."

"I tried," Vivian says weakly.

"Quiet!" an old man grunts from across the table. "This is the reading room." Vivian looks around. Mary has gone.

CHAPTER 21

1 9 9 5

THE WINTER CAME and went, dumping more snow than usual. But apart from the constant pain of Dad's absence, things seemed to go back to normal. Then the rain came, Mr. Peterson died, and everything changed.

The rain pounded the ground, but the old man at the Inn said the snowmelt brought the water up. The door to the bar was open a crack, so Elena peeked inside. The old man was the only one there. Mamma must've been on a break. Elena decided he was the very oldest of Frank's regulars, ninety at least. His name was Vince. He was nice and he liked to talk. He passed her a half empty packet of dry roasted peanuts and he spoke so slowly that she had to weigh up her impatience against the chance he might eventually say something interesting.

"In the winter ... the snow builds up on the moun'ns, but if it gets too hot in the spring ... well it melts ... real quick ... and the rivers ... can't handle ... all that snowmelt comin' at 'em ... so ... they ... overflow."

"Will my house get flooded?"

"Could do," he said. "No way ... to know for sure ... what the river'll do."

Elena didn't want to leave Stapleton but the threat of being separated from her home seemed to be lurking just around the corner. The pressure was building like hot air before a summer storm and everybody felt it. If Kathryn's family couldn't survive here anymore, how would her own family ever find a way to stay, especially without Dad? He would be home soon though, she reminded herself. He would never leave them here. She would tell him proudly that she always knew he'd come back.

Vince's glass was empty, striped with lines of white foam. He loaded his pipe and gently tamped down the tobacco before adding more. He singed the tobacco at the top of the pipe with his lighter until it seeped smoke. He lit it again and cradled the bowl in his palm, sucking on the end of it. She liked the smell, sweeter than cigarettes. The air in the bar was mostly old smoke.

"My brother smokes."

The old man's lips pressed against the pipe a couple of times and little clouds escaped from his mouth. "He'd probably 'preciate it if ... you ... kept that to yourself."

Elena paused. "Can you blow smoke rings?"

He opened his jaw and moved his lips into a circle. He brought his lips closer together and apart and together again, until a few wavering smoke rings rose. He was one of the coal miners, she reckoned, who came here long ago. She could imagine him, a young man in those museum pictures, going deep underground in a rickety shaft with a headlamp and a pickaxe, coming back with his face covered in the stuff he was being paid to dig up. His rough cough was the coal dust trapped inside him, rattling around forever.

"Why do you come here all the time?"

"Got no one ... to talk to ... at home."

Elena shuffled halfway off her chair and craned her neck so she could see if anyone was coming down the hallway. "I'm not supposed to talk to you."

"Your mom's rules?"

She nodded, keeping an eye on the doorway. Vince grunted. Elena looked into his filmy eyes and wondered why he didn't have any friends.

∽ Dad always said Mamma didn't appreciate what they had. "Aren't you glad I bought this view, Elena?" he'd ask her when they were all outside on a hot day. "People pay millions for a view like this."

Elena would nod. "I love our house," she'd tell him, and she meant it. Mamma would roll her eyes.

If Dad was in a really good mood he'd say: "The only thing that could make this place better is a few flowers. Wouldn't hurt to plant a few flowers, would it, Giulia?" Mamma would tell him to plant his own damn flowers and he'd laugh loudly. Mamma couldn't help smiling.

Elena passed the gas station on her way home from the Inn. There were sandbags stacked up outside. She watched people pull in and load them into their trucks as she wheeled around the gas pumps on her bicycle. Dad said their house would never flood. The river never got that high, he said. She hoped he was right.

∽ Mamma was working all day Saturday, so she put Rob in charge. He told Elena they were going to the park. It was better than sitting at home. He abandoned her as soon as they got there, with strict instructions. She wasn't to leave the park or come and talk to him under any circumstances. Elena watched him from a distance. He was with a girl.

Red hair, freckles, bracelets and rings piercing her ears. She looked very different from Ashley, Rob's ex-girlfriend. Mamma didn't know about the new girl. She used to know everything about everything, even the things they tried to hide from her.

Elena didn't recognize this girl. She wasn't from Stapleton, unless she'd been living under a rock. She could've come from one of the neighbouring towns, but how would she have met Rob? He wasn't old enough to drive. Maybe she could, or maybe she was home-schooled and grew up on one of the ranches and lived in the semi-wild. Maybe she rode horses and knew how to shoot guns. Lots of people in Stapleton knew how to shoot guns. Dad tried to take Rob out hunting a few times, but he never showed much interest. Elena wasn't asked but she didn't mind. You had to be quiet if you went hunting. Elena didn't like being quiet.

She walked around the edge of the park while Rob and the mystery girl hung out.

"Hey. Elena."

The low, rumbling voice came from behind her. She spun around and stepped back in surprise. It was Audrey. She had come back.

"Did ya miss me?"

"Yeah."

"I've been lookin' all over for you. No one was at the house. I figured you might be here. How's your mom holdin' up?"

Elena looked down at her sandals. It was only barely warm enough to wear sandals, but all of her other shoes were too small. When Dad was still around, Mamma would've noticed by now.

"She's fine," Elena said.

Audrey didn't seem to hear. One hand was clutching her

handbag and the other was shaking. She spoke too quickly and she kept looking around like someone might be watching them.

"Listen, Elena, who'd ya tell your little theories to? About your Dad's disappearance and the cover-up?"

Elena didn't like Audrey's tone, or the word "little". She was definitely nervous about something and it was starting to make Elena nervous, too.

"You need proof before you start saying things to people or you get yourself in trouble."

Elena looked down at her sandals in response.

"Who'dya tell?" Audrey asked.

"I said a few things to Mary."

"Mary. Who's Mary?"

"She runs the museum."

Audrey considered it. "She doesn't seem like the talking type. Who else d'ya tell?"

"No one. Why?"

"Who else, dammit!"

Audrey was right. She had told someone else, but she didn't want to admit it now that Audrey was angry.

"The councillor. I talked to her ..."

"Vivian?"

Elena nodded. "She came up to me when I was leaving school."

Elena remembered the powerful smell of her perfume and the silk scarf wrapped around her shoulders. Elena didn't know her but knew she was an important person in Stapleton. It was strange that the councillor was waiting for her outside the school gates but she seemed nice enough. She just wanted to help. Not many people wanted to help.

"What did you tell her?" Audrey asked.

"She was worried about Dad and she wanted to know if I knew anything. So I told her what I thought happened."

"I should've told her something more believable," Audrey muttered. "I didn't think she'd do her own dirty work."

"What do you mean?" Elena asked, confused.

"It doesn't matter now."

"She said it was safe to talk to her," Elena said, "because it's her job to look after the whole community, including me and Dad. She just wants to make sure we find him."

Audrey scrunched her eyes as though she had a terrible headache but when she opened them again her whole face had changed. There was a brightness in her eyes and she put on the smile-scowl that had frightened Elena when they first met.

"We don't need to worry about her anymore. I got some amazing news." Audrey leaned in and whispered in her ear: "We found him. We found your dad."

Elena stepped back and looked at her. "Really?"

Audrey nodded. "He's in the forest ... laying low."

Elena couldn't quite let herself believe it. "So you actually saw him?"

"Jim did. Tracked him down. Made sure he was doing okay. But I can't tell you where he is, just that he loves you and misses you. He wants you to be strong for your mom and your brother."

Audrey's words and her fake kindness didn't feel right, but Elena had to believe that what she said was true. He was still alive and he was going to be fine. Everything was going to be fine. Tears welled up in her eyes.

"Have you already told them?" she asked.

"Who?"

"Mamma and Rob."

"No. They wouldn't believe me. It's our secret for now, okay?"

"Yeah." Elena's voice wavered. We found him. He's in the forest. He's still alive.

"Your dad can't go to prison. He's not the prison kind. He's better off living in the bush the rest of his days than being locked up. Now, me and Jim are gonna to do everything we can to clear his name and make sure he gets back to you, but that might not happen for a while ... maybe a long time. So you gotta be strong and keep goin' and keep this to yourself. And your dad said he doesn't want you getting involved anymore, alright? He was very clear about that. It's too dangerous."

"Okay," Elena said, nodding. She couldn't imagine not saying anything to anyone. This was the best news they'd had in a long time. At the very least, she had to tell Rob.

"Elena, I'm serious. You gotta promise me you'll leave this alone now. Don't say anything to anyone, don't follow anyone, don't accuse anyone. Keep your head down."

"I promise."

Audrey gave her a hard stare. "I gotta go."

Elena gave her a goodbye hug but Audrey stood stiffly. It was like she was trying to be happy and trying not to cry at the same time. Elena had never seen her like that before—in pieces.

As soon as Audrey left, Elena looked around for Rob and the girl. They'd gone off somewhere, which meant Rob probably hadn't even seen Audrey. Elena walked around the park a few times and allowed herself to imagine Dad in the forest, thinner than the last time she saw him, surviving on berries and leaves, rabbits, deer and grouse. He was thinking of them just like she was thinking of him, and he was safe. He was coming home, hopefully soon, but maybe not for a while.

She sat on a swing and rocked herself back and forth until Rob appeared. He smelled funny, a sour sweet smell, and his eyes looked tired. He talked slowly. She told him about Audrey, and about how Jim had found Dad, and he was doing fine. Rob just laughed and laughed and laughed.

~ It was late when Mamma came home. Elena didn't look at the time, but her eyelids were still heavy with sleep. She had been woken by the sound of Mamma in the kitchen, opening cupboards and scraping back a chair.

Elena pattered into the room in her nightie. Mamma was sitting at the table staring at the empty cupboard that used to be crammed with dried goods like pasta and rice. The makeup Mamma had put on before her shift was running down her cheeks in quivering black lines. Elena hugged Mamma, who pulled her in closer.

"What are we going to do?" Mamma whispered.

"About what?" Elena asked softly.

Mamma wouldn't say. She assumed Mamma was referring to Dad. His disappearance hit them at odd times. A deep sadness could surge up in Elena's chest out of nowhere. It would sit there inside her all day and there was nothing she could do to get rid of it. Sometimes she didn't want to get rid of it. Missing him had become part of her. If she let go of that, there'd be nothing of him left.

~ "I'm going out. I'll be a few hours."

Mamma peered into the kitchen as she slid earrings through her lobes. Rob glanced at her before picking up his cereal bowl and draining the last of the milk from it in one long slurp. He didn't seem to care about Mamma's plans.

Elena studied Mamma's face, perfectly made up, not like the night before. She was wearing a pant suit, the only one she owned, and she looked very professional.

"Where are you going?"

"I'm going to look for a new job."

Rob dropped his bowl onto the table. "What about the Inn?"

"Frank had to lay me off. Business is slow. There was nothing he could do. But don't worry. Someone will be hiring."

Mamma smiled as if this was good news and disappeared into the hallway. Elena and Rob looked at each other. Elena didn't want to be like Kathryn's family; she couldn't imagine her home boarded shut. They belonged in Stapleton.

Mamma hummed a little tune to herself as she checked her hair again in the hallway mirror. "Frank says we should leave town but I told him we'll stay until your dad gets home. I can find work here."

As soon as Mamma left, Rob said: "It doesn't matter where she looks. She won't find anything."

⌁ Mr. Peterson was seriously injured in the explosion. He had severe burns to most of his body. Elena didn't know him or his family. His boys were much older, almost adults, but he worked shifts with Dad, and she'd seen the two of them acknowledge each other in passing.

The Petersons were a rough family. Elena had never heard anything about a Mrs. Peterson, but Mr. Peterson and his sons came up sometimes in gossip at the café or in the playground. People said Mr. Peterson poisoned his neighbour's dog because it wouldn't stop barking, and his youngest son was arrested for breaking into a house on Spruce Drive and throwing a party there while the family was on vacation.

Elena heard Mr. Peterson wasn't doing so well. His was one of the names people brought up when they talked about the explosion, whispering about how unrecognizable he looked and how many surgeries he was having. People only spoke about him sympathetically now. They called him, "that poor man."

Mamma had been out of the house all afternoon. She was busy plastering the neighbourhood with flyers advertising her cleaning services and she came home with a stack of them still in her hands. She called Elena and Rob into the living room. Elena hoped she had something to say about Dad.

"Mr. Peterson passed away this morning," she said.

Mamma paused, and then she explained very gently that he had gone in for another surgery and this time he hadn't come out. Mamma was talking so delicately that Elena wondered if she should be feeling upset about Mr. Peterson. It was sad that he'd died but she didn't know him. It took Mamma a while to work up to what she really wanted to tell them.

"His family is obviously heartbroken, and they need time to grieve. If you see his sons around, just avoid them for now, okay?"

"I hardly ever see them," Elena said, still confused.

"Well that's good, but if you do see them, try to stay out of their way," Mamma said.

"But why ..."

Rob interrupted. He was good at getting to the point when Mamma wouldn't. "They think Dad killed him. They think it's Dad's fault Mr. Peterson died. Mom's worried about what they might do to us."

Elena looked over at Mamma wide-eyed.

"Rob!" Mamma said. "Don't scare your sister. I just don't want either of you getting into any confrontations with that family. The last thing we need is more trouble."

Elena wasn't actually scared. She didn't believe the Peterson boys would want to hurt her, even if they did think Dad was responsible for their dad's death. She and Rob were just kids and Mamma always overreacted.

Mr. Peterson's death was followed almost immediately by another big local story, one that did make Elena anxious. The news came from Ken again, but this time he didn't bother coming around to tell them in person. Mamma's frown deepened as she listened to him over the phone. She hung up and turned away from them for a moment.

"Ken says there's a rumour going around the café … that Dad has been seen in Stapleton."

Elena's eyes lit up but Mamma was quick to crush her hope.

"This isn't what it seems, Elena. If he was here, he would come home."

"Then why did someone say they saw him?"

"I don't know. Maybe they saw someone who looked like him, or maybe they just wanted to cause trouble."

She thought about telling Mamma what Audrey had said, that Dad was safe and hiding in the forest. She could have told Mamma about that earlier, but she always stopped herself. Mamma would tell her it wasn't true.

The cops came by the house again, two men this time, and they didn't pretend to be kind. Even their doorstep introductions sounded like threats. They took Mamma into the kitchen and closed the door. They didn't stay long, probably because Mamma didn't have anything to say, but Elena caught what the dark-haired one said as they left. "Be careful who you help, Mrs. Reid. If you lie to us, you won't see your kids again."

Mamma held Elena tightly as they stood by the living room window and watched the cop car pull away. Mamma said they could intimidate her all they wanted but all she could give them was the truth. They couldn't take her kids away for that.

COPS APPEAL FOR INFORMATION

~ It never took long for gossip about Dad to appear in print. The next morning, the local paper was encouraging people to contact the police with any information they might have about a possible sighting of Curtis Reid. He had been spotted near the secondary school when all the kids were in class. Elena was getting so used to seeing his name in print it almost didn't seem like him anymore. Curtis Reid wasn't Dad. Curtis Reid was some guy reporters liked to talk about.

What really upset Elena about the article was that it had little to do with Dad. The journalist quoted one person several times; Vivian Lennox, the councillor. She had seemed so concerned about Dad when she approached Elena outside school, but she was a different person in the paper.

"It's absurd that while the victims and their families are still grieving, the main suspect in this investigation appears to be free to come and go whenever he wants and has no trouble evading the police. The people of our community deserve answers. We've suffered enough."

She had trusted the councillor. Vivian said it was her job to look after them, Elena and Dad, because they were members of the community too. Elena actually thought there was one person, somebody important, who believed as she did, that there was something more to the mill explosion. Rob took one look at the article and said it was all bullshit, a word he chose because Mamma wasn't in the room. Either way, it was all coming back up again, rising quickly like the river water.

⮑ Mamma had left the house by the time Elena got up the next morning. She was giving an elderly neighbour a free trial of her cleaning services and she had told them she'd be gone for a few hours.

Elena rubbed her eyes as she studied the view beyond the kitchen window. The hills looked the same as they always did but the river had crept over its bank and was lapping the edge of their lawn. She called Rob over to take a look, and a few minutes later they were both dressed and heading across the yard. The river was higher than they'd ever seen it, pushing against the edge of the grass.

"Don't go too close," Rob said, pulling her back.

The far end of the yard was spongy and the muddy water squelched up around their shoes. It was coming.

⮑ Rob and Elena biked over to the gas station. Rob thought he could buy a few sandbags with his remaining paper route money and give someone a few extra bucks to drive them to the house.

The attendant appeared, a scrawny guy a couple of years older than Rob, and Rob swaggered up to him like he was the boss. "Where are the sandbags?"

"We're sold out. We're getting more in on Thursday."

Rob huffed. "What a joke."

By Thursday, Elena imagined, the river would've swallowed their house whole. It was only one storey high and not very wide.

"Frank might help us," Elena said. Rob huffed again. "No one's going to help us." He wheeled his bike off the gas station lot and headed home.

Elena went to the Inn. She still didn't know whose side Frank was on but that meant there was a chance he'd be willing to help, and he was the kind of guy who knew how to get hold of things.

Elena pushed through the side gate and balanced her bike against the fence. Frank's jade cutting device was in pieces in the far corner and the boulder was gone. Elena wondered if the blade had managed to cut through the rock or if the boulder had won and broken the blade, but then decided that she didn't care about Frank's projects anymore. The powder blue truck was parked in the same spot with its hood popped up, and Frank was standing behind it. There were a couple of other people back there with him, disguised by the curved truck body.

She crept through the long grass, carefully avoiding the half-hidden metal scraps as she approached the vehicle. The other two were young men; one wiry like Frank, with dull blonde hair that lay flat until it ended abruptly at his chin. He wore a blue plaid shirt over a t-shirt. He was speaking.

"... can't just get rid of 'em, Frank."

"I know that, but we need to do something."

The blonde guy replied but the wind blew his words away. Frank's voice again, more forceful than usual, but she couldn't make out his response.

Frank and the blonde guy could probably both fit in the third man's biker jacket, festooned with chains over ripped jeans. She pictured the two strangers standing outside the trapper's cabin, the skinny one stepping forward trying to detect Rob among the trees. They could have been the same men she'd seen in the forest but she wasn't certain.

Their low voices petered out and they were on the move, the two strangers heading towards the gate. She tried her best to backtrack through the junkyard but she wasn't quick enough.

The big one stomped toward her, crushing everything in his path. "Whatcha playin at? You spyin' on me?"

His words weren't lazy like Frank's. He wasn't joking around. Elena locked her eyes onto his and tried to look defiant. That's what Dad told her to do if she ever came across a growling dog. "Make yourself big. Don't run."

Frank was coming around the truck, wiping his hands on a rag as if he'd actually been doing some work back there. The big man spoke under his breath.

"Go play with your fuckin' dolls before you get yourself into trouble."

He glared at her again but she couldn't run. She was stuck.

"Elena! Get over here!"

Rooted to the spot, she blinked twice and then raced toward Frank without looking back as the other two left the yard.

"Were you eavesdropping?"

She didn't answer.

"Some of my business is my business."

Anger and disappointment in his voice. Elena didn't know what to say. It didn't seem fair that he could keep all his secrets and also be annoyed with her.

"Who were those men?"

"Old friends."

Those boys were too young to be Frank's "old friends." Maybe what Frank meant was, they'd worked together before, around the time of the mill explosion, for instance.

"What happened to my dad?"

"I don't know Elena. Why are you asking me?"

"I heard one of your friends talking about getting rid of people."

"When?"

"Just now."

"Nobody said that. You shouldn't have been listening in the first place. Your mom raised you better than that, didn't she?"

Elena didn't like being scolded by Frank. She wanted it to go back to how it used to be, when he cracked jokes and told stories. But they could never go back because she knew he was hiding something.

"We weren't talking about your dad. I told you before. I had nothing to do with that."

Frank took a five-dollar bill from his pocket and pulled it taught to straighten out the creases. "Go buy yourself something and stay out of my yard." She took the note but not because she believed him. Frank stared at her as she tucked it into her jacket pocket.

"A few of my albums have gone missing. I'm not accusing anyone, I just wondered if you might know anything about it."

"No."

Frank waited for a moment, but Elena didn't offer him anything else.

"Ah well. They'll turn up."

Frank stumbled back toward the powder blue truck and lifted things from his toolbox. Elena wandered halfway back to her bike before remembering the sandbags. She called over to him.

"Can you help us find some sandbags to stop our house getting flooded?"

Frank didn't even look at her. "Not right now ... got business to deal with. Your house won't flood if it hasn't already."

The way he spoke it was almost like he controlled it, when the river rose and fell. The Stapleton Inn loomed behind him; his family's legacy, the town's heritage. Mamma never trusted Frank and his ways, but even she had been sucked in for a while.

"How do you know?"

"I listen to the news. The water levels have peaked. The river isn't gonna get any higher without some serious rainfall. At most, we might get a few light showers."

Elena wasn't going to take his word for it. She couldn't trust his opinion on something as important as their home.

~ By the time Elena got home, Rob was pulling furniture out of the kitchen door. She dashed into the middle of the yard and jumped up as high as she could. The ground spewed water when she landed. Bits of mud clung to the edges of her jeans.

The powerful river awed her. The neighbours who hadn't lost their homes to the bank already had sandbags neatly piled against their fences.

Elena and Rob pulled out the kitchen table and tipped it on its side. Mamma never liked it that much anyway. They dragged it onto the grass, positioned it so it faced the river, then secured it with big rocks. Beside it they stacked the garden chairs, also pinned down with stones. There was a pile of leftover firewood. Rob could carry more pieces, faster, so that soon became his job. Elena did her best to line up the wood so the water wouldn't seep through the cracks. She stuffed the holes with fistfuls of grass or the crushed beer cans she'd found within throwing distance of Dad's garden chair.

The yard got mushier and it started to rain; little drips that soon became big ones. Yet it was hardly a downpour, as Frank predicted. Rob trotted in and out of the house, alternating between passing her more logs and moving valuable items to safe places. Rob hadn't said anything, but Elena knew as soon as he started working indoors that he thought their barricade would fail, and the river would come into the house. "Finish the wall and don't go any closer to the river," he said. "It's deep at the end of the yard."

Rob brought over the last of the logs and Elena examined the remaining gap between their makeshift wall and the fence. There weren't enough logs, even if she only made one tier out of them. She'd have to space them out and then find other things to cram between them. There were some stones Dad had used to build a fire pit at the bottom of the garden. She could see a couple of them sticking out of the water close to the willow tree.

Rob went back inside and thumped around, stacking pieces of furniture atop each other. Unplugging all the electronics. Putting the things that would suffer the most damage on top of things that didn't really matter.

The wind had started to whip the old willow tree, water sloshing its trunk. She stepped over their makeshift barricade and moved toward the fire pit stones, icy water slopping around her ankles. She leaned down and pulled at a stone, but it didn't budge. It was too heavy. Rob could probably manage that one. There were a couple of smaller ones that she could lift but they were submerged.

She looked back. Everything was there, in that house. All her memories, her things, the secret spaces that hid her diary, her desk with the stationery that made her feel grown up, Mamma's old photos of Italy, photos of her and Rob since they were babies. That house was their home.

Rob burst out of the back door. "Elena! Get away from there!"

⁓ Reluctantly, she headed back. The rain stopped but they'd run out of items to reinforce their wall. Rob said they might as well take a break, at least until they came up with another idea. Elena went through to the living room only to find that Rob had unplugged the old TV and dumped it on top of the sofa.

Through the living room window, she spotted Mamma coming down the road dragging a blue tartan bag on wheels. It would do for her cleaning equipment until they got the truck back.

The bag clunked along their gravel driveway, Mamma steadying it as tipped from side to side. She was almost at the front door when the patrol car drove up and stopped. Mamma turned around and one of her cop dramas unfolded right there on the gravel.

Two male officers got out of the vehicle and quickly accosted Mamma. Elena knew this time they hadn't come for a chat. Mamma stretched her arms out in front of her while a young, blue-eyed officer cuffed her wrists. Elena pushed her fingers flat against the glass, willing them through it and onto Mamma's, pulling her into the house. The older cop spotted Elena watching from the living room window. Mamma noticed her then and took an instinctive step towards the house but the older cop held her back. She wore her despair like a trapped animal. Mamma mouthed something at her but Elena couldn't catch it before the officers tore her away from their home. Mamma was disappearing, just like Dad. All Elena could do was watch, tears slipping down her cheeks. Mamma made Dad's absence bearable, but only just, only because Elena knew he was going to come back. They couldn't take Mamma away, too.

"Rob!" she shouted, voice trembling. She banged on the

living room window hopelessly. He rushed in, jaw dropped, and looked.

"What ...?"

He started toward the front door but a second car pulled into the drive. This one had no lights on top. A middle-aged couple, in suits, marched up to the front door and knocked loudly. Elena looked at Rob.

"We have to let them in," he said, "but do exactly what I say, okay?"

Grey suit and grey skirt and hair specked with grey. Rob opened the door and Elena hovered behind him and the grey couple smiled and showed them name badges and the woman said they were going to help them while Mamma was away, but Elena didn't understand.

"Are you here to help us with the flood?" she asked.

"No. They're going to take us away," Rob said abruptly.

She might have attempted to run then but Rob seemed to sense her panic and latched a hand onto her arm. Hard.

"There's absolutely nothing to worry about," the woman said softly. "We've got a couple of really nice families in Stony Creek who are going to take care of you until this is all sorted out."

She said families. Plural. They were going to be split up. She couldn't be on her own. It was bad enough without Dad. They couldn't do this to them. When she looked up at Rob, she could see something in his eyes the grey people couldn't. Defiance. He wasn't going to let this happen.

"Me and Elena have some things we want to take. Can we get them quickly?"

The grey couple exchanged looks.

Rob pleaded with them. "The river's flooding. If we don't get our things now, we won't be able to."

The woman loosened. "Quickly then," she said and she nodded to her companion.

The man followed them into the home while the woman waited by the doorstep. As soon as there was enough distance between them and the stranger, Rob whispered one word in Elena's ear.

"Dubov's."

⮑ They filled their backpacks while the male social worker hovered in the hallway outside their bedrooms, doors open so he could see what they were doing. There was no way for them to escape as long as he was standing there. Elena shoved in some clothes and her nail polish and her diary and heard Rob start up a conversation with the grey man about sports. The man said he was a Canucks fan, so Rob showed him into the living room and pulled out a radio from the bookshelf and put the game on with the volume up.

Elena sneaked out of her bedroom and into the kitchen. She slipped across the vinyl in her socks, grabbed the too-tight sneakers that were sitting by the back door and turned the handle as delicately as she could. She darted across the damp grass in her socks, not wanting to slow down long enough to put her shoes on. She climbed over the low fence, squelched her wet feet into her runners and waited for Rob in Mrs. Dubov's yard.

Rob scrambled over the fence a minute later and they ran through the yards and down a back alley until their chests burned with the cold air.

"Don't look back," Rob said. "It'll slow you down."

A treed area broke up the homes and popped them out into another quiet residential street. Elena almost sprang into a hedge when a vehicle approached. It was white and much larger than the grey couple's car. Rob led them into another alleyway. Dogs barked and a woman yelled at her pets from behind a tall fence.

"Come on, Elena. We're almost there."

Almost where? she would've asked him, if she'd had any breath to spare. He led her through a small neighbourhood park that connected another set of houses. Finally, the back-yards opened into a large ranch that wound around the base of one of the surrounding hills.

This is it, she thought, their big escape. When Rob hit his teens, he had become obsessed with the idea of leaving. He wanted to get a job in Stony Creek, a place of his own and a car. Mamma said it was part of him becoming an adult, needing to be independent. Elena had never wanted to leave, and now that they had to, her heart lurched with every step. She wished she had a deep root like the sagebrush, anchoring her deeply in the ground, but she remembered they only had shallow roots so it was easy to be swept away.

"Just a little further," Rob said.

The fields nearest the road had been tilled and green shoots broke out of the soil. There were large greenhouses further down the road, but the pair ran in the opposite direction, where they were less likely to encounter other people. They scrambled up the hill in tracks carved out by dirt bikes and ATVs. Beyond them was uneven scrubland that took a gradual incline toward the forest.

"I need to stop." Elena's chest was burning so much her stomach churned. Her legs shook. Rob was on full alert. He permitted a break but insisted they crouch down. His head swivelled like an owl's.

"Where are we going?" she asked as her body began to recover.

"Stony Creek. But we can't go yet. It's too risky trying to hitch a ride when everyone's looking for us. We'll have to stay in the forest for a few days until the social workers leave. Then we'll go to Stony Creek."

"What about the bears?"

"Don't worry. They aren't interested in you."

He sounded just like Dad, except Dad would say it with a goofy grin. Now that Rob was getting bigger, he looked a lot more like Dad.

~ The problem was, the real reason things fell apart was, Rob wasn't a man yet. He was going to be, but he wasn't yet. He didn't think of all the things Dad would've thought of when they escaped the social workers at the house. It was dusk when they crept into the forest without food, water, matches or enough warm clothing. It was early spring and the nights still got cold. Luckily, they'd both packed sweatshirts but those didn't keep the chill off their bones once the sun had left the sky. They huddled together into the shoulder of a large rock. Elena's feet were wet, toes crushed inside the shoes she'd outgrown. She pulled off her sneakers and thought her toes might freeze off as the wind circled them. Her back hurt after a while so she lay down on the pine needles while Rob kept watch.

Neither of them could sleep. Elena rolled around and complained of being hungry, then thirsty and then both. Rob told her to stop being a baby but he wasn't doing much better. He twitched every time a branch creaked.

"We should go back home." Elena whispered, as if the conifers that surrounded them might be listening.

"We can't. They'll find us."

"No, they won't. They'll be at home in bed by now. We

can sneak in and get what we need for a few days in the forest and leave before they come looking for us in the morning."

"What if they're watching the house?"

"We can go in through the yards again. If we're quiet, they won't even know we're inside."

Rob's stomach growled.

"There's food in the house," she said. "We should pack as much as we can if we're going to be out here for a while."

Elena couldn't see his expression in the dark but she could tell he was thinking about it. He got his flashlight out and scanned the trees and then he stood up. It was decided. Elena squeezed her sneakers back on her aching feet and he led the way back to town, downhill this time and at a slower pace. It was comforting, seeing all the familiar houses between the streetlights.

Her legs felt so tired by the time they reached their lane that she just wanted to run inside and crawl into bed but Rob stopped her. They scooted into a neighbour's yard, one of the boarded-up houses, and made their way carefully back toward Mrs. Dubov's house. Water seeped into Elena's shoes again, but the river didn't seem any higher since they'd left.

When they reached their own yard, Rob was especially cautious. They had to make sure there weren't any cops or grey people hiding in the bushes. When Rob was finally satisfied the house was empty, they ran through the yard and unlocked the back door. Rob was still paranoid about attracting attention so they left the lights off. Even a nosy neighbour could give them away. The floor was dry; the river hadn't oozed into the house, at least not yet.

They found bread and honey in the cupboards and ate in silence on the living room floor. Rob said he was going to set his alarm for 4 am. That would give them enough time to sneak back to the forest before the sun came up. It was midnight already. She heard him go into his room and close the door, and she dragged her own tired legs slowly to bed.

∼ She smelled it in her dream, the fire. The mill burst into flames and bits of it landed in her house. Red hot limbs of broken machinery, blackened lumber and falling ash. Tiny pieces fell into her mouth, sticking inside her throat, choking her. She heard shouting; her name, Rob's voice, but it wasn't terrifying until she woke up and discovered the smells and sounds were not dreams.

A loud crack had woken her but she couldn't see where it came from. She shot upright, inhaled a lungful of smoke and tried to cough it out. But it became a thousand tiny razors in her throat, scraping and scratching and making her cough harder.

Covering her mouth with her pyjama sleeve, Elena crouched and crab-walked to the door. The handle was hot and scalded her palm. She leapt back, cradling her hand. Rob's shouts sounded distant through the fire's noise.

Pushing and pushing against the stiff window lock with her burned hand, she screamed hoarsely in relief when it flew open, admitting a rush of cool air. She heaved herself through the frame and hit the ground, hard. It knocked the wind out of her and she lay gasping, throat on fire. It passed. She had to find Rob.

She stumbled toward the river, toward their makeshift barricade, desperate to spot him among the dismantled pieces of their home. Clouds had rolled in; she couldn't see him.

Heat and smoke at her back. She turned around and watched their home crumple like the paper house Mamma always said it was. The curse had finally found them. Rob couldn't be in there; he must have escaped to the road. She had to get back to the road.

The yelling man came out of the blackness, charging toward her, his face hidden under his big jacket and hat. He was screaming like a maniac, coming to get her. She clambered over the firewood section of their barricade to get away from him and the grass squished beneath her feet and the shouting got louder and their lawn became the river. She tripped over the fire pit stones by the willow tree and fell. The water pulled her in.

She moved with the muddy river and it dragged her back. Weeds loomed from its rocky belly. She merged with them like a fish. It took Elena no strength at all to move downstream. The powerful river carried her where it wanted her to go.

Someone else splashed into the water behind her and she thought it might be the yelling man, but the water made his shape black and blurry. His movements were heavy, arms and legs attacking the river, and she realized he was trying to reach her.

Everything was dense underneath. That person grasped at her body, but the river separated them. It propelled her onward, faster and faster until the other person's flailing shape became distant and she knew she wouldn't see anyone if she could look back. They were both part of the river now.

CHAPTER 22

"**V**IVIAN, YOUR SON'S here to pick you up!"

His voice is too soft. Vivian distrusts men with soft voices.

"He's going to take you for a nice afternoon drive. Would you like that?"

The attendant hauls her upright out of her armchair, holding her until she's steady on her cane.

The figure standing at the front entrance is not her son. This man is tall and dark-haired and the look in his eyes frightens her. She opens her mouth to object, but there is never enough time to get the words out. The attendant lowers her into the stranger's car and she grips his bare arm with all her might. Seatbelts click. The stranger is sitting beside her. The attendant brushes her hand off his arm like a fly.

"Have a lovely time! It's gorgeous out."

The car door closes. The attendant waves. Vivian stares helplessly through the window like a trapped insect.

A city surrounds them. They weave through trucks and cars and noise, slowing down beside a hotel and an Indian restaurant. The lights change and the world whizzes by too fast for her to identify anything.

"I'm taking you home, Vivian."

He reminds her so much of an old friend, except she knows, somehow, this man is not a friend. This man is dangerous. She steals a sideways glance. He's facing forward watching the traffic, both hands on the wheel.

"How exactly did you get a sawmill built on contaminated land?"

"No," she shakes her head firmly. She pulls on the door handle, but it won't budge. She yanks it again.

"Stop, we're moving. You don't want to get away from me that badly, do you?"

He grins. She resolves not to look at him. Suburban homes meet the road. A pregnant woman manhandles two small children into an SUV. Vivian doesn't shout. No one can hear her. Where's Tim? No, Todd. Why isn't he protecting her?

"I don't have any illusions about who my dad was," the man says calmly. "He was a criminal, a liar and a coward. But I believe he died with regrets. Do you have any regrets?"

He's driving far too fast, making her sick. The houses are further apart now, set back from the road.

The sky becomes large and blue and the land is hilly and empty. Some time later they turn onto a smaller road. They enter a desperate place with older homes and more boarded-up businesses than functioning ones. It upsets her, the broken glass and graffiti, weeds where the lawns should be.

"Do you know where we are?"

She doesn't answer him. She doesn't like these games. They're always out to trick her, all of them. They are making her crazy.

"We're back in Stapleton. The town you ruined."

∽ Now they are close to the river. There's a little row of mobile homes with an overgrown gap in between them. The vehicle stops in front of the gap. He lifts her out and takes her by the arm, a thin folder in his other hand. She couldn't manage the uneven ground without him but she doesn't like being so close.

The gravel of an old driveway crunches under her feet, grass sparse between the rocks. He points out a concrete slab in the middle of the derelict lot. "The house used to be over there."

Hundreds of tulips are flowering along the riverbank. Bright reds, yellows and oranges bursting out of the sandy soil. She refuses to take the one he picks for her.

"When Giulia Reid lost her house …"—he looks back at the empty lot behind them—"… Frank took her and Rob in. Rob moved to Stony Creek as soon as he finished high school but Giulia stayed, as you know.

"Giulia started planting flowers here during the trial of the two Peterson boys, the kids responsible for burning down her house. A few locals noticed she would take regular walks to the riverbank to care for her flowers. They began adding to her collection and over the years it's become quite the spot to visit in the springtime. People come here to reflect and enjoy the flowers and watch the river. Someone even put a bench just over there. The locals call it Elena's Place."

The river is wide and full. Vivian wishes she could rush quickly by like the water. Instead she lets him lead her to the bench. She doesn't want to sit here. This is the very last place she wants to be. There is no beauty in these flowers or this river, not today. She wants to get away from him but knows she can't. So she sits quietly and frowns.

~ It shocks her, to see Mary of all people, standing on her doorstep with tear tracks on her cheeks. Hair dishevelled, a complete mess.

"How much did you pay those boys to do it?" Mary's voice wobbles, wavering between anger and grief.

Vivian retreats into her house and tries to close the door, but Mary jams it with her foot.

"You're upset," Vivian says calmly, "but why you would think I had anything to do with it ..."

"Because you always do. It always comes back to you."

"Surely even you must realize I am not responsible for everything that goes wrong in this community."

Vivian waits for a vicious comeback. Instead, Mary looks at her with utter disgust. She can't forget those eyes.

"You cared about that girl," Vivian says, "but her family had issues. If the mother hadn't got herself arrested, that terrible accident never would have happened."

"Accident?" Mary spat. "Two kids burned their house down."

"I believe that's speculation at the moment."

Mary lunges towards her. Todd breaches the gap and takes the impact, pushing the woman back. He slams the door shut.

"Was she really such a threat to you?" Mary shouts from the step. "She was just a child!" Vivian tries to stop the quivering in her hands.

Quiet outside and Vivian takes a heavy breath. "You're a monster!" Mary shouts as she retreats down the road. Todd grips Vivian's shoulder as she hovers by the door. He looks into her eyes and asks in a whisper so quiet she pretends she hasn't heard: "What have you done?"

She slips down to the hard ground. I didn't mean to; a weak sentiment in a weak moment. The tangled threads unravelled too quickly. She thought that as the creator of the piece she was in control of it, but she wasn't.

Is it minutes or hours later, when Todd finds her again? In bed, fully clothed, blanket over her head, pillow wet with tears.

"The Mayor's on the phone. He's been asked to make a statement."

Vivian collects herself, finds her politician's words. Dries her face, straightens her blouse, checks her pearls, strides defiantly past the portrait of Father on the mantelpiece and picks up the receiver in the living room.

"Do you have a pen? Our community is in shock today ..."

~➤ Dean opens up the folder, pulls out a couple of old newspapers and places them on her lap. He traces the headlines of the first paper with his finger. Familiar words, painful ones, but the context escapes her.

"This is the story that fell out of your pocket that time I saw you at the gas station. Do you remember?"

STAPLETON STRUCK BY TRAGEDY AGAIN.

She throws it on the ground. He doesn't retrieve it. He picks up the other clipping and starts reading to her.

"This is the follow-up article. These are the names of the dead, just here," he shows her. She reads the black print. Elena Reid. Ken Melnyk. "Their bodies were washed up where the river broke its banks a short distance downstream from here."

Vivian wraps her long cardigan around herself as though defending herself from a chilly breeze.

"There was one survivor: Roberto Reid. Both kids escaped the burning house but in the confusion Elena fell into the flooding river. Ken Melnyk appears to have run after her, presumably to try and save her."

He pauses and looks at Vivian.

"Do you understand anything I'm saying?"

She did know them, once. They bring up that dreadful feeling that she has spent years pushing down. It wasn't supposed to be. None of it was.

"Mike Peterson's sons confessed to setting the house on fire as revenge for their dad's death, but they also kept insisting they were told the house would be empty that night. I read the court transcripts. They said Ken Melnyk encouraged them to do it, but you can't cross-examine a dead man. The jury was convinced by the prosecution's argument that the boys hadn't given a second thought as to who might be inside, and Ken was a hero who happened to be passing by when these two delinquents decided to burn down a family home."

"Who is Ken?" she mumbles. The young man whips a rock into the river, grabs her arm and leads her back to his car.

⌁ They are standing outside the Main St. Café. The young man has a key. Brown paper covers the large front windows. Peeling white paint.

Inside has been hollowed out. Gone are the tables and chairs, the counter holding baked goods and the other one stocked with ice cream. The stranger flicks a switch by the door but nothing happens. All that remains are the items that could not be picked up and taken away; linoleum peppered with black scuff marks and scraped walls with cobwebs clinging to the corners. As Vivian looks closer, she spots a couple of tiny nails where picture frames used to hang. She remembers the photographs. One featured a fly fisherman casting a line into a river, and there was another of a majestic bull elk.

"Wild and free," Vivian says casually as Ken draws the blinds, preparing to close shop. "Couldn't be more different than life at a correctional facility."

Ken won't look at her. He pulls down the other blind. "They'll leave town eventually. We don't need to push them out."

He keeps on fighting her. It's as if the explosion has left a terrible ringing in his ears and he can't hear her well-reasoned explanations. The whole affair has sucked the life out of him. The café is dead and it's not just because people are short on cash. Ken spends all day looming over the counter looking about as welcoming as a snarling grizzly bear.

"Ken. That girl keeps asking questions and sooner or later, someone will actually listen to her."

"Why can't you ask someone else? I've done enough."

He hadn't complained in the seventies. Ken was in his 20s then, thicker hair and thinner around his torso. He took pride in his new business, but those first years were tough for him, the town having shrunk so much since the closure of the coalmine. There was also a restlessness about him that Vivian knew would be useful. Some men like to keep a few secrets while remaining, for all intents and purposes, "decent guys."

"Good money for good work," Vivian called it, and Ken happily accepted the bribe to help push Vivian's mill proposal through council. Soon enough he was offering to "do whatever is needed to help the town." He pitched in several times over the years, no complaints, and he was always well remunerated.

"You and I are in this together, Ken." Vivian stands in front of the fly fisherman photograph. "Involving more people increases our risk. And you know the Peterson family. The boys will listen to you."

"They've been through enough."

"Oh, come on. If they're smart, they'll get away with it. If not, those two are heading to prison sooner or later anyway. The older one has spent more time in juvenile detention than he has in school."

"That doesn't make this right. And what about Giulia? Curtis was my best friend. I can't do that to her and the kids."

"This is what's best for them. There's nothing left for them here. Curtis isn't coming back. Giulia won't get another job in Stapleton. This way, they can start fresh with the insurance money, which is more than everyone else is getting."

Ken grumbles and Vivian leaves him to consider his options. In the end, Frank talks him into it somehow. Frank can be very persuasive.

"Melnyk was one of your guys, wasn't he, Vivian?" The young man is watching her as she stares at the tiny nail protruding from the empty wall.

"When things started to go wrong, he was in over his head. It didn't matter that he was Curtis's friend. You found a way to implicate Ken and Frank and whoever else was involved in the scam you pulled to get the mill built. They had to help you cover up its destruction if they wanted to avoid prison."

Vivian raises her eyebrows as if to say: "That's quite a story you've dreamed up." A small action, but effective. He reaches over and rips the nail out of the wall. Vivian stares at the scar.

Ping; he flicks it to the ground. He clutches her shoulders. There's so much anger in his eyes but he holds his voice steady.

"One of the nurses at your home told me that familiar places and objects from the past can trigger memories in dementia sufferers. I know you remember something, even in this empty room. I can see it in your face."

His expression is desperate. But she can't give him what he wants. Some secrets are supposed to be buried.

"A man named Vince Thomas left a statement with the police. He said Ken was at the Inn that night. When someone mentioned the Reid kids had gone missing, Ken left his pint at the bar and ran out of there. The prosecution argued he wanted to help find them and he thought they might have returned to the house. But Ken knew what the Peterson boys were about to do, didn't he? Giulia was in police custody, the kids were taken away, supposedly. The house should have been empty, but it wasn't."

Vivian closes her eyes. She's old now. When she closes her eyes, people get blocked out, people go away. There is quiet, when her eyes are closed. But he just won't be quiet.

"My father controls everything," she mumbles, eyes still closed. "Talk to him."

She can see Father now, in front of the wide fireplace at their grand Stapleton home. Whiskey in one hand and a watchful eye on her. Not loving. Controlling. Mother tiptoes around him, so weak she doesn't even catch his attention anymore. She offers him another glass or something else to eat. He won't dignify her with a response. It's all part of his game. He wants them to believe they are less than him, but Vivian knows she is not. She will succeed. After all, she is his daughter.

She opens her eyes. A man is dragging her into his car. She tries to resist, but she isn't strong enough. She tries to call out, but Main Street is dead.

"Maybe you'll talk to her," he mutters.

⁓ They pull up outside the Inn. The long veranda shadows the entrance and the ground level windows. They should bulldoze the whole thing. Why keep such an ugly piece of the past? She shakes her head as he unbuckles her seatbelt.

"I don't want to go in there, Frank. We can talk somewhere else."

"Why don't you want to go in there, Vivian?"

He's taunting her. He knows exactly why.

"Are you afraid of Giulia Reid?"

She doesn't like that name. Giulia. Even the sound of it. Joooo-lee-ah. Like a sneer. She scrunches her eyes closed and turns her head away from the man who won't be quiet.

She won't let him pull her out of the car. She won't. She goes limp. He pulls her out effortlessly. He practically carries her into the building.

It's dark inside. It takes her eyes a moment to adjust. The bar is empty. He sits her down at one of the tables and Vivian glances around helplessly. There she is, that woman, looking back at her, like a ghost.

"Do you remember Giulia?" he says.

She does. She does remember. But before she was beautiful. Now she is skeletal with hard edges.

"She needs to leave," Vivian says.

"Why don't you want to talk to her?" Frank says. He gestures to Giulia and she drifts slowly towards them. She doesn't speak. Her feet don't make a sound on the old boards. She isn't quite alive.

"She needs to leave."

"Why?"

"You know why, Frank."

"Tell me again."

Vivian glances at Giulia. "I can't tell you in front of her."

The man leans forward. "Is she dangerous?" he whispers to her.

She refuses to acknowledge him. She's looking at Giulia, watching her, remembering. The little girl. The little girl who was paying too much attention. Elena. The family had to leave town. "A clean break," she mutters. Frank doesn't want to hear it. "She doesn't love you, Frank. Stop being so damn sentimental. Fire her and she'll leave. They have to go." Giulia wants to leave, she just needs a push. She'll go when she has nothing left to stay for. The kids will go with her, and the little girl will stop asking questions. That's all Vivian wants.

She leans towards Giulia who is now sitting across the table. "You'll find somewhere in Stony Creek," Vivian tells her.

Frank speaks. "Giulia's daughter is dead."

Vivian's hands tremble. She fumbles for her pearls. They aren't there. Where is Todd? She grips the edge of the table and pulls herself up to her feet. Where is her cane? He legs feel weak.

"Who caused the explosion at the mill?" he asks.

Giulia rests a hand on the table and her wedding ring looks heavy against her thinness. Frank speaks for her. "It wasn't Curtis, was it?"

Curtis. Vivian doesn't remember his face, but she knows the name. She knows exactly.

"Did you frame Curtis Reid?"

"You framed Curtis Reid," Vivian says, staring at him, "because you're in love with his wife."

Giulia looks at him, with what—guilt? Shock? She doesn't speak.

He starts again. "Are you saying ... Frank framed Curtis?"

Vivian doesn't answer him.

"How did the explosion start?"

Vivian slams her fist on the table, surprised that it hurts. She leans away from him. He's too close.

"Pete Bernier died in the explosion. He was Frank's former brother-in-law, wasn't he? Was he involved?"

Frank suggested Pete. He would get it done. He would wait until the shift change and start a fire far away from the main exits. The employees would be evacuated. No one would get hurt. Frank said that, she remembers him saying that.

"No one gets hurt!" she shouts. Frank shrinks back in surprise, but Giulia doesn't flinch. Vivian isn't thinking about them. She's thinking about what Frank said. Pete knew exactly how to make it look like an accident. A mechanical malfunction combined with excess dust. If anyone were to shoulder any blame, it would be the mill company. Vivian was satisfied. She had to be; there was no one else she could trust to be discreet with a situation as delicate as this.

Frank tries again. "Did Pete cause the explosion?"

Vivian refuses to look at him but it's rushing around in her mind as though it happened yesterday. She looks at the veins running through her wrinkled hands. Half the time, she doesn't recognize the world she inhabits now in this old skin. But there are pieces of the past lodged in her brain that she cannot shake out. Pete started the fire too early and it caught too quickly and the fool blew himself up. Frank didn't admit to Vivian until afterwards that his dependable friend had been a nervous wreck the whole time.

They are waiting for an answer, but she doesn't give them one. When Giulia finally speaks, her voice sounds as weak as her body looks.

"Is Curtis dead?"

Vivian looks directly into her eyes. "I don't remember."

Giulia curls her head towards her knees, hugging her

body tightly. It is a necessary lie. Vivian will not let them beat her. She will not be dragged down by them, not now. Anyway, she wasn't there. Frank was there. She only has his word to go on as far as the truth is concerned, and if anyone can stretch the truth, it's Frank.

"In a letter my dad left me ..." The young man pulls out a piece of paper. "He says: 'Giulia needs to know Curtis is gone. He's not coming back. I'm sorry. There was nothing I could do.'"

The young man puts the paper down and waits for Vivian to explain. They don't seem to understand, either of them, that she will not give them what they want. She will not willingly give them, or anyone, power over her.

And Frank wasn't so helpless, after all. He knew that the mess at the mill needed to be cleaned up. He did that all on his own. Pete was Frank's guy. If the cops suspected Pete was involved in the explosion, they would find their way back to Frank sooner or later.

Curtis Reid was Frank's solution. She wasn't there, was she? But she remembers the smell, the burning, the chaos as if she had been there. It is very clear now; Frank waiting in the parking lot, listening to Bob Dylan's caterwauling in his truck, expecting an evacuation and then the flames. But it didn't happen that way. The blast came first. It shook Frank out of his seat, shook him too his core. Something had gone badly wrong and someone other than Pete Bernier would have to take the fall for it.

Frank found Curtis Reid's burned body in the parking lot. Frank said he couldn't find a pulse. That's what Frank said. Vivian chose to believe him.

Other men were running out of the building but in all the mayhem, no one saw Frank hoist up Curtis and half drag, half carry him to his truck. Vivian never asked how he got rid of the body. She didn't want to know. Frank moved Curtis's truck to make it look as though he'd made an escape. He sent his guys back a couple of days later when the military activity had died down to plant more evidence. If the cops were looking for a suspect, they had one.

Vivian glances over at the widow. So much hate, she sees it now, in those eyes. She will never understand; neither of them will. They've never had to make such difficult decisions.

The bar door opens and daylight streams in. She squints and when her vision comes back, she sees a frail old man who has been by her side for most of her life, his face contorted with rage.

"I called the nursing home, and they told me my wife was out with my son. But I knew it was you. You kidnapped my wife! I could have you arrested!"

The young man jumps to his feet, propelled by his own fury. "What about what she's done? When's she going to pay for that?"

"Don't drag a sick old woman into your sad little conspiracy theories."

"You tell me the truth, then. I'm sure you know what she did."

Todd shakes his head in disgust. "Do you know what my wife would say to you if she could?"

"What?"

"She'd tell you that some people like to play the hero, some people like to assign blame and others actually get things done."

After a minute or two of watching them posturing, Vivian can't remember why they are arguing. Her husband and the young man. He's such a nice young man. Charming. Well-dressed. Well-spoken. He looks a lot like someone she used to know.

She smiles at him, the young man. He would make an excellent mayor. "We should talk. We can make that happen."

She winks at Todd, who frowns. Perhaps he's jealous. The young man is very handsome.

"We have big plans for this town," she says. "It'll come back. It always does."

Vivian closes her eyes and dreams it. Dreams the future she has spent so long planning. She has come up with a solution to all of Stapleton's problems. It is nothing short of a stroke of genius. You won't even be able to see the trash. These days they build it up into grassy hills, everything hidden underneath. Just like Stapleton. They'll use the old mill site. Hide the contamination. Vancouver's waste needs to go somewhere.

Todd helps her out of her chair and takes her away from that dark place. She doesn't look at them as she leaves, Frank and the widow. She doesn't want to see their faces and she doesn't have to. They can't make her look anywhere, anymore.

Todd drives her home. He slips her shoes off and removes her thick cardigan. It's too warm in here, he should turn down the heating. He leads her to the nearest chair and lowers her gently into it. As she sits, she realizes things aren't right. Father is not hanging over the mantelpiece. There is no mantelpiece. In front of her is a large television and beside her are white-haired people she doesn't know. Why has he brought her here? She tries to get up, but she hasn't the strength. He puts his hand on her shoulder, reassuring her. "It's alright, Vivian …"

He sits beside her as a nurse comes over. "Time for your medication," she says cheerfully. Todd squeezes her hand as she stares at the tiny yellow pills. She looks at him, and he nods gentle encouragement. The day has shaken her; the anxiety pulsing from her chest has subdued her desire to fight. She gulps the pills down with water so they don't stick in her throat.

She is very tired now. Todd is sitting beside her and they are watching television. She should get on with her knitting. Doesn't she have some knitting to do? She turns to ask him about it but he has picked up the remote and turned up the volume.

The TV screen is full of tiny yellow pills. Dropping out of a chute into medicine bottles. "Breaking news" the ticker reads. Female news reporter in a fitted red suit. She's talking.

"GBA Pharma has admitted that its dementia drug Cefegana not only increases the speed at which dementia takes hold but can also trigger a range of other side effects, from nausea and frequent nosebleeds to increasingly erratic behaviour and heart failure. The company only yesterday defended its claims that the drug delayed the spread of the disease and increased periods of lucidity for most dementia sufferers."

Nose bleeds. She gets nose bleeds. It's the dry air. She should ask Todd if he gets them. She turns to him. He's busy at the moment, watching something on the TV. She tries to focus on the woman in the red suit. The reporter talks quickly and is difficult to follow.

"GBA Pharma CEO Zac Fuentes has stepped down amid allegations of corruption. The government announced today it is launching an inquiry into the shortcuts the company took during the research and manufacturing process for the drug, allegedly in an attempt to boost profits. Fuentes claims the shortcuts were designed to make life-changing medication available to dementia patients as quickly as possible."

Todd cannot seem to remove his eyes from the screen. The little yellow pills pop up again. She has seen those before. Ads follow; for sunscreen, fast food and more pills. Then a family discusses something animatedly in their kitchen while the husband makes pancakes. Every few seconds there's laughter, though not from the family. No one on the screen is laughing. Vivian quickly loses interest in the nonsense.

She looks down at Todd's hand, tightly holding hers. He's worried about something, she can tell. "Come into the garden with me," she says. "I want to look at the flowers." His eyes are watering and he's pressing his handkerchief into them. He helps her up and walks her over to the window where they gaze at the blaze of colours. He has planted tulips. They look so pretty, blooming in pots on the patio. It's getting dark now. Perhaps they'll go out and admire them tomorrow.

Acknowledgements

I have been writing stories ever since I can remember. They weren't always very good. Thank you to my first readers who persevered and encouraged me: Elaine, Duncan and Patrick Boxwell, Diane Diggle and Michelle Riches. Thank you also to David Keppel-Jones and Nina Johnson for their expert opinions, and to Steve and Hilda Hummel for their support, especially during the final stages of this process.

David Bergen's mentorship as part of the Humber School for Writers' Creative Writing Correspondence Program was invaluable in developing a first draft. Thank you to my editor, Lindsay Brown, and the team at Guernica Editions for taking my manuscript and turning it into a novel.

Finally, thank you to my partner, Erica Hummel, for bringing me to the little corner of British Columbia that inspired this book.

About the Author

Josephine Boxwell writes fiction and creative nonfiction. Her work has appeared in several magazines and anthologies. Originally from the UK, Josephine lived in Ontario and British Columbia prior to a recent move to Alberta. This is her first novel.

josephineboxwell.com
Instagram: @joboxwellwrites